Gathers
bucked fo
tension.

Leach felt his gut twist in old familiar pain.
He went for the gun strapped to his side, but
he saw no one, nothing but the fog drifting
along the roadbed. The mist came on them
quickly, like a living thing. It tied the car in
thick tendrils, stealing the air.

"Get out!" Too late, Gathers brought the car
to a lurching halt at the edge of the ditch by the
roadside.

Something cold touched Leach's mind, and
he felt pleasure that was not his own, that fed
on his dread. Darkness swallowed him whole,
but he did not lose consciousness—it was an
absence of light, not an absence of awareness.
Jonah, in the belly of the whale, and the whale
was laughing at him. Then, suddenly, Leach
felt the thing pressing him down, seeping in
through his skin, wrenching him inside out,
until it tore him from his body. . . .

**Innovative, evocative DAW Fantasy Novels
by Camille Bacon-Smith:**

EYE OF THE DAEMON

THE FACE OF TIME

THE FACE OF TIME

Camille Bacon-Smith

DAW BOOKS, INC.
DONALD A. WOLLHEIM, FOUNDER
375 Hudson Street, New York, NY 10014

ELIZABETH R. WOLLHEIM
SHEILA E. GILBERT
PUBLISHERS

Copyright © 1996 by Camille Bacon-Smith.

All Rights Reserved.

Cover art by Jean-Francois Podevin.

DAW Book Collectors No. 1042.

All characters and events in this book are fictitious.
Any resemblance to persons living or dead is strictly
coincidental.

If you purchase this book without a cover you should be
aware that this book may have been stolen property and
reported as "unsold and destroyed" to the publisher. In such
case neither the author nor the publisher has received any
payment for this "stripped book."

First Printing, December 1996

1   2   3   4   5   6   7   8   9

DAW TRADEMARK REGISTERED
U.S. PAT. OFF. AND FOREIGN COUNTRIES
—MARCA REGISTRADA
HECHO EN U.S.A.

PRINTED IN THE U.S.A.

THE FACE
OF TIME

CHAPTER 1

"Something's wrong."

Detective Chief Inspector Geoffrey Leach glanced up at the young sergeant who leaned over the open passenger side door of the unmarked car. He swallowed his first response, an observation about hinges and the effect the weight of the officer in question would have on them, and gave the narrow street a quick scan. Midday, and the only movement came from half a dozen men in work clothes near an open sewer access partly obscured by a public service truck. Should have made it a road crew, he figured. They could have mended the potholes while they were standing about looking conspicuous as hell at taxpayers' expense. But Gathers waited, his breath pluming in the damp chill.

"What something is that, Sergeant?"

The young man shrugged. "Someone's watching us," he said.

"Ah." Astute, Leach admitted to himself. "Jacobs and Bannister, second house down and across the street."

Gathers raked the fingers of one hand through hair the color and lay of a thatched roof, and Leach suppressed an inward sigh. The sergeant was one of Chief Superintendent Hadley's disappointments, a rising star dropped on Leach's desk when the kid had turned down the accelerated track for reason or reasons unstated. So far this didn't look to be one of Gathers' shining moments. Leach tried a different tack.

"Look, Col, I said it's Ben and Jack. They've been stuck in that grubby bed-sit for the last week, and no one has come near number eleven since the last of the cell left two days ago. So what's bothering you now?"

"It doesn't feel like Ben and Jack."

"I can't take your 'feeling' to Hadley." Not the right answer—Gathers' face closed down like the blinds snapping shut all up and down Edmond Place. "What does it feel like?"

"Not a friend. Not friendly, either."

Leach did sigh then, and Gathers' polite subordinate mask dropped in place; the lack of expression made it clear that Gathers took his point.

"There are probably half a dozen locals peering between their curtains, Col, and they doubtless wish us to perdition for mucking up their street and scaring their cats, but number eleven is empty."

"Right." Gathers pushed off the car door, contained frustration ghosting across his face. "We're ready, then."

Leach nodded and levered himself out of the car to watch as the sergeant moved toward number eleven, motioning the constables dressed as workmen to follow him into the abandoned terrace house. The house was rumored to hold the local stash of small arms for a half-baked terrorist cell with its eye on Harrods. Word hadn't made the group out to be above stupid, but Leach had a bomb squad standing by. Gathers knew he was to pull his squad out and leave it to the experts if they found any sign of explosives— the usual drill.

Still, apprehension pricked at Leach's skin. Just Gathers, giving him the willies, he told himself. But he couldn't wait out here in the silence of a chilly afternoon with his imagination working overtime and the drawn shades at number eleven showing him nothing. Leach started across the street, feeling four kinds of a fool. The sound of a gunshot caught him halfway, and he started to run. Jesus bloody fucking Christ, what a cock-up. The house was supposed to be empty. None of his men had guns. . . .

He was inside, then, and didn't know how he had gotten there, didn't stop to think that he was unarmed and somebody inside the house had a gun. The stairs were in front of him, and the body—Col Gathers—on the landing, right leg folded under, left held by the heel caught between spokes of the banister. Leach took the steps two at a time, missing the broken riser by chance, and stopped, shocked dead in his tracks by the blood on the landing—more blood than he had seen in twenty years, more than he'd ever seen a man survive. It dripped with a sodden inevitability into the puddle forming on the step below the landing, and Leach's heart picked up the rhythm of its fall. His fault, his fault. Should have listened, no matter that Gathers hadn't a shred of evidence to give him. *This can't be happening, not again,* and oh, dear God, he had to stop the bleeding.

"Sergeant. It's me, DCI Leach. Can you hear me?" Leach stepped over the body, wedging himself in the corner where he could see Gathers' face, and the wound in his chest.

Gathers moved his head, just enough to show he was conscious and still tracking, but his eyes glazed with shock. The pain hadn't hit yet, Leach knew. It had been like that in Derry: first the surprise, then the pain—or death. God damn it, he was not going to lose another soldier—no, not Derry, Gathers was a cop, down, and Leach realized that the radio was in his hand and that he'd been giving instructions for an ambulance and a weapons squad while his mind reeled in old places, breathing in the smell of stale blood with the mildew and fear-sweat and fresh blood flowing from a wound in Colin Gathers' chest. Stupid, stupid, with the danger of explosives in the building, but he was running out of instincts except the one beating need to keep Colin Gathers from dying on that stair landing.

No handkerchief, nothing to stanch the flow—God in heaven—he clenched his fist against old memories of blood on his hands.

"This is going to hurt," he said, and pressed the palm of his hand down hard on the wound. Fresh blood welled between his fingers, and Leach fought the revulsion.

"Oh, shit." Gathers coughed on a bubbling wheeze of pain and surprise. Well that hadn't been a lie—it hurt like hell—and Leach resisted the compulsion to draw his hand away when Gathers plucked weakly at his wrist with blood stained fingers.

"Help is coming," he answered the accusation in Gathers' eyes. "Help is coming, you'll make it." And Leach prayed silently that the ambulance would come, the ambulance would come. Policemen with guns were moving past him, and a paramedic took Leach by the arm and gently lifted his hand away.

"We've got him now, sir. You can let go."

"Don't let him die," he said, as if the decision lay in the hands of the medic, and didn't say what he felt— *my fault. Why didn't I listen? And to what?* his own mind answered. *How could I have stopped this?* "Don't let him die!"

"Sir. DCI Leach!"

Geoffrey Leach awoke with a start and looked

around, confused: no terrace house, no blood, just the darkness and the motion of the car in the night. "I must have been dreaming."

"I know. You called out. Didn't sound like one of the better kind."

Gathers was silent then, while Leach pulled his scattered thoughts about him. Hard not to state the obvious—you survived then. Gathers was very much alive in the driver's seat, and Leach didn't think the sergeant would appreciate revisiting the bad old days. Besides, he knew what had brought the nightmares on again; the reason lay on his lap. He opened the file and examined the forensics photos, eight by ten glossies he still couldn't look at without a shudder. Six corpses—four men, two women—all eviscerated. Something had laid open the bodies from throat to crotch, exposing bone and entrails. Each victim had been gagged to silence by a large stone jammed between broken, bloody teeth. They'd taken a long time to die.

Killers were all bad, but the mad ones were the worst. No way to guess which direction they'd jump. Looking away, Leach found his own face staring back at him from the side window of the Fiat. Approaching middle age with no distinguishing features—if he'd been a villain, that's how they would describe him—hair thinning, a few extra pounds stretching the lines around his eyes. Before she left him, Margaret used to nag him about his weight. About the nightmares, too. Then she just got tired of it all. Standing in the front hall with her two suitcases and three boxes of wedding crystal, the lines around her mouth part bitterness and part sorrow, she absolved him of the crime she could not forgive. Too late for children, she told him; she couldn't fight the competition any longer. A man could devote himself to only one wife, and his bloody memories left no room for the garden-variety comfort she had offered.

An honest policeman, he could not deny the allegation. Guilty, guilty. Even now, a stark reflection in the Fiat window, memory painted bloody images on the night-dark M1 falling behind at 65 miles per hour. Fizzing up his sinuses like the afterbite of cordite and teargas, the old nightmares clawed their way out of the backbrain, pushing adrenaline through his system. He hadn't seen carnage like this since two pounds of C4 took out Sunday Mass at St. Albans in Derry.

The similarity ended there. Not bombs and politics, but a single madman had murdered the archaeologists digging just outside the village of Thorgill. Probable weapon—Leach grunted at the use of the term. Improbable weapon was more like it—a flint ax, and recently chipped. Forensics had found flecks of volcanic glass in the wounds. So far, thank God, there hadn't been any children. Still, the case seemed likely to add to the repertoire of shadows haunting his sleep.

He closed the file on the photographs with an emphatic snap and pinned Sergeant Col Gathers at the wheel with a thoughtful stare. Evidence. For two years they'd worked together, had come to trust each other with small confidences—Gathers had a weakness for kung fu movies and dark-eyed women with big breasts—had come to know each other, Leach had assumed, in the way men who worked long hours under stressful conditions together reveal themselves by glimpses. Lately, he'd begun to realize that he knew only as much about the man as Gathers wanted.

Twenty-six, and young for the job, Col Gathers seemed to have not one but a series of masks to show the world. He'd caught Hadley's eye in spite of the "old gaffer" country burr he couldn't quite hide in his speech. Gathers had the straw-colored hair and sprinkling of freckles that made him an easy target for the stationhouse comedians, but the sergeant seemed to rise above it all with a steady, almost stolid fortitude. Only a few of them had seen the endurance sparked with anger in eyes that seemed to know too much—not stolid at all, then, but a be-damned refusal to let on what he felt about any of it.

The man was smart as a new suit, no question about that, and he moved like a trained . . . something. Not martial arts, not dance, but he sure hadn't learned that quiet, contained economy of motion sitting on a tractor. Whatever it was, it hadn't been enough to sidestep a bullet. Past and present images kaleidoscoped on the windowpane: pale shadows moving across stained wallpaper, Gathers picking his way lightly up the rotting staircase that became a tumble of brick in Derry, then the stair landing, and Gathers falling, bleeding, falling onto broken pavement with chips of flint glinting in the wound—No!

Leach opened the window, obliterating his reflection, and took a breath. A man had died a bloody death under his command once before, and he didn't like the feel of coming that close again. But this time it would be different. Shifting his weight in the cramped seat, he felt the government-issue Browning semiautomatic drag at his side. Hadn't kept the naturalness of that weight, one more thing he'd let go since he'd left the army. Mea culpa, mea culpa. Mistakes in this job were measured in pints of blood hung above a hospital bed.

"You should've told the chief you weren't fit for active duty yet." Accusation weighted the words.

"I didn't have a choice."

No explanation, just another blank mask, and the wind pressing on Leach's eardrums.

"What do you mean, no choice? They pulled you off

holiday, *and* you came off the limited-duty roster just two weeks ago. You could have come to me if Hadley gave you any grief. I'd have taken your part."

"So Hadley owes me one. I'll catch up on my reading some other time."

Gathers was tired, bleached out beneath the scattering of pale brown freckles. He still had the pinched look of somebody who had grown wary of breathing too deeply—a bullet in the chest did that to a man. The memory of finding the sergeant in a pool of his own blood still drove Leach from the depths of his nightmares screaming for the sergeant to answer him, to live in spite of too much blood on the floor.

They'd found the shooter, arrested and convicted him, too. No older than Colin Gathers himself, the bastard would be an old man before he saw daylight again: small comfort when they were driving from bad to worse in the middle of a fogbound night.

"Col—"

Appealing to their tenuous friendship wasn't going to work. Leach tried to force the words past the sergeant's impassive mask: "What do you know that you're not telling about this one, Sergeant?"

Gathers did not glance over. "You read the file." Leach wondered that the words didn't freeze-crack the windscreen.

So the man wanted no part of him. They were both here anyway, in spite of their best efforts, and they were going to work together however much the sergeant resented his presence. If Col wanted it by the book, that's what he'd get.

"Yeah, I read it." Frustration tightened Leach's voice. "It's left a few things out, like why you fought Hadley about coming up here with supervision when you had good cause to turn the assignment down flat."

"It's not that simple. Once Hadley was involved, I didn't have a choice. But there was no need to bring anyone else into it."

"Doesn't tell me anything," Leach glared at the sergeant. "Most especially, it doesn't tell me why you haven't looked at the map or asked for directions once on this trip. This Thorgill's not one of your major landmarks but, I swear, you've been driving like you could find it in your sleep."

"I grew up here. That's why they requested my presence at this little picnic. You know that."

"So why you? There's a lot of policemen between Thorgill and London. What makes you so special?"

Gathers sighed. "Here, as in Thorgill, DCI. I grew up in Thorgill."

Bitter emphasis marked the last word. Leach still couldn't figure out how talking to his sergeant about the current mass murder had turned into the interrogation of a hostile witness.

"You know this Powell?"

"Never heard of him before Hadley called me in this morning. I expect he got my name from Constable Tuttle in the village."

"I suppose Constable Tuttle does know you, then."

Gathers surprised him with a laugh of real humor. "You could say that. He arrested me for teasing Sally Mayhew when I was eleven, sentenced me to an hour in the slammer and three weeks after school working her dad's farm. If I'd had a better solicitor, I'd have gotten off, there not being a trial and all, but Granny Finlay rejected my appeal."

So Thorgill had a Granny who'd been a holy terror. Gathers must have liked the old biddy too. Leach recognized the tone—lightly ironic—from a time before the shooting at Edmond Place. The sergeant had never been free with his confidences, and Leach grabbed onto this bit, one more piece of the puzzle clicking into place, starting to make sense of the sergeant's chancy moods. Those pictures in the file were of strangers to Leach; he hadn't considered the possibility that Gathers may have known the victims. Now he was just glad that the name Sally Mayhew hadn't been among them.

"Hell raiser, were you?" he asked, trying to keep the suddenly lightened mood.

"You could say that." The sergeant grimaced at some secret memory. "According to Tuttle I never outgrew it, leaving Yorkshire for the fleshpots of London and all. But he does have a certain degree of respect for New Scotland Yard."

"Well, that may help, but Powell is the question. Forensics report looks thorough, preliminary crimescene report looks solid. He's not going to like us playing in his sandbox."

"You're right there. According to Tut, DCI Powell did not express jubilation about bringing in the Met's finest."

Leach stared sharply at him, the self-conscious camaraderie gone. The story did not add up, not with Col Gathers protesting he knew nothing one minute and admitting he'd discussed the case with the local authority in the next.

Col seemed to read the confusion on his face. "Tut called last night. He wanted me to take some time off and come up on my own, unofficially. I said no, thought it was done with. I underestimated his determination, it seems. The good constable refused to work with Powell unless he brought me in." Col was taking them deeply into ironic territory now, treading the paths of old arguments Leach hadn't been privy to. "Short of giving up the force, I don't have much choice. At this point, I suspect, neither does Powell.

What he'll make of you, well, I warned you not to come."

"Not your call, Sergeant." Leach hit the last word hard. Rank had meaning in the service, any service. It had to, or the whole system fell apart. But something had almost set rank aside in Chief Superintendent Hadley's office this afternoon, and nothing but the Department's ironbound rule not to send a junior officer into a major crimes scene alone had put Geoffrey Leach in the passenger seat.

"No, it wasn't my call." Gathers' expression had shut down again, the moment of shared confidences ended with another bland mask slipping in place.

Bloody hell. Six dead outside their jurisdiction, the DCI in charge was unhappy about their presence, and the local constable seemed to be running them all on a short string. So what else could go wrong? But he didn't voice the question. Leach had the uncomfortable feeling he'd find more answers than he cared to know in the little town. He stared out the windscreen at the night rushing toward them, trying to shut out the danger warnings that buzzed in his head.

"Trouble." Gathers pressed the accelerator and the Fiat bucked forward. A pinched frown betrayed his tension.

Leach felt his gut twist in old familiar pain, the forensics photos etched in his brain. He went for the gun strapped to his side, but he saw no one, nothing but the fog drifting along the roadbed. The mist came on them quickly, like a living thing. It tied the car in thick tendrils, stealing the air.

"Get out!" Too late, Gathers brought the car to a lurching halt at the edge of the ditch by the roadside.

Something cold touched Leach's mind, and he felt pleasure that was not his own, that fed on his dread. Darkness swallowed him whole, but he did not lose consciousness—it was an absence of light, not an absence of awareness. Jonah, in the belly of the whale, and the whale was laughing at him. Then suddenly, Leach felt the thing pressing him down, seeping in through his skin, wrenching him inside out, until it tore him from his body. Sensation touched him from a distance, unreal; Leach felt himself choking, and then the force that had invaded the car seemed to cut him free. A twinge of regret pulled at him when he looked down on the figure of the sergeant slouched over the steering wheel. Should have felt more, knew he once *had* felt more at the sight, but twisted logic told him he couldn't see Gathers from this angle unless he were dead himself.

In seconds the mist receded. Leach's body drew him, as if the fog, in passing, had left a vacuum where his awareness should be. He knew he was really back when his head started to pound.

Stirring cautiously, Col Gathers rubbed the back of his neck. "What happened?"

"I thought you could tell me the answer to that one, Sergeant. This being your home patch."

Comprehension dawned before caution shuttered Gathers' eyes.

"Oh—"

"Not quite the answer I was looking for," Leach pointed out.

"Anris."

The word seemed to mean something to Gathers. The sergeant restarted the motor in silence, and the tension thickened as the fog had minutes before. Finally, he offered a grudging, "We've had company."

"Not good enough, Sergeant." Leach didn't like the feeling he'd had from the start on this case, that he was flapping bare-assed in the breeze. One way or another, it was going to end now.

"From the minute Hadley called you in this afternoon, you've been acting like this was your personal file instead of the case file"—He shook the folder in Gathers' face, refused to look down when the photos scattered across his lap and drifted to the floor.

"Whatever has got up your nose, get over it. We've got a job to do, a killer to find before he does it again, and an officer in charge of the investigation who is not pleased that we are here. And since you seem to have the key to this tea party, I think it's time you did a little sharing, before we all wind up dead."

Leach had stopped expecting answers, and he almost missed the words Gathers whispered, as if to himself.

"He doesn't want us dead yet. He's testing our limits, seeing what it takes to scare us. He wants that—sucks up the fear of his victims like it was Newcastle Brown." Something vicious crossed Gathers' face. "Why couldn't you stay out of this one? You're a weakness I can't afford here!"

Anger met anger, too close to the surface and waiting to explode; Leach grabbed a fistful of Gathers' jacket, and the sergeant braked the Fiat, throwing it into park under a sign that said "Welcome to Thorgill" as Leach shook him, hard.

"Do you think I want you dead, Gathers, or that I'm just too incompetent to keep you alive?" Jesus God, he was over the top and out of control. Hadn't meant to drag that into the open here and now, with no time to work a way back to where things had changed on that stair landing. Not with an unhappy DCI and six dead bodies ahead of them, and deadly mists plaguing them in the night. He opened his hand and waited for Col Gathers to pull away.

"Hadn't considered it until you tried to run us into a tree just now," Gathers snapped.

"I made a mistake," Leach explained, "Didn't out-think the crazy bastards, never should have sent you in without a gun, and then I didn't listen when you warned me. But understand this, Sergeant Gathers: I do not make the same mistake twice. I will not lose another man on my watch, ever."

He felt the tension drain from knotted shoulder muscles, realized he'd been tensed for a blow for the past three months. The truth lay between them now, made real by the words, out where they had to deal with it. "I can't keep you alive if I don't know what we're heading into." Slumped against the backrest in the confined space of the Fiat, he waited.

"I never blamed you for that." Gathers stared at him like a man suddenly awakened to discover he's been sleeping on the wrong train. "We both did what we had to do, and for however long, we're both here to tell the tale." He shrugged, letting it go. "What more can we ask?"

Not a lie. In the few seconds of Gathers' confusion, Geoffrey Leach saw that clearly—trust and friendship and regret all running across features quickly brought under control. But darker things still festered at the black centers of those too-knowing eyes.

"If it's not me, then what are you so afraid of?"

"Not here." Masks gone, the memory of a bloody death he'd cheated by inches stamped itself in the tight-drawn lines of Col Gathers' face. "Do you trust me?"

Leach didn't stir, barely breathed the answer: "Haven't always, to my loss," he admitted, because they needed truth between them after that . . . thing . . . had taken a walk through his head. "But, like I said, I don't make the same mistake twice."

Gathers seemed to measure that answer for a moment before he went on. "While we're in Thorgill,

I'm asking you to put aside rank and do exactly what I say."

"That's—"

"Crazy?" The sergeant quirked him a humorless grin. "Before this is over, you may be sure of it, but you have to believe that I know what I'm doing."

Leach swallowed the protest about senior man present. A wise man defers to local knowledge any day, but: "How can I believe that when you haven't told me what you know?"

"You'll get your answers in Thorgill," Gathers promised. "Right now you just have to take my word that this is more dangerous than any case we've ever handled."

Leach knew the sergeant followed the drop of his eyes, knew he was thinking of bullets in the chest and life leaking onto the floor. But Thorgill had six dead already, and they'd asked for Col Gathers.

"Soon," Gathers promised. He pulled the car back onto the road, sunk in a silence that felt almost like church, somebody else's church, to Geoffrey Leach.

CHAPTER 2

Gathers turned left past the White Rose Inn. Thorgill. He felt the presence, waiting; he couldn't draw breath and wondered that Leach didn't seem to notice. Turn around, turn around; London is home now, let someone else take care of Thorgill. Death laughed at him—no going back, and never had been. He was a Finlay, *the* Finlay by birth, like it or not. The village would have its way, Anris would have his pound of Finlay flesh, or the village would die. Which he would cheerfully leave it to do, except that Kate had come back, and Tuttle had stayed, and he couldn't live with their blood on his conscience.

Geoffrey Leach was a silent presence at his side. Not patient, no. Electricity crackled in the passenger seat, an explosion building behind the inspector's set mouth. Leach couldn't hide the bewilderment that tensed the lines around his eyes, or the anger rising to confront it. The man dealt in facts, in things he could see and write up as evidence in that little leather-bound casebook he carried. No help from that direction; Col realized he'd have to deal with Leach soon, but he was at an absolute loss as to how. Wasn't even sure he could keep the DCI alive past the next hurdle—Tuttle. But all choices narrowed to one here; he left at the crossroad his last desperate hope that he could somehow avoid Thorgill's call—breathe in, breathe out, dammit—and pulled the Fiat around the curve of road that circled the village green.

The village drew him in, filling the suddenly empty places with its own needs and purposes again. Morgan's grocery still had the sign turned to "open," waiting for him, but Laura's Tearoom was dark. The few tourists they might have this early in the season would be gone, frightened away by the murders or by the nervous locals. Those same locals would be home tonight—fires burning in the fireplaces, doors and windows protected with a scattering of salt. Or they'd be praying in the little green Methodist church with the tin roof, lights still shining on the village green through the plain glass windows. They'd stay lit until the end, he knew, in the strange syncretic fashion that marked life in Thorgill.

He braked in front of the police station, a stone cottage indistinguishable but for a small painted sign over the door. No time to back out now.

"This is Thorgill," he announced.

"Seems a quiet place to host a mass murder," Leach remarked as he exited the automobile. The wary way he scanned the green belied the words.

Gathers shook his head. "What happened here was murder, all right, and it isn't over yet." Actually, he didn't think Constable Tuttle would kill Leach outright. Didn't count out a bit of maiming, though. He ushered Leach into the two-room station. Constable Tuttle's desk and several file cabinets were covered with paper. Gathers would have bet those surfaces hadn't been exposed since Tuttle took the job when his uncle retired—Col had been ten years old then. The neolithic chipped ax sitting like a paperweight in the middle of the desk was a new addition but, like the town itself, nothing else here ever seemed to change. A few chairs were scattered about, and the door to the lockup in the back room was closed.

The constable looked up when they entered the room. He hadn't changed much, either. Once stocky, Tuttle had run to fat a while back, and his bald head glistened with a fine sheen of sweat in the overheated room the way it had when Col was a boy. Tuttle still had chips of stone for eyes when something displeased him. At the moment, something displeased him quite a bit. Col ignored the warning signs, and made the obligatory introductions.

"DCI Leach, Constable Henry Tuttle, the Thorgill Police—"he nodded with bland formality—"Constable, DCI Geoffrey Leach, New Scotland Yard. He's come to offer his valuable assistance in your ongoing murder investigation."

Tuttle slid a glance as hard as the obsidian ax sitting on his desk over the inspector. That one look dissected then dismissed Geoffrey Leach as unworthy of further consideration. He faced Col Gathers with mournful disappointment blunting the edge of his disapproval.

"We sent for you, Colly, not some City brass. Don't need outsiders mucking about in business that doesn't concern them."

The inspector's jaw tightened. Before Col could think of a way to stop him, Leach answered for himself: "You requested the assistance of London Metropolitan Police with a murder investigation. London sent me as senior officer to assist and to coordinate our resources with the local authorities."

He smiled a bureaucratic smile that didn't fool Gathers one bit. "Sergeant Gathers and I are both at your disposal."

"Fine," Tuttle agreed too easily. Then, "I'm disposing of you now. Stay the night in York—Maude Farley runs a top-rate B and B—and you can be back in London by late morning. We'll send the lad back when we're done with him."

With that the constable turned a too-familiar paternal frown on Col Gathers. "Kate arrived this morning; she's expecting you at the cottage. We were a little worried last night when you said you wouldn't be coming, Col, but I'm glad to see you made it after all."

Gathers glared at the man, feeling eleven years old again, and hating it. "You never could take no for an answer. You've compromised my position with the department. CID will want a report—what am I supposed to say?"

"Use your imagination," Tuttle snapped. "If you weren't so stubborn, we could have kept the whole thing off the record."

"Not bloody likely," Gathers countered, "Not when you've got six corpses and the National Trust breathing down your neck. Did you plan to introduce me to the local investigation as a tourist with a general interest in murder?"

"We'd have come up with something, you know that. Who else were we supposed to call? Powell is a good man, but he's no match for Anris. And your DCI Leach here—what's he supposed to do, read Anris his rights and put the cuffs on?" Tuttle shook his head. "You owe Thorgill, like your granny and her father before her back to the beginning."

"Anris. You said that on the road." Leach, icy anger heating up and aimed at Col Gathers—no question, Col figured, that he'd escape the wrath of the DCI unscathed. He'd left too much unsaid, or said too much, or just hadn't had the good sense to die at Edmond Place and remove himself from the question. Whatever. Leach was going to make him pay for the drive up here in the dark in more ways than one.

"You've known who the perp is from the start?" Leach asked through gritted teeth, adding the obvious: "That is not in the file, Gathers.

"Has anyone told the local investigators? Or Superintendent Hadley, who might like to know why, if there is no investigation to conduct, are we here?"

"Knowing who was the easy part," Col said, "Stopping him is something else entirely. I'll explain later."

Leach did not look placated, but he'd have to wait his turn. Tuttle had first dibs on his hide. The constable's logic was irrefutable. Anris had been a Finlay problem for five thousand years. They'd trapped him, bound him to his tomb, and hatred for them would fuel his insanity still. Col knew all that, had since he was a kid. That didn't mean he could stop it. "I told you last night I wasn't in it any more. Haven't played these games since I joined the Met, don't even know how anymore."

"This is no game, Col. He's already killed six times, seven if you count the suicide. I'm not strong enough to take him on—none of us are. The Finlay has to do it—you know that. Do you want to leave it to Kate?"

Tuttle crossed to an electric urn set on a filing cabinet and filled three mugs while he talked. He shook his head, and Gathers felt a twinge of guilt. The man was only doing his job—he simply didn't have skill enough to handle it. Kate might just manage it, but on her own, his sister would never survive the battle. The idea of Kate beaten to death against Anris' insanity left a cold knot in the pit of his stomach.

The constable seemed to read his mind. "Kate's strong, I'll grant you that, but she's not *the* Finlay. That makes it your responsibility."

Which left the question of Col Gathers hanging. Finlay or not, he had neither the will nor, he suspected, the ability to do what Thorgill expected of him.

Leach interrupted then, with no sign of patience in his voice. "What the hell's a Finlay?"

Gathers had almost forgotten Leach's presence, couldn't afford the distraction now. Cutting off Leach's protest with "Later," he turned his attention back to Constable Tuttle.

"I don't know that I can do it, Tut. It's been a long time." He settled himself into an uncomfortable chair and took the chipped mug that Tuttle offered. The tea was as bad as always—tasted as though it had been stewing since morning. Leach took a mug but did not sit down. Instead, he took up a position behind Col's chair—Col felt the brooding presence there for what it was, backup, and didn't know whether to laugh or cry. No good, Inspector. Your kind of vigilance can't save us here—

Tuttle read him as easily now as he had years ago. "You'll manage." He gestured toward Leach with his mug of tea. "But what about this one? Shall we lock him up for the duration, son, or will you pack him off home, and no hard feelings?" The constable's eyes glinted cold and hard in Leach's direction.

Col felt the sudden tension behind him. Leach put his mug on the desk very carefully, and Col held his breath, unsure whether to warn Leach or see the confrontation through. Leach gave him no time to decide.

"I may not understand everything that is going on here, but I know why I've come. You've got a maniac who gets his jollies killing people—slowly and very messily—wandering your quiet village." Leach matched the constable's cold tone.

"You seem to have known Sergeant Gathers for quite some time, and I respect your faith in him. It's not misplaced; the sergeant is damned good at his job, but Chief Superintendent Hadley and I agree that a more experienced senior hand is needed here. None of us wants to lose a fine young officer through lack of experience."

Leach had touched on a sensitive nerve there, but the constable didn't flinch. "The lad'll do what he must—it's not your place, or mine, to say what that will be."

Tension pulled Col's shoulders together, instinctive self-protection and about as useful as standing under a tree in a lightning storm. Tuttle's irises dilated, holding Leach trapped in the black-eyed stare locked over Gather's head. Power built around them. Electricity crackled up Col Gathers' spine and along his arms while the room spun and colors smeared into a murky rainbow. He grounded automatically, a simple trick Granny Finlay had taught him when he was seven, to drain off the energy dancing on his skin and feed it harmlessly into the ground beneath his feet. But Leach had no such training. Col turned and saw pain and disbelief clamped firmly behind Leach's implacable rage, but the inspector held his ground.

"Enough." Col moved to his feet, gathering power. He gestured sharply at the constable, and the voltage snapped and disappeared. Warning lights glinted in his eyes, but he grinned lazily. "Like riding a bicycle," he conceded.

"Knew it would be." Tuttle shook his head. "Doesn't answer my question, though. He doesn't belong here."

"What the bloody hell was that?"

Leach. Gathers recognized the tone—explosive. And he still had Kate and the rest of the town to deal with. His own short fuse, held in check for too long while the village and the force bartered his life away, got the better of him.

"Not now! I'm trying to keep you alive long enough to meet the enemy." He dismissed Leach's objections with an impatient glare.

"He's my problem, Tuttle. I'll decide what's to be done with him."

"He has no defenses, Col, none at all."

Again Leach started to object, then fell silent. He stood at parade rest, watchful and alert, jaw clenched tight. Remembering the fog? Tuttle was right. Leach had to know it, but it wouldn't change his position. He'd made that clear already.

The constable continued: "Our old enemy may not kill him outright, but I'm betting Inspector Leach will wish that he had before this is over."

Gathers knew it was true, hated it. "If that happens, I'll take care of him."

"And if you're dead?"

Gathers saw the narrowing of the DCI's eyes and gave in to a shiver. Leach was not the only one who remembered that stair landing with grim horror, and Col wanted a repeat no more than the Inspector did. But being Finlay carried a price tag. He didn't like it, but Col recognized it, lived with it in Thorgill. He couldn't spare Leach this truth either.

"If I'm dead, I can't very well stop anything you do." His smile held no humor. "Including murder of the senior inspector from London. Until then, no one touches him, or I'm gone. Understood?"

When Tuttle dropped his head in agreement, Gathers relaxed into his chair again. Leach would find a way through this, he was sure of it. Right now, however, he didn't have time to coddle outsider sensibilities. He reached for a folder on the desk.

"Let's see the file you didn't send to Scotland Yard."

Leach did move then, intercepting the file. "The

sergeant will not be dying today, thank you. And I am still in command."

The constable shrugged and handed Leach the file, but he spoke only to Col Gathers: "You knew this would happen if the Finlays left Thorgill."

"Don't try to make this my fault, Tut."

"Who else, then? Not more than six months after Granny Finlay passed on, the damned archaeologists had permission to dig out the barrow. Came directly from the National Trust. With the rest of you off in the city, we had no way to stop it."

Gathers didn't need the accusation in Tuttle's voice. "Who besides Granny even believed in this stuff anymore?"

Until the folks from the museum broke through Anris' prison and the killing started, at least. Then the village dusted off the old stories, the old obligations in a hurry. He knew what Thorgill expected of Finlays, and he couldn't give it—couldn't leave London, couldn't leave the work that made sense of the obligation to serve that Granny Finlay had impressed upon him so long ago. And sense was the key. Nothing in Thorgill made sense, especially what the town expected of Kate and Colin Gathers, whose mother's name was Finlay, and whose father's name was never spoken in the town.

Well, dying never did make sense, and that much he owed them. But not his life. He held the constable's gaze, projected his own hostility into the silent exchange, and turned back to Leach, holding the file. Tuttle went on with his explanation.

"They breached the main chamber about dusk the day before yesterday. In the morning, we found two of them dead inside and one in the tent they have up there for their gear. A fourth had thrown himself down the mine shaft."

The details of the case drew Gathers in. "His body killed the other three?"

"Climbed a two-meter fence to lose his footing in the dark otherwise. At any rate, there've been three more since then. Kate arrived last night, and that quieted things down a mite. She's up at the cottage now, told me to have you stop at Morgan's grocery. She gave him a list this morning.

"Frankly, Col, I'm in over my head. I can calm the neighbors when the local kids start chucking the crockery about in their poltergeisting phase, pull a few parlor tricks like the one earlier with your friend here, but Anris is beyond me."

"I know it, Tut, but we'll think of something." Now, when he stood between Thorgill and the village's destruction, he had to believe he'd be strong enough to stop Anris. But the memory of death still clung to Gathers like a shadow.

"Yeah." Tuttle gripped his shoulder in a moment of silent encouragement. "Now that you're here, I can start to believe it."

Gathers rose to leave, but Tuttle stopped him. "One other thing—you weren't stupid enough to bring a gun into town, were you?"

"Not me." Col opened his jacket to demonstrate. Both men turned to the inspector.

"Leach . . ."

"Don't you ever learn?" Leach pronounced each word slowly, as if to a stubborn child, then loosed a staccato burst of rage and frustration on Col Gathers. "If you'd been armed three months ago, you'd have gotten that bastard before he shot you.

"It may not matter to you that you came this close to dying, but it matters to me—" Forefinger and thumb pinched together, the inspector pushed his hand into

Col's face, and Gathers ducked, reflexes reacting to a blow that never came—"I won't let it happen again."

"It matters." Col wrapped his hand around the fist Leach clenched in his face and forced it down. "I know what I'm doing. I've been getting ready for this fight since I was ten. And I'm not unarmed, not in the way that will count this time." He gave the inspector a grim smile. "We will win this one, but our way. The old way. Give Tut your gun."

Leach's eyes darkened with stubborn fury. Col knew he could force it—a little posthypnotic suggestion and he could even make Leach believe it was his own idea. Tuttle expected it, but the thought revolted Gathers. He let the moment pass, absorbing the anger and confusion of the other man. Time. They just needed time. . . .

"We've learned all we can here." Leach pivoted in place and headed for the door as if the past five minutes had never happened. "We should take a look at the crime scene."

"Not tonight," Col objected. "It's not safe." He nodded in the direction of the moor looming a darker black above the village. "Too dark. We'd never find the dig this late at night." No point in mentioning the real danger—Anris on the loose and a gun at the hip of a nonbeliever. None of them would survive that nightmare. They'd be lucky if they survived the one he had planned.

The fight seemed to leave Leach in a sudden, explosive sigh. "Right," he said. "We'll get some sleep, start asking questions in the morning."

Not yet. They still had Kate to face, and Barbara. Col hoped that confrontation would knock some sense into Leach's head, but common sense told him the Finlay women would just make the Inspector more certain that the whole village had gone mad. Too much inbreeding—he flinched away from that thought and rose to follow the inspector into the street.

A low grumble reminded them they were not alone. "Sure you don't want him tucked up safe and sound in the lockup till this is over?"

"Give it some time, Tut." Col turned to face the constable, more tired than he should have been. He hoped Leach was wrong about how ready he was to take on the scourge of Thorgill. Dying was one thing, but failure was quite another. "We'll talk again tomorrow."

"I hope you know what you are doing, Col."

Col Gathers stopped. "So do I, Tut. So do I."

He left without a backward glance.

CHAPTER 3

Geoffrey Leach stared at the low, dark bulk of the stone cottage. None of this case had made sense thus far. He'd thought he'd passed the limit of his capacity for shock in Tuttle's police station, but this splinter of a former century sitting at the edge of the Yorkshire moor stopped him cold. That was real thatch for a roof, and the faint light in the window flickered like candle flame. Either someone went in for electric verisimilitude, or they were walking into a firetrap. Col Gathers didn't even pause.

"Duck your head, the doorway is low," he'd said, and then passed inside, a twenty-pound bag of rock salt balanced with one hand over one shoulder, a sack of assorted oddments that made no sense to Leach, but that Gathers had ticked off with a satisfied grunt at the general store, gripped in the other hand. Leach suppressed a shudder at the doorsill. A reality he wasn't ready to face, that included the night's visitations and the fact that Colin Gathers had not been surprised by any of it, waited, he knew, on the other side. But it was dark, and he could think of no earthly reason not to, so he followed the sergeant into the cottage.

More than a century out of time, Leach figured. He half expected to hear the lowing of cattle in the side room. Dresser, settle, fireplace, a table, a few spindle chairs softened with pillows that looked handmade to match the curtains drawn away from the smoke-fogged windows: the place could have been a bloody living museum. A branch of candles stood on the table, and two smaller ones stood on the dresser, casting a soft yellow glow on the room. The night was warm for April, but a fire burned in the big fireplace. Leach wondered if they would survive the night or burn to death in their beds, a fitting end for an old army man who knew better than to volunteer.

"Is the whole village like this?"

Col glanced around, as if noticing the room for the first time. "Not even the whole cottage. Don't rightly know why Granny never renovated the parlor, but she seemed to think it was important."

He dropped the twenty-pound bag of rock salt on the dresser. "Kate, are you here? Barbara—" He gave an abrupt nod to the woman who appeared in the back doorway. "You're early."

"Not early enough, obviously, or we wouldn't have seven dead. I was wondering how many bodies we'd have to accumulate to get you back here." She stopped suddenly, a single eyebrow raised in an expression Leach couldn't quite read, except that it wasn't friendly. "Who's he?"

"Detective Chief Inspector Geoffrey Leach. London sent him to liaise with York on the investigation. Geoff, this is Barbara Finlay, my half sister."

She was almost as tall as Col, with black hair that fell in sharp architectural lines to curve precisely at her shoulders. Leach figured it didn't dare do otherwise. Clear blue eyes glinted daggers in a fine-boned porcelain face. Leach offered his hand, but she ignored it. "What is he doing here?"

Behind him, he heard the sergeant reply, "Couldn't stop the bloody fool, could I?"

"Didn't try too hard either, I reckon."

Leach would have left the room discreetly if he'd had a place to go. He most definitely did not want to know about Col Gathers' difficulties with his family. Didn't see that this was exactly the time to dwell on them, either. "His guvnor didn't give him much choice about it."

"And you'd know that because . . . ?"

Leach smiled unctuously, but Gathers cut off his response. "He's my boss. So be nice to him, or I'll lose my next raise in pay for uncooperativeness."

The woman, Barbara, glared at him, and Leach wondered briefly how fast he could get a wagon up here and whether he could have the woman arrested for obstructing justice. Before he could pursue the thought, another of Gathers' female relatives burst into the front parlor radiating fury.

"I won't have that man in my house!" The woman shoved her face into Leach's, glaring up at him with scorn and something more dangerous just leashed behind her eyes. "Didn't Hadley have enough sense to assign you to someone else after he got you shot?"

The question wasn't for Leach, but it struck at his own fears: that he didn't have the judgment anymore and, since the shooting, maybe didn't have the stomach to send men into danger. But she was just starting on him. "Come to finish the job this time?" she asked.

"That's enough, Kate." Col would have stopped them, Leach knew, but something about the woman, whoever she was, demanded answers he didn't have. She looked like a smaller version of Col Gathers—hair redder and long, with a bit of a wave to it but the same eyes. She hadn't Barbara's icy beauty or Col's contained economy of motion; she might have been plain if not for the fierce warmth of her. He thought suddenly of warrior elves and guardian angels. She roiled the murk at the bottom of his soul, and suddenly he longed to tell her secrets he never would have shared with Col Gathers—things he'd been afraid even to think since Derry. Leach found himself responding to her challenge with all the anguish of his own unanswered questions.

"I know I failed him. Don't think I haven't seen him bleeding in my sleep every night since it happened. I've played it over in my head hundreds of times, and I still can't find anything I could have done, any way I could have moved faster."

"You could have issued guns." Barbara entered the fray with a direct hit. Leach dropped his head, admitting defeat, but to the newcomer, not to the woman who sliced him into little pieces with those ice-blue eyes.

"We had men watching the house. It was supposed to be empty." And he knew they were looking for explosives, should have issued sidearms. But the stakeout was solid, the house was empty. Except that one man they'd never seen enter the building had been waiting. Thank God he'd only had a twenty-two—an assassin's gun, no good for moving fast or shooting at a distance. A nine millimeter would have ripped a hole the size of his fist in Gathers' chest. A botched job from beginning to end—the gunman's friends never did come home to the roost, and Col Gathers spent a week in the hospital and two months in rehab for Geoffrey Leach's error in judgment.

"And this is Kate, my sister." Gathers drawled the introduction with heavy irony. "Say hello, Kate."

They glared at each other until Kate Gathers softened, the hurt flitting quickly across her face. "You didn't fail him. In my saner moments, I know that. Sometimes it's just easier to blame the charm for not working than to accept that some things are beyond our control." Her tone shifted into irony: "Even for a London DCI."

Leach found himself responding to her absolution, and that scared him more than the thing that had come upon them on the road had.

Kate Gathers seemed to read the fear and longing in his eyes. She touched his forehead with her fingertips, and suddenly Leach felt the power in her to take away his pain. No one but Margaret had ever had the power to make him feel clean the way this woman did—and even Margaret couldn't manage it by the time he left the army. He knew he should be afraid of this woman's knowledge, but he found himself longing for her words to be true.

"Only you can forgive your sins, Mr. Leach." Her sad smile was all for him. "We don't, any of us, need them anymore."

The exchange lasted only a moment, and then she was brisk efficiency, speaking to her brother: "You know he's going to pull the Earthbound like nectar pulls bees."

"Not until midnight, I think. We'd better have this place secured by then." Col's temper seemed to have evaporated, leaving behind a residue of stolid acceptance. He hoisted the bag of salt onto his shoulder again and led the way into the back.

Kate followed with the paper sack from the grocer, but Barbara Finlay stayed behind. "Go home, Inspector." She chilled him with the same obsidian glare that Tuttle had turned on him, and he settled his balance more firmly over the balls of his feet, waiting for the room to waver as it had in the station. But Barbara Finlay shook her head, as if reading his mind and refusing some challenge she read there. "If you stay here, you will die. It's that simple." She turned her back on him then and followed the Gathers siblings through the doorway.

Leach waited long moments alone in the center of the room, not forgotten, he knew, but dismissed as irrelevant to the task at hand. He was getting bloody tired of all the obscure references and oblique threats to his life. No wonder Col never spoke about his family—they were all insane. But Kate had seen something in his heart, he knew, and somehow, she'd offered him something of herself in return. If only he could figure out what it was. Finally he went in search of the murmuring voices of Col Gathers and his sisters.

It was a planting shed. Gathers stood with his back to the door, his hands on a long worktable. Above the table, jars and crocks were arranged on shelves. Now and again Gathers reached for a jar, opened it and sniffed its contents, or shook it gently, all the while measuring with a connoisseur's air.

"Not nearly enough of anything if this goes on long," he muttered. "We'll have to pull him in soon. For now, though, let's get this place sealed up—I don't want to fight Anris on Granny's doorstep."

Gathers split the bag of salt with a short curved knife, and the two women filled silver bowls from it. Barbara disappeared into the front room, but Kate remained behind to sprinkle salt across the doorways and on the windowsills, then in the corners of the workroom.

"It will be all right," she stopped to assure Geoff. "Col knows what he is doing." She smiled, and he suddenly realized how tired she looked. Then she was gone, and he heard the two women talking softly together in the front room.

Geoff prowled the workroom's perimeter, touching a bunch of dried herbs tacked to an exposed support

beam, brushing fingertips over the leaves of plants growing in pots on a shelf beneath a wall of windows. He gave the rocking chair a nudge, and he realized with a start that he hadn't seen it until then. Nor had he seen the small girl sitting curled up on the seat until the sound of her quick indrawn breath caught his attention. She stared at him out of Col Gathers' eyes—ubiquitous in this neighborhood. He guessed she must be nine or ten. Not likely to be Gathers' kid, then. "What is your name?" he asked in the tone he saved for interviewing frightened witnesses.

She seemed about to answer when a potted plant fell off the shelf behind him. Geoff ducked and reached for his sidearm. He managed to stop the draw against the broken clay pot, but he couldn't quite control the cover reflex when another plant teetered in its place and crashed to the floor, scattering dirt and potshards on his shoe. "What—" he began, and grabbed a third plant making a suicide leap to freedom.

Col Gathers just shook his head and swept the little girl into his arms. "It's okay," he crooned softly, "Inspector Leach won't hurt you, Katy."

"Mummy says he's going to get us all killed."

Gathers hesitated long enough that Leach knew the girl was telling the truth. So much for trust. But he'd known that from the beginning. He didn't need it; he could do his job either way—had done it without more often than the other. But he remembered Kate Gathers strolling through his soul just minutes before; he hadn't realized it would hurt quite this much to give up the illusion of forgiveness so soon.

"The Inspector would never hurt you on purpose, Kitten." He gave her a quick peck on the cheek and set her on her feet. "He's come to help us. Now go find your mum and help her with the wards."

The child gave Leach a last thoughtful stare, then

stepped carefully over the scattered salt in the doorway. He heard the sharp staccato of her footsteps running on the bare wooden floor until he lost her in the murmur of women's voices beyond.

"Talk, Gathers." Leach set the potted plant on the workbench, well back from the edge, and crossed his arms over his chest. "What the bloody hell is going on here? Why does that child think that I have come to town to kill her and her family—" and why does she have your eyes, he almost asked, but stopped himself in time. Not his business, and Gathers didn't look like unburdening his soul at the moment.

"Kate doesn't think you mean us ill, Geoff."

So, she was Kate's kid. Kate, with eyes just like her brother's. He kept his expression blank while Gathers collected a broom from the corner and swept the scattered debris onto the heap of broken pots and other planting remains beside the garden door.

"But—" he prompted.

"But the people around here aren't used to strangers, don't trust them. Nobody wanted those archaeologists here—didn't want them dead, but didn't want them invading the town, either. Now they are dead, the first murders in Thorgill in at least a hundred years. To the people who live here, strangers woke the murderer when they interfered with things they didn't understand. They believe that more outsiders—even policemen from the outside—will bring nothing but more bad luck."

"That's not it." Leach fought the urge to pace out his frustration. He stood his ground, using logic where he sensed orders or anger would drive the young officer into his impersonation of a brick wall.

"Or not all of it. You forget, I was with you on the highway tonight. They used a powerful narcotizing agent on us out there, so they aren't amateurs at this.

And you knew who it was, half expected it. You're expecting them here, tonight. What is it, Col—a hostage situation? Has your Constable Tuttle told DCI Powell what you are facing here?"

"No," Col answered, cold, so cold his tone, with death in it, that Leach remembered, and knew the sergeant saw the same stair landing from a different, almost fatal, angle. "Nor will he. This is Thorgill business. We'll handle it, and Barbara will give him what he needs to close his report when we're done."

Leach shook his head, but it didn't help. He'd made a lot of guesses about Col Gathers in the past two years, but in none of them had he pictured the man as a closet vigilante with aspirations to Rambo-hood.

"You know better than to try to keep the police out of it—or do you think you can take them out with just Tuttle and a couple of women? You didn't even bring a gun, for Christ's sake! Tell me who it is, what they want. We'll get the SAS in if we have to. Just tell me what we're up against!"

So much for logic. Gathers stared at him for a long hard minute. "I was afraid it would come to this." He ran his fingers through his already disheveled hair. "Sit down, at least," he said. "I have to work while we talk, and this may take a while."

Leach dropped into the rocking chair and allowed himself the luxury of dropping his head into his hands for a brief moment. Nothing since that first overheard conversation in Hadley's office seemed real. Certainly not being dead—drugged, maybe, but it felt as though he were dead—even for seconds. Not being threatened by a constable with the body of the Michelin Man and the eyes of a tomb. Not Col Gathers calmly filling little burlap sachets with salt and odd bits from the kitchen while the world went quietly mad around them.

"None of this makes any sense."

"I told you not to come. Knew how it would be if you did. This is an old problem for us, Geoff. We have old ways to solve it." As Col Gathers spoke, his fingers found by touch what he needed. Two iron screws, an unbroken clove of garlic, a sprig of sage went into each sachet, Leach inventoried, topped off with a full measure of salt.

"Don't be a fool if you can help it, Sergeant. You've already told me that you haven't had a murder in this village for over a hundred years. Now you've got six, maybe seven, and what's your answer? Rock salt? Works fine on snails in the garden. Believe me, it does nothing to stop mass murder."

Gathers set down the sachet he was working on and turned. He set a hand on either arm of the rocking chair, and Leach felt uneasily like a prisoner beneath his stony glare. "I said our ways were old, Geoff. Not a hundred years, but thousands of years." His voice was distant, bitter; Leach didn't know if Gathers directed that bitterness at him or at that gray distance that seemed to grip him in this place.

"But you're right. The wards won't stop him. With luck they will slow him down until we're ready for him."

Leach shook his head. "You talk about this killer as though you know him. Is that the problem? Are you trying to protect a local who's a shade more paranoid than his neighbors about strangers in the area? That's collusion. A crime, remember?" It struck him then with claustrophobic clarity that Col Gathers had given him no explanation at all. He was alone with this man in a village that wanted him gone, a village in which all the other outsiders were presently dead. And Gathers didn't sound as though he planned to take the killer into custody.

"Or are you planning murder?" Leach forced the words out, so softly that Gathers had to lean in to hear them. Not the smartest thing he'd ever done, perhaps, but Geoffrey Leach had faced death before, and he needed to know where he stood now. Death was in Col Gathers' eyes all right, but not Leach's. The man backed away, his face gone so cold that Leach wished for the warmth of the fire in the next room.

"Do I know who is killing people in Thorgill?" Gathers asked the air in front of him. "Oh, yes. As for murdering him, I only wish I could.

"I am trying to protect my people from something you can't even begin to understand with your rules and regulations. I was born for this fight, literally, and if the past is anything to go by, I will die in this fight. They expect it. I accept it. The faster we do it, the fewer innocent people we'll lose in the battle. But," he paused for a moment, shook his head. "How do we keep you, and your damned gun, safe while we work?"

"You can explain who is really killing the good people of Thorgill and its visitors," Leach suggested, "and trust me to act on it like a reasonable man."

Gathers looked at him sharply then, as if taking his measure. Then the tension left him so suddenly that he slumped on the edge of the workbench. "Just remember, you asked for this."

Leach settled back in his chair to listen.

CHAPTER 4

"His name is Anris." Col Gathers paused to collect his thoughts a moment, then: "Do you know what an earthbound spirit is?"

Leach shook his head. "Only what I've seen on the front page of the *Sun*—spooks, ghosts, bumps in the night, that sort of thing."

The corners of Gathers' mouth twitched in a half-smile made dangerous by the cold anger in his eyes.

"Not the most accurate description, but yes, he's a ghost, if you like." Salt, sage, lavender, garlic, iron: a pinch of each went into a leather bag smaller than a keycase. Col filled the bag and tied it off with a leather thong, picked up the next. Kate would have his hide if he didn't get the warding charms done while he talked.

"Sometimes people become so attached to places or things in this life that they can't give them up; other times, they are so afraid of dying that they don't really believe they're dead. They can get a bit rowdy if they're crossed, but you can usually convince them to move on without much trouble."

"Didn't much like being dead, then, this Anris?"

Gathers caught the sarcasm, knew better than to ignore it. Leach liked all his i's dotted, his reports on time and checked for spelling. But in spite of the stolid rationality, Col had caught the occasional glint of something haunting the man. Ghosts of his own, then.

"I know, it doesn't make sense. That's why I left. The old stories, training for a battle that never comes, didn't seem to wash anymore. But some things drag you back, no matter what you want. Finlays have been guardians of Anris' tomb for five thousand years."

He sighed, and couldn't keep the yearning for innocence he'd never known out of the sound. Leach tilted his head, a startled expression twitching briefly across the policeman's expressionless exterior, and again Col wondered what resonance his own weariness had struck in the older man. Perhaps he wasn't the only one of whom fate had asked too much, but whether the shadow of that memory would bind them in their purpose, or destroy them all, he could not guess.

"Anris was a magician during the time of the first Finlay king. He wanted what the Finlays had and would stop at nothing to get it."

"Rich back then, were they? Going to introduce me to the king of Thorgill?"

"No, they weren't rich—likely had some cattle and a bit more land than most, but nothing special that way. Wasn't a job like now, more like being magistrate, except that you were likely to get chucked off a cliff if the rain didn't come on time or the well dried up. They had respect, though, and some power.

"Anris wanted the Finlay land, but more than that, he wanted the power. Maybe at first he wanted the people to love him as well, but only because he didn't understand. Nobody ever loved the Finlays. Needed them, depended on them, but never loved them. Only equals are free to love, and the Finlays had no equals, not in what they were called on to do."

The words drifted into silence. Needed but not loved. It summed up the life of a policeman, too.

THE FACE OF TIME

Maybe that's why he'd gravitated to the work after university. History for its own sake didn't seem so important when there were people out there who needed help. The wound in his side still caught him unawares at times, reminding him of cliff tops he'd faced in his new life as well. He frowned, pulling back from the grim and lonely place his mind had wandered, and found Leach looking back at him with a too-knowing expression.

"Fairy story or not, they knew what they were talking about, those old Finlays," Leach offered: not belief, but a way that he could make sense of it all. It was a beginning. Col knew he'd need a lot more if any of them were going to see London again on this side of the grave.

Slowly, his voice still distant, Col picked up his explanation. "Anris never understood the power. They call it magic today and make it seem mysterious and irrational. It was different when Anris first challenged the Finlays—science, religion, philosophy don't begin to describe it. Things like walking in the woods, and building your house so that the doors faced in the right directions, and knowing all the different kinds of rain and when they would fall came together to make meaning out of the power of earth and air and water.

"It may sound daft, but almost anyone can learn to nudge the cosmos a little, with caution. Some, like the Finlays, spend more time training not to do things accidentally than learning how to make things happen."

Gathers waited, knowing his voice had betrayed him, exposed too much, and Leach was too good a policeman to miss it.

"You mean, you are some kind of magician?" Leach

drew out the words, carefully, as if Col might somehow mistake their meaning otherwise.

When Leach had insisted on coming to Thorgill, Col had feared for the safety of his people first and for his own career second. He hadn't expected Leach to accept him as he was, without the barriers he needed to protect the part of him that was Thorgill from the rest of the world. But he had let the tiny hope fester in the back of his mind that they might defeat this thing together. Now he faced it, make or break, and so he answered, "Some kind, yeah."

"And anybody, even I, could be a magician too, if I wanted, right now?"

"You've had a lifetime of unconscious training in denial." Col answered with grave consideration. "So it would take you some effort. But yes, you could. I could teach you how, if you wanted. Kate would do a better job of it, but I'd suggest you stay away from Barbara. She doesn't suffer . . . students . . . lightly." He couldn't help the wry smile. Barbara Finlay's methods were rough on the self esteem, but they did work.

"I'll grant that you believe in this—" Leach stopped, and Col watched as he picked carefully through the minefield of words between them. "—but it doesn't explain why you think this dead guy is killing your neighbors. I mean, if you believe anyone can do this stuff, why not someone actually alive, with something to gain?"

Army man, Col reminded himself. Anris was Thorgill's monster, but he wasn't unique as a type. You could find that kind of evil in a blood-soaked line through history—Hitler, Stalin, Pol Pot. It still went on—Leach had seen it and carried around the marks of his own battles, knew that evil at the level of Anris existed. So maybe you didn't need to be from the unbroken line of Thorgill's defenders to understand, under the skin where the rational gave way to a man's basic need to protect those weaker than himself, what they fought and why they could not afford to lose. Which would help them about as much as day-old spit if Gathers couldn't convince Leach that Thorgill's murderer didn't come with a beating heart.

"There are two routes to tapping the power of the cosmos, Geoff," he explained. Good and evil weren't particularly useful categories in Col Gathers' world, but they might help Leach. And if anything fit in a category called "evil", it was Anris. "One way finds the direction the cosmos is going and sort of hitches a ride. 'Don't Tamper' is the first rule you learn. The other takes the power of the cosmos by force, if you like. You can do more with it if you have the strength, but that kind of power feeds on itself, until you need more and more just to stay even. And the only place to get it is to steal it from other living beings.

"Anris took the second road, force. He turned to coercion, to murder, to sustain his power. They say he killed thousands before the war, and thousands more died to stop him. Finally, the Finlay trapped him inside his tomb and killed him there. The family has guarded it ever since. Now he's out, and it looks like it's all begun again. A bloody *déjà vu*."

If dust had a sound, Gathers heard it in his own voice—the dust of the tomb gaping open on the moor above them. He paused, thinking of the morning.

"And I suppose you're a Finlay somewhere along the line, right?" Geoff asked him. Crossing all the t's, Col noted.

"Gathers is my father's name. My mum is a Finlay, and that makes me a guardian."

Leach stared down at his hands for a moment, and when he looked up, Col found only sorrow in his expression. "It makes an interesting story for a rainy night, Col, but you can't expect to solve the case with it. What happened to those people was as real as it gets and, face it, it took at least two hands, if not an accomplice as well, to slice those people open."

"Anris is real, too, Geoff. Believe it or we're dead." Gathers stopped a minute, thought, and corrected himself. "No, we're probably dead regardless. If you can't learn to accept, you may take the town with us. You can't imagine what he is capable of."

Leach shook his head. "Don't have to imagine it, old son. Our perp had the physical power to tie down and tear the living insides out of six healthy young archaeologists and the technological know-how to drug us in our car on the way into town. Oh, don't get me wrong—" Leach raised a hand, and Gathers waited out his objection "—I know there are people out there with some strange ideas, and I don't doubt that a place like this, remote as it is, may have a few old legends clinging to it.

"But you're not some farmer who's been no farther than the market in the next town. The ax that killed those people is real, and ghosts don't wield axes, even stone ones."

They were all going to die. Col focused on the charms he was constructing at the workbench for a moment while he tried to wipe the knowledge off his face.

"You're right," he agreed. "A ghost has no body of its own. But sufficiently motivated, an earthbound spirit can make use of the bodies at hand. And an archaeologist can chip an ax out of flint and gut his teammates before he takes the long fall down a mine shaft. Farmers and shopkeepers can do the same to their neighbors, and when Anris is done with them, they have to live with the memory of the murders he's made them commit, or they die themselves, penance for crimes their bodies committed while their minds cowered in whatever corner Anris drove them to."

Col dropped the charm he was working on and faced Leach, his fists clenched to keep from shaking the man where he sat. "Can't you understand?" he demanded. "Human beings release a lot of energy under stress, and dying by torture is as stressful as you can get. The more he kills, the stronger he becomes, and the more energy he needs to maintain his strength. He won't stop killing, won't ever have enough in this world or any other. The feel of that power is like an addiction, like the perfect orgasm that doesn't have to end as long as there are victims to draw on. He has to kill not only for the power that transforms his will into existence, but for the pleasure that he takes in the pain and destruction he causes."

Gathers opened his clenched hands like a sigh, and made a dismissive pass in the air between them. They were out of time, and he was running out of patience.

"You saw the photographs. You know what Anris did to those people." Gathers let all of his cold dread power the death in his voice. "He almost wiped us out five thousand years ago. It took a war to end his killing. He'll finish the job if we don't stop him now. Imagine how it will feel when he does it using your body, your gun. Imagine how it will feel to have no control when he uses your hand, your skill, to kill Kate and Barbara, to murder Katy and Tuttle.

"I remember when I came back to duty after the shooting. You could barely stand to look at me. Imagine how it will feel to stare down the barrel of your service pistol at me and pull the trigger while he laughs in your head."

"You want my gun." Leach hesitated, held out his

hand as if the pistol lay balanced across his palm. "I can't. I'm sorry."

"Change your mind soon, Geoff. Or go home. We're running out of time." An ultimatum. Col was tired going into this fight. Probably not fit enough yet, either, and he certainly didn't have the reserves to wait out the stubborn, righteous old bastard in the rocking chair. He picked up one of the charms he'd left strewn on the workbench and held it out by its leather thong.

"Humor me, okay? Put this around your neck." When Leach had done as he requested, he added, "Don't take it off until Kate tells you. And one more thing. We're not alone in this. Civilians are coming into Thorgill right now, and some of them have been in this fight for generations. They are as dangerous as the thing we are hunting. If they're not, we've already lost. *You* are an outsider—an amateur—to them. They are going to be nervous, and a flip remark will get you killed.

"If you do exactly what you are told, and keep your skepticism to yourself, I may be able to keep our side from chucking you off a cliff just to shut you up. But while you are in Thorgill, don't forget that you are in danger from everyone you meet. And Geoff, if we run out of time waiting for you to come around, I will be the most dangerous of all."

Col swept up the charms he had constructed by their leather strings and headed for the murmur of voices in the main room. "We've got company," he noted, and stepped over the trail of salt at the threshold, leaving the inspector to follow.

CHAPTER 5

Leach scuffed through the salt that crossed the threshold and Barbara Finlay, watching from the center of the room, glowered at him. "Your death wish is going to take a lot of people with you if you're not more careful." She turned her venom on Col Gathers, who sat back motionlessly in a rocking chair, the twin of the one in the workroom: "And it will be your fault for bringing him here if he does."

"He brought himself, Barbara," Col answered her. "If I'd had my way, neither of us would be here."

"You can't hide from your duty that easily, brother—not in London and not behind your DCI either."

Leach wasn't quite sure what he'd done to bring the harpy's wrath down on his head, but Barbara Finlay did clear up one mystery. Leach now understood where Gathers got his martyr's complex. The man might be quick to stretch himself out on any available cross, but he could count on his family to supply the hammer and the nails.

"No one brought me, Ms. Finlay." Leach intruded on the private conversation with the tone he saved for reluctant witnesses. "And I am not leaving until we apprehend your murderer. The faster we do that, the faster I will leave your lovely village, so you serve your own best interests by cooperating."

Geoff scanned the room full of people, all looking back at him. He recognized Barbara Finlay and Kate Gathers, who sat on the settle, little Katy drowsing with her head on her mother's lap. Tuttle, the constable, held up the wall just inside the front door. More than a dozen strangers milling at the center of the room paused to stare at him with suspicion. The light of dozens of candles that seemed to have appeared out of nowhere glinted in their watchful eyes and cast an uneasy golden glow on the shapeless robes they wore. A few wore intricate embroidery at the neck; others could have been wearing industrial strength flour sacks for all he could tell. One thing was certain—they hadn't been in the room when he'd arrived.

He grimaced his disgust: a spastic gorilla could have taken out the whole front room and he wouldn't have noticed while Gathers was talking. The Met's finest? They'd be lucky if the vicar didn't walk off with the silver while they were on watch! Except that, not surprisingly, the vicar seemed to be the only one missing. But Gathers had known, Geoff realized. While he talked, the sergeant had moved simultaneously and apparently without effort in this world and another, distant, reality. Geoff wasn't sure the realization made him feel any better.

Danger prickled at the back of his neck. Geoff scanned the room quickly from where he stood in the doorway to the workshed; his attention snapped back to Barbara Finlay with a nervous intensity that set his teeth on edge. She was the center of the moment, and he didn't trust her. A quick look at Col Gathers told him there'd be no help from that direction. Without consciously willing it, Geoff's fingers curled slightly into loose fists; he shifted his weight almost imperceptibly over the balls of his feet, wishing abstractedly for something to happen, something to set him in action or break the unbearable tension. Gathers watched, with a look that said, "I warned you."

For a moment he thought no one would move at all—that they would stand that way, a tableau of accusation, until Thorgill's murderer walked in the door and slit their throats where they stood. Then Kate Gathers shifted the child off her lap. "He didn't know," she pointed out, "since nobody's told him anything that would make sense out of what we're doing."

"He knows," Col answered, "but he doesn't believe it."

"I'm sure you gave him the family history, Col." Her glance was more rueful than accusing as she repaired the damage Leach had done to the line of salt across the threshold. "But did you tell him anything useful, like what to expect when we go after Anris? I didn't think so."

The indulgent warmth in her voice took the sting out of the words, and Geoff realized that she was defending him against her family. Maybe he had an ally in this madhouse; he let her take his hand and lead him to a chair by the window. She didn't let him go, and he flushed slightly, though her touch was strangely comforting. Col Gathers watched from his place by the fire; Leach noticed that the people in the room seemed to turn toward the man as if warmed by his presence, the low-burning coals in the fireplace a mere afterthought. In that room, separated from London by the centuries, it seemed, as much as the miles, Leach could almost believe his sergeant was some kind of pagan king. In the faces of the strangers, he saw Gathers' words come to life: "Needed them, depended on them, but never loved them." The bitterness in the voice returned to haunt him: Gathers didn't want to be here, didn't want the burden of these people's belief.

One person did seem to love Col Gathers, though. Kate Gathers looked toward her brother, support and understanding in the silent request for permission to go on. He gave it, Leach noted, with an almost imperceptible nod of his head, a gesture she returned.

"Katy, come sit with me," Gathers coaxed softly, and the child walked solemnly to the rocking chair, sparing a fleeting glance of wide-eyed suspicion for Leach when Col lifted her to his lap. She curled into the crook of his arm, and Gathers set the chair rocking gently.

When the child had settled, Kate Gathers took up her explanation. "The salt forms a barrier. Anris can't pass it, and if the barrier is strong enough, he can't force a physical body to pass it either. The fire in the fireplace is to keep Anris from coming in through the chimney. I know it sounds strange, but remember, he doesn't have a body to get stuck in the flue.

"The charms protect individual people: the salt keeps Anris from taking possession of the wearer's body, the garlic and iron are protection against less direct forms of attack as well as from possession. Each ingredient has a symbolic meaning that reflects its magical use. The sage, for example, is for wisdom. That means you should be able to recognize Anris when you see him, and you can avoid his more basic traps."

When she mentioned the charms, Leach glanced up and noticed that the newcomers were distributing the little sachets on their leather thongs that Col had made in the workroom. Each put the charm around his or her neck, let it settle in plain view above their hearts.

"You don't have to believe for the charm to work," Kate explained, "but you do have to wear it. We're

worried that you'll forget and take it off. Under
normal circumstances you would only endanger yourself—even with your body, Anris can't touch someone
protected by a charm. The gun complicates things—
we think he may be able to kill from a distance, using
your hand and your gun."

Murmurs of agreement circled the room like an
echo. Kate Gathers released his hand and went to
stand behind her brother. Col added his own blunt
warning to the explanation.

"The fact that you have killed before will make it
easier for him, and the charm was designed to stop a
ghost, not a bullet."

Leach paled, the words falling like a blow, and he
willed himself to be stone, to show nothing, while
everything he'd eaten on that short-ration day threatened to make a reappearance on Col Gathers' front
room floor. Visions of a child bleeding in his arms rose
up to gag him. Had to shoot, had to, with one man
dead and a second Molotov cocktail with a fistful of
nails in it in the boy's upraised throwing hand. He
hadn't meant to kill; smoke and the blood dripping
from his forehead into his eyes had obscured his aim.
And the boy had bled so much, so fast, there was
nothing he could do. Not his fault. They'd cleared
him, no blame attached, then sent him home with a
clean slate while the storm of it seethed on Derry's
uncertain streets. But God, "How did you know?"

"I'm not blaming you Geoff. I know you well
enough, at least, to realize that you would never, of
your own volition, deliberately kill anyone if you
thought you had a choice."

Full of qualifiers, Col's words did little to reassure.
No wonder they didn't want him here, a child killer in
a town beset by death. "How did you know?"

Col shook his head. "I haven't been hacking into

your file or talking about your private affairs with Hadley, if that's what you are asking. The real answer, well, you're about as ready for that as you are for any of this."

From her nest on Col's lap Katy gave him her solemn consideration, and he wondered if they'd told her what he'd done, if that was the reason she thought he would kill them all. "It's the shadow that sits on your soul. Dark," she said, "not scary, really, but very sad."

Leach stared at her, and Gathers smiled, kissed her on the head. "Smart girl," he said. "That's it exactly." He turned his attention back to Leach. "It's part of the training, to see past the outside of people when necessary."

"No," Katy corrected him, "Mommy teaches me not to look and not to tell when I forget and look anyway. Privacy."

"Yes, privacy," he agreed, and amended as he might a lesson for the girl, "but sometimes, when you really, really need to know, to save a life, it's okay to look."

"And so, we looked. We don't know who or what or why, Leach. No one back in London is gossiping behind your back. And we don't blame you for it—as Katy says, we see horror on your soul, not satisfaction, and no pleasure in any of it. But the experience is there, never far from your thoughts, and Anris will gravitate to it; he can use it, and your skill, to kill again and go on killing, while somewhere inside your head the Geoffrey Leach who killed and mourned and never let go of the guilt will scream to be allowed to die. And when he is done, when all of us are dead, Anris will set you free with all those memories."

Kate Gathers softened her brother's accusation with a milder warning: "That's the worst damage you can

do. Little things like scuffing through the house protections, or just ignoring the warnings that the charm
will give you can be dangerous as well."

"With Anris, you don't get a safety margin." Barbara Finlay's voice cut with icy disdain. "You haven't
a clue about what we are up against here. You don't
believe a word we say, and you are still hoping you
can get Col to carry a gun. Frankly, we're running out
of time, and we can't afford your pride—"

She made a grasping gesture in the air, and Geoff
felt the gun fly from the holster on his belt. The
Browning automatic flew across the room and fell
deep into the fire as if he'd thrown it there. Geoff
pushed through the circle of robed strangers and
lunged for the glowing coals, heedless of the heat. He
only knew that he could not lose the gun.

"No." Fingers closed around his right wrist. He
strained toward the fire with his free hand, and that
too was held fast. Col Gathers fell to one knee in front
of him, forced him to look up into fierce gray eyes bur-
nished silver in the firelight.

"Col—" Whatever coherent thought he may have
had fled then in a surge of pain so astonishing that he
could not draw breath. His hands, his hands. Upheld,
they burned like twin torches, turning Col Gathers'
eyes into blood-red pools: deep pools of flames
reflecting Leach's pain. In the eyes that looked back at
him or in the hands upraised before him, he could not
tell anymore, but, oh God, the pain, as flesh burned,
crackled in the flames of Col Gathers' eyes. The child
Katy stood between them, solemn but not afraid, and
Leach wanted to run, wanted to hide the grotesque
sight of his burning hands, wanted to smother the
screams he heard from where? Who?

"Illusion, Geoff. It's not real." Slowly Col Gathers
slid his fingers around Geoff's right hand, closing the

burning stubs of bone with his fist, and the pain cooled.

"Illusion." The word reached Geoff like a mantra, distant, cool, and slowly the pain faded, the fire went out.

"Look," Gathers commanded, and Geoff saw his hands, flesh intact, the skin not even pink from the experience.

"Touch." Gathers pressed Geoff's palm onto the cool butt of the gun, folded his fingers down, to curl around the weapon. "It was an illusion." Gathers' voice repeated, reassuring, "Illusion."

He stood and drew Geoff after him. Geoff felt some of the tension drain from his shoulders and found that his hands were once again free. He rubbed his wrists, though Col hadn't held them tightly enough to hurt— he needed to wipe away the feel of those minutes suspended over the fire, becoming fire.

Barbara Finlay turned to her brother with ice in voice. "He's defenseless. Get rid of him before we all die," she said, and took her place among the strangers at the center of the room.

"Go home, DCI Leach." Kate Gathers took Col's place at his side; her words were no less damning, but she spoke gently to him, holding his hand lightly, as she might a bird. "We can't protect you here. We need all of our energy to protect ourselves and do the job."

Geoffrey Leach stared into her eyes and saw her brother there. He felt the woman measuring him, weighing Col's safety in the quality of his response. He didn't like it, but he didn't resent it from her, either.

"I can't leave him here alone."

"Alone!" Barbara Finlay snorted, but Col Gathers silenced her with a gesture.

"I told you that's what he'd say," a familiar voice drawled from behind him. Tuttle, shifted to a chair by the window. He set a bottle of ale on the table at his elbow and grabbed a sandwich from the plate. "Not that it will stop him from doing something stupid if given half a chance."

"I know." Col waved in the general direction of the table. "Sit down, Geoff. Don't talk, don't move." A bitter smile with no humor in it passed like a memory across his face before he added. "When this is over I'll put myself on disciplinary report for insubordination, if we make it that far."

He'd never seen that cold look in Col's eyes before, didn't think he could have stood against it if he wanted to. But Leach's gun had flown into the fire at a gesture from Col's half sister, and his hands had burned. The flames may have been imaginary, but the pain had been real; he flinched away from the memory of it, even knowing that it had happened only in his mind. He could not doubt the power that had torn away the illusion. So he found a chair at the table from where he could watch the room, and sat.

Col nodded. "We should get started."

The strangers moved quietly in the old cottage, setting candles in windows and on the table and the dresser. More candles already burned on the mantlepiece, and the fire on the hearth was stirred up in spite of the heat in the room. A small group inscribed a circle on the floor while an elderly woman told the rosary, and Tuttle drank his ale.

Geoff took in the faces but turned away from the flames darting on every side. He stared at his hands, trying to believe what he had almost done—what, for long moments, he thought he *had* done. He'd seen men with burned hands frozen into scarred claws and forced himself to imagine it: never to wrap his hand around a pint or feel the skin of a woman through his fingertips. Thorgill's insanity was contagious.

"It's all these city ways, now." The constable did not look at Geoff, but no one else was close enough to hear him. Geoff grunted a noncommittal acknowledgment. He noted the bitterness that tinged the man's voice when Tuttle gestured with his chin at the group circling in the center of the room.

Leach watched the child crawl through the circle, adding a five-pointed star within it while the robed figures set white candles at each point. When star and candles were set, Katy left the circle, careful to step over the chalk lines, and joined hands with the adults who chanted something just below the level where Leach might distinguish the words.

"That borders on child abuse, Constable." He tilted his head in Katy Gathers' direction. "Someone ought to put her to bed, not fill her head with hocus pocus and mass murder."

"Then why don't you step right up and do the deed, DCI?" Tuttle mocked him, he knew, but still he sat, unable to act against the drone of slowly moving figures at the center of the room. Beside him, Tuttle sighed.

"Don't put any stock in it myself, Inspector Leach." Tuttle pointed to the star in the circle. "Not the old way, you understand, but city folk with new magic, later than Anris for sure. And they pull the power in the land, wake up the dead with their chanting. Archaeologists come out from the city, breaking into tombs not even knowing what they may be rousing. And where are the Finlays when all these city folks are stirring things up here in Thorgill? They're back in the city, pretending they don't have an obligation old as time itself to protect this town. Granny Finlay's dead in her grave only six months, and already Anris is out.

"So you take what help you can get when those who are supposed to protect the town abandon it. You learn how to accept that help gracefully. It's not a bad thing, after all, to learn respect for someone else's belief. Not that it will matter in the long run, of course. If Colly doesn't stay, you'll see Thorgill dead before Katy reaches her next birthday."

Geoff dropped his head and contemplated his ale. He never got close to his men: didn't want to know more about them than he needed. Were they good at the job? Col Gathers was damned good. Could you depend on them? Sometimes Gathers had seemed like a second right arm, the work ticking in the give and take of suspicion and evidence and perpetrator. The man never forgot a thing, and his intuitive leaps, carefully leashed with the DCI's demand for proof, logic, evidence, had taken them to more than one success he couldn't have achieved without that input. Thorgill was more proof than he needed that knowing too much could destroy two years of carefully built trust.

But stay here? Leach couldn't see it. The place fit Col Gathers like a hand-tailored straightjacket. He tried to imagine walking away, leaving Gathers behind forever, but he couldn't make it real. Only the blood on the carpet a few short months ago had substance. He stared at his hands and tried hard not to think at all, but the gun weighed heavily at his side. Whatever else happened, the damned fool wasn't dying on his watch.

A sound at his side drew his attention. Tuttle stretched and yawned. "Better be on my way," he announced to the room in general.

Col looked up at him, letting his glance slide briefly over the DCI. "We've a patch of floor for you here if you want to stay."

Tuttle shook his head. "Got my rounds, and after, I think I'll sleep in the jailhouse. If there's trouble, folks should know where to find me."

Gathers nodded and followed him to the door. "Be careful."

Tuttle nodded. "DCI Powell will be back in the morning. I'll meet you first thing, up on the moor. I've gone over everything with him already, but you may as well get it straight from the horse's mouth."

"Thanks."

Leach saw the troubled frown as the sergeant watched the man go out the door.

"Problem?" he asked.

"Probably not," Gathers answered slowly. "Just thinking."

"You're too tired for heavy exercise." Leach said it like a joke, but he meant it. Gathers looked drawn in the candlelight that lost its hold over the darkness at the open door. Maybe it was a trick of the shadows, but Leach thought not. "You may have these people believing you are indestructible, but it doesn't take a fortuneteller to see you are out on your feet."

"Soon," Gathers promised. And, in fact, the circle at the center of the room was breaking up. Robed figures returned the candles to the table and filed out with a respectful nod to Col at the door. When the last of them had gone, Leach realized that Barbara Finlay had gone with them; he was alone with Col Gathers, Kate, and the little girl already half asleep again on the settle.

Leach began to relax. A few more minutes of family good-byes and they'd be on their way to York and the sanity of a modest hotel for what remained of the night.

Col picked up Katy and disappeared through a side door, returning a few moments later. The expression on his face unsettled Leach, but he didn't quite know why. It was just a softening, a warm, family-type look that had warned him he was in for snapshots and teething reports in the squad room, but it didn't sit well on Col Gathers.

"Time to go, Sergeant," he said, "We'll want to get an early start tomorrow, get a look at the crime scene as soon as we have the light."

"I'm staying here, Geoff, in Granny's workroom, to guard the back door. It seems a likely target if Anris is about tonight."

"Ah, come on, Sergeant! If he's a ghost, you've got your hocus pocus. If he's a killer, you've got locks on the doors. Unless you have reason to believe he's coming after you personally, I think you can take time off to sleep."

"It is personal, sir." Col put more emphasis on that last syllable than it needed. "That's why I am here, after all."

Kate Gathers interrupted the brewing argument. "Laura Simms, who runs the tea shop, has a room or two she lets to tourists during the season," she said. "If you wouldn't mind staying here tonight, she can have a room ready for you tomorrow morning."

"I can't put you to any inconvenience," Leach objected, and the objection went heart deep. Bad enough he had to see this relic from a past age that Col Gathers called home—he did not want to sleep under the man's roof. But Kate Gathers gave him no out.

"Nonsense," she said. "You can have Granny Finlay's bed. She won't need it."

"Don't be gruesome, Kate." Col threw an arm around his sister's shoulders, a wry smile easing some of the tension in his face. "But she's right—you won't find your way back to Pickering at this hour, and I can't take the time to drive you. And Granny is safely dead and much too much a lady to haunt a sleeping gentleman."

Since Leach had no idea where Pickering was, this

seemed quite likely. "All of this is highly irregular," he pointed out, and added, "I seem to be a prisoner of your hospitality, ma'am." If he was giving in, it would be to the lady of the house, not to the sergeant who had put him in this position and who would have hell to pay once they got back to London.

Kate smiled and took his arm. "This way," she said, and showed him to a boxed staircase he hadn't noticed until then. "It's at the top of the stairs. And Granny had her own lavatory put in, so you'll have everything you need."

She left him there, and Geoff stared into the shadows with trepidation until Col reached around him and flicked a switch. A light went on at the top of the stairs.

"Good night, sir," Gathers said, and the brief, sardonic glint in the man's eyes told Leach the man knew what the DCI expected—no lights, no heat, no running water, and a straw-filled mattress. He didn't need the heat, but in the end Leach found that Granny had done okay by the tiny upstairs room. The thatch was real, all right, and low enough that he could reach up and touch it at its highest point. But the light at the bedside was electric, the water ran hot, and the mattress was quite modern and in excellent condition.

CHAPTER 6

Early morning sunshine filtered through clouds before dribbling past the workroom windows. It drenched Col Gathers with watery light but no heat. The light didn't awaken him, however—the dreams had. They'd been bad this time.

Over and over again he'd smelled the dust of the derelict terrace house, heard the sound of running feet where no one was supposed to be, then turned and stared death in the face as the bombers' lookout darted around the corner of the upper landing and shot. Always it seemed to happen in slow motion, until the jolt of the bullet shattered his sleep. This time when he turned to face his killer, he looked into the eyes of DCI Geoffrey Leach at the other end of the gun.

Gathers knew where that dream came from; Anris wouldn't win that easily. He replaced the images with his own memories. They'd gotten the guy who shot him and gotten the explosives they'd gone in for. Geoff had been there, holding onto him until the ambulance arrived. When unconsciousness wouldn't come, and the sharp pain from the bullet was nothing compared to his fear at the bubbling froth of blood at his lips and the liquid obstinance of his lung refusing to take in air, he'd held onto Geoff's hand and followed desperate orders to breathe, damn him, breathe. To stay alive.

He'd seen Leach's own fear written so plainly on the man's features that he didn't dare die because of what it would add to the ghosts Leach carried. Geoff would back him against the devil himself to atone for that one second when the sound of a bullet told the DCI that this time a tactical error might cost him Col Gathers' life.

No, Anris might try, but he could not move Col's faith from that one certainty. Not even now, when an error in judgment could kill them all. The man just needed time; he couldn't help it that time was the one thing they didn't have. Geoff would give him the gun. Col Gathers would wait until the DCI was ready. Somehow. Shaking off the last of the morning cobwebs, he went in search of breakfast.

Kate stood at the dresser, cutting slabs of bread that she spread with fresh butter and marmalade. Tea steamed in a pot at her elbow.

"You look awful," she said, handing him a cup of tea.

"Dreams," he explained, and she nodded her understanding. The bloody images Anris fed them wouldn't go away until they'd put him back in his tomb, or until he'd killed them.

"Barbara was in a few minutes ago. She says the village is worried."

"That's a bloody surprise," Col noted, and sipped the hot tea.

"Katy's been alone too long. She needs a brother. They're afraid the line will end now, with Anris being out and both of us as likely as not to die bottling him up again."

Kate didn't look at him, just sliced the bread, and

the thud of the knife on the cutting board became the sound of a bullet impact. Again. Again.

"Don't you think you've cut enough bread?" he asked, and she looked down, at the loaf in thin slices on the dresser.

"It'll feed the birds," she said, but she set aside the knife. "I don't like this any more than you do, Col. Hell, it's going to play havoc with *my* life, not yours. But they won't go on until it's done."

Col set the cup down carefully, the muscles in his hand rigid with the effort not to smash it against the wall. "Maybe it's time we put a stop to it, dragged Thorgill out of the Bronze Age and into the twentieth century. Here. Now. We can do like the Americans say, and just tell the good citizens of Thorgill, 'No.' "

"And Anris?" she countered. "He'll kill us—all right, maybe he would anyway. But think of Katy. Think of what he could do to her. See her, Col, with blood on her hands and Anris' smile on her face. Without the village, we've got no chance; without an heir, we've got no village. Barbara has set it up for tonight. Just make sure the Detective Chief Inspector is out of the way and occupied, or you'll have more to explain than the seven dead bodies on our hands."

"Leach." Col wiped his hands across his face, but he could not erase the marks the dreams had left.

Her frown was answer enough, but Kate told him what he already knew. "I saw him hurting you and enjoying it. Are you sure you trust him?"

"You know who sent the dream—it's Anris we have to fight, not each other."

"Not going to answer the lady, Sergeant?"

Geoff stepped out of the box stairwell from Granny Finlay's bedroom. He looked more rested than either of the Gathers, but you never could tell with him. More disturbing was the way he moved: light on his feet, his eyes narrowed, watchful. No confidences about dreams here.

"You know I do. Just *be* there—I hate looking the fool."

"Anything you say, Sergeant." Leach drawled the assurance with a broadly false cockney twang that emphasized the usurpation of authority, but Col Gathers heard the fear and confusion behind it. Anris had crawled into more than one bed last night, and Col wondered what horrors the earthbound spirit had teased out of Leach's memory to feed back to him in a closed loop of blood and terror.

"Trust me for just one day, Geoff." The words came out somewhere between supplication and an order. "Give me tomorrow, and we've got him."

"Maybe," Leach temporized. "And maybe tomorrow I'm going back alone, with your death certificate in my pocket. I'm not planning to take out any of the locals, Col. I didn't come here for vigilante justice, and with any luck the damned gun will never leave its holster. But we've got too many bodies on this one to go in unarmed."

Gathers shook his head. "I hope nobody has to die to convince you, Geoff." He kissed Kate on the forehead. "Set it up, then, but be careful."

He headed for the door to the workshed, turned with his hand on the latch. "Tuttle should be meeting us at the tumulus. I'll see you there."

"Wait," Leach called out, and Gathers stopped. "How will I find it?"

"Hard to miss," Col answered, "but Kate can bring you up after you've finished your tea. You'll want to start asking questions when we're done up there— Tuttle will have a list with him."

He closed the door and made his way through the workshed. For once the smell of the place, herbs and medicinal flowers, moist earth and the musky scent of growing things, gave him no peace. He missed Granny Finlay, badly. He still couldn't quite believe the stern old biddy was gone. She'd been their anchor and purpose, and she'd wielded the power of the Finlay with firm authority through all the years of Col's life. He left the workshed and, as he moved out into her garden, he could almost see her there in her long dress and apron, kneeling amid the rosemary and the thyme. The breeze teased at him, and he heard Granny Finlay's soft voice echoing hard truths in his mind: the history of Thorgill, of Anris, and his duty. He remembered her serene face, carved with the deep lines of age even then, when he was as young as Katy, and her indulgent sigh when his temper sent dishes and potted herbs flying. She made him clean them up again and take longer practice sessions of calming meditation. Being the Finlay was all about control she told him over and over again.

His grandmother had known what he would become and had worked longer and harder with him than with any of his cousins to teach him the discipline he would need. Gradually, five thousand years of duty had seeped into his soul. Col Gathers had sworn to protect Thorgill as had all the Finlays before him, but he hadn't expected the call to come in his lifetime. He wasn't ready, but he figured the original Finlay hadn't been ready either.

Why me? Why now? He asked of the garden, but no answer came to him while the mist burned away overhead, leaving a sky of pale-washed gray and the shoulder of the dale rising at his back door. Enough. Passing through the patch of herbs, Col easily found the old path up through the multilevel flower garden built around the stones and old railroad ties to keep the dirt in place and the wild out. Back farther, where the path wandered left to the rivulet at the bottom of the dale, he took the right fork, up past the gnarled old oak tree clinging to the gentle slope, up, as the path grew steeper, to the break in the stone wall at the crest. Suddenly, the carefully manicured patchwork of the dale was behind him, and the end of creation opened up to the horizon.

Curlews called as they wheeled overhead, and a rabbit scampered at his feet in the bracken that rose almost hip-deep in places. Barren sticks now, by the end of the summer the heather would bloom in billowing folds like a crumpled blanket. In the late spring death rested on the land—no, not dead, but waiting, the skeins of creation left in an unmade tumble for the late summer. He picked his way through the tangle of low-growing branches, watching for the springs that turned the land marshy underfoot. As he moved deeper into the stark wildness of a world unmade, the old call filled him, and he moved faster, away from civilization and careful growth and saying good morning to your neighbors.

Here, he let the wildness swell in his heart, felt the moors draw him back as surely as the dale below drove him away. The moors bred the wildness into his bones. The dale tried to tame him, control the wild reach of him. They wanted creation, but he felt in himself the powerful sweep of destruction, the drive to unmake the universe and all its rigid order. Here, wrapped in the mist, with the sound of the bees and the bleats of the few rugged sheep grazing on the marsh grass and bark, he felt his kinship, not with the Finlay but with the earthbound spirit. Had Anris felt this draw of the unmaking of creation as well? Had five thousand years in his tomb festered an insanity made more acute by the need for chaos that churned in his soul?

What would it be like, trapped in that narrow tomb, inescapable, constrained like the oak that struggled for survival on the lip of the dale. Better to die here, Col thought, free, than to beat himself to madness against the darkness for eternity. He reached for the charm at his heart and held it tight.

"Here I am," he said, and smiled.

CHAPTER 7

Gathers closed the door, leaving Leach alone with Kate. For the moment, at least, Geoff reminded himself.

"Where is Katy this morning? I thought she'd be up with the birds," he observed.

"She was. She went down to the village to spend the morning with some friends." Kate offered him a cup of tea, and Leach took it with a stiff nod of his head.

"Thank you, ma'am. Is Ms. Finlay about?"

"Barbara? She's in the village as well, checking on some of the neighbors."

"I see." Leach drank, watching her cautiously over his cup. "You're worried about Col," he concluded after a moment's observation, and could have kicked himself for stating the obvious like it was a grand revelation. But his next words surprised him as much as they did Kate Gathers: "I'll send him back to London this morning if you think he's in danger, have him send a few of the lads to take the brunt of the legwork."

"Too late, Inspector." She shook her head, a grim smile crossing her features, "Too late by about five thousand years. Are you finished with your tea?"

Geoff put his cup down and followed her through the workshed. Once outside, he stopped, his mouth slightly agape, and looked at the shoulder of the moor lifting over the tiny cottage.

"The tumulus is right up there." Kate Gathers pointed to a low mound of grass-covered earth and stone on the moor above them.

A stone fence about waist high marked the line where the side of the dale crested at the moor. Leach wondered why they had built that wall, what monsters its long-dead builders meant to keep out, or what they meant to shut inside the tiny green hollow. He couldn't imagine Col Gathers staying on this side of the fence, ever, and the thought of the sergeant as a small boy made him profoundly uncomfortable.

"Shall we, then?" He turned and gave her a professional smile. She answered with a smile of her own, and he wondered if she'd somehow read his thoughts in his expression. Whatever she saw, she did not mention it, but led him through the garden to a gently sloping path that covered the side of the valley at an easy angle.

The sound of a tractor drifted toward them from across the dale, and somewhere down nearer the bottom of its bowl, where the cluster of the village rested, the motor of a car with a faulty muffler rattled loudly with the rip of gears.

"When Col and I were growing up here, you could go all week and never hear a motor," Kate said. "The world seemed to move only as fast as children wanted it to do back then. Col spent most of the summer on the moor, exploring. He couldn't get enough of it. We'd go looking for him long after dinner was over— we could never find him, but he'd always be waiting in Granny Finlay's house when we came back. He'd hide out there, knowing Mum would tear into him for scaring her so. Granny wouldn't ever let anyone scold

Colly for roaming, though—she said it was part of what made him king."

"Spoiled, then, was he?" Leach asked. He didn't really want to know, but he thought the confidence required some sort of comment.

"Not at all," Kate laughed. "Granny was right. We all knew Colly would follow as the next king."

"Some king," Leach mumbled, thinking of who called whom "sir," in London, and who gave the commands.

Kate shook her head. "The title hasn't meant anything politically since before Magna Carta, and as for wealth, well, what there was went to the British Museum a generation ago. Today, I guess the closest description would be a religious title. Col told you about the natural power, didn't he?"

"You mean magic, hocus pocus stuff, like voodoo," Leach corrected her carefully. This was where the whole thing got weird.

"Not exactly," Kate corrected in her turn. "Being king means that the person descends from the direct line of the Finlay and that he or she still possesses the power of the original of the line. It doesn't confer any authority over the village anymore. You could think of it as being a reservist subject to call up if the need arises. The need has arisen, and we have returned as required, but Col has the greatest responsibility. Between us he was the stronger, and so he was named king." She smiled then; her eyes grew distant, unfocused, and Leach wondered what memory she saw. When she spoke again, her tone carried the promise of shared confidences. "Granny really had a job of it bringing him under control. We sometimes wondered if the village would survive his geisting time. He could break windows from one end of the dale to the other when he was upset, and he once accidentally set three of Jesse Morgan's haystacks on fire trying to light Granny's fireplace—good on power, our Col, bad on location accuracy!"

Leach felt her eyes on him, questioning under the playfulness in her voice. It sounded crazy. It was crazy, but she seemed to be waiting for some kind of response. She wasn't giving away any clues about what she wanted from him, though.

"Look," he said, "I sincerely doubt that you are telling me family stories about Sergeant Gathers' strange behavior as a child just to pass the time. So why don't you tell me, straight out, what you want me to get out of this little tale. And while you're at it, you might tell me what you think it has to do with mass murder of archaeologists."

"Why do I need an ulterior motive, Chief Inspector?" she asked, but the laughter had gone from her face. She stood a few paces above him on the slope, looking down into his eyes with an expression that would have been at home on the face of a judge. Or, given the circumstances, a madman.

A light drizzle began, shrouding the moor above them with unnatural dusk. Leach shivered and tried to put it out of his mind; ghosts existed only in the fertile minds of the gullible. He rested one elbow on his right knee, bent for balance on the rise of the slope. *No challenge—just the facts, ma'am*, he thought. But when he started to answer her question, he found he could not look into her eyes. Instead, he stared at the tumulus, its outline obscured by the drizzle above them on the moor.

"Since I entered this little town," he said, "I've been dead, briefly, the gun I carried has mysteriously flown into the fire and reappeared at my side when I reached to fish it out again. I can find no reasonable explanation for these facts but the possible use of an hallucinogenic gas and its aftereffects. The same residual effects could have caused the strange dreams I had last night—" he stole a glance at her then. "You knew about the dreams, as well as the other, didn't you?"

She nodded. "Not until you came downstairs this morning," she added, "I could tell by the way you looked at my brother. You killed him, didn't you? In the dream, I mean?"

He did not grace the question with an answer she already knew. "Do you know the principle of Occam's razor?" he asked instead.

"The simplest solution is likely to be the correct solution, if I recall, Inspector. I'm a teacher, you know, not a . . . whatever you may have thought."

Leach left that one hanging. In truth, he hadn't known what to expect of her, and he still didn't. With an effort he picked up the thread of his explanation. "Exactly. The principle is an important one in our line of work, you see. If someone has the motive, the opportunity, and the ability to commit a crime, then we investigate that person more thoroughly, to find whatever evidence supports the suspect's guilt or innocence. We don't waste time on those suspicious characters who could not have committed the crime for one reason or another. And policemen have what you might call Occam's corollary: suspect anyone who tries to spin an explanation more complicated than the circumstances require."

"Going to put the cuffs on now, copper?"

She drawled the words, her hands held out to him, wrists together and Leach grew very still.

"Are you confessing?" he asked, so softly he was not sure she heard.

But she had. "Are you making an accusation, Inspector?"

"Not yet." Leach gusted an explosive sigh and ran

his hand through his damp hair. Damn it! He couldn't read her, couldn't tell whether she was laughing at him or trying to tell him something.

"Six lives ended brutally just outside your idyllic little cottage, Ms. Gathers." Frustration made him angry, and he didn't try to hide it from her. "Young lives, with fathers and mothers who will never see their children again. Jerry Monk, one of the dead, had a wife and two children who were to join him here next week. They will never see their husband or father again, not even in his casket, because your local murderer made such a mess of his body.

"Now, I have two possible solutions for this crime. One, that somehow a hallucinogenic material has been introduced into the environment of the village of Thorgill, producing the symptoms experienced here last night and, in all likelihood, the madness of your murderer. Or two, a ghost is flitting about town trading parlor tricks with the locals while killing off strangers.

"The rule of Occam's razor tells me the correct answer is the first. The policeman's corollary tells me that the person or persons most invested in the alternative, more complicated explanation must have a motive for that explanation that needs investigating.

"This is where we stand today, Ms. Gathers. Someone murdered six outsiders, and your house is the closest structure to the crime scene. In your home, and in the automobile of your brother, the effects of this hallucinogen manifested themselves most strongly. And you and your family, with the aid of your local constable, have gone out of your way to put forward a completely preposterous alternative theory for the murders. This does not seem, to me, to be a fitting matter for levity."

"No, Inspector, you are correct. Call it gallows humor, if you will."

Leach gave her a long, thoughtful look. What was she covering? He found it hard to suspect her—after all, she was the only person he had spoken to directly in this town who had not threatened him. He could easily believe that Barbara Finlay had the icewater nerves it took to murder with impunity. He would not have thought she had the physical strength to overcome and vivisect four strong young men and two women in the space of thirty hours, any more than Kate Gathers did. But if Col hadn't stopped her last night, she might have . . . no, stay clear of that image. But the vision returned with the smell of fear and burning flesh, his arms plunging elbow-deep into the fire, burning like torches. And she hadn't needed to raise a hand to make him do it.

Tuttle had the physical strength, and he'd wanted Leach gone as well, had even taken advantage of the hallucinogens still in his system to frighten him away. But he'd felt the effects of the drug first in Col's presence. The unanswered questions from that ride from the York police station in the borrowed Fiat came back to him then. "Where did your brother go on holiday, Ms. Gathers?"

Kate looked at him blankly. "What holiday, Inspector?"

"Hadley called him back from holiday for this case. Do you know where he went?"

"Not here, if that is what you are asking me, Inspector." She didn't look at him but turned instead to face the village below. "He doesn't come home anymore, almost wouldn't come to Granny's funeral. Mum shamed him into it."

"But you don't know?" He didn't want to think it, but he couldn't ignore Col's strange behavior since the beginning of the case. He couldn't ignore the fact that Col had been present at all three incidents of the hallucinations and he'd been on holiday when the murders had occurred. He considered the one solid objection he had: physically, Col still suffered the aftereffects of the shooting. The sergeant simply didn't have the strength to overpower and kill those people.

But Leach seemed to be the only one with any doubts about Gathers' condition. The docs had cleared him, Hadley had sent him. And the night before, Barbara Finlay hadn't needed to overpower Leach physically; she'd controlled his mind so completely he'd have sliced himself open if she told him to.

He closed his eyes for a moment, but the newborn suspicion would not go away. Col Gathers had the opportunity. With the hallucinogens, he had the means; Barbara Finlay had taken advantage of the drugs in Leach's system, but only Sergeant Gathers had been present for all three of the hallucination attacks. And Kate Gathers had given him a motive. Col hated the village, hated the claims made on him by his family and neighbors. And somehow, he'd tied those feelings into the legends about the tomb above his home.

"Did your brother do this, Kate?" His voice almost broke on the question. He'd dealt with dishonest policemen, knew that crimes of passion did not respect a uniform. But the police stood between an innocent public and the insanity of a world without rules. If the police were insane, what hope did any of them have?

"If he's guilty, he's a sick man. We can prove that, get him help. But we can't let him go on like this. He has to be stopped, before he kills again."

He would not let his real question shape itself in words: if Col Gathers was mad, what chance did Geoffrey Leach have to control the madness hiding behind his own memories? "It could be you next time, or the child." No time now to mourn a child bleeding on a Londonderry pavement. "Tell me what you know, and we can stop this thing, together."

Kate stared at him for a moment as if he had suddenly grown a second head, and then she laughed softly, with tears gathering in the corners of her eyes.

When she looked back at him, her expression had turned hard and grim. She almost seemed to grow taller in front of him, and he found himself unable to move. "My brother is guilty of two things, Inspector. He abandoned his responsibilities to this village, for which he may pay with his life. And he has tried to keep you alive, for which he seems to be paying with the loss of your trust.

"Occam's razor, indeed," she whispered, looking up at the top of the slope, not at him. "When you have lived all of your life in the shadow of Anris' tomb, the obvious answer may differ from that of a London policeman. I suppose that can't be helped, but if we survive tomorrow, I will make you eat those words."

He would have handed Kate Gathers his doubts then, and the beating heart from his breast, but she passed a hand across her face and something faded from Geoff's perception of her. He could move again, and did, striking out for the top of the slope as fast as he could. The policeman in him mocked him for running away. But his only explanation—that he had sat with Gathers' blood warm on his hands, had felt sorrow, but no evil in its touch—made as much sense as Col's stories about ghosts and long-dead kings. He needed proof. And then he needed to do his duty. How he felt didn't matter.

CHAPTER 8

"Col? Colin!"

A voice, he recognized it as Kate's voice, wormed its way past Col Gathers' resolve. And Leach walked beside her. The DCI would learn more about him than either of them wanted him to know this day. He sighed and waited where he stood, not quite able yet to let go of the charm at his neck. It would be so easy . . .

She saw him then; he heard it in the panic that pulled him back from his own private abyss: "Colin, don't!" and he let go, thinking of clifftops, his body broken but his soul free at the bottom of the fall. When he looked up at her, he knew they shared the meaning but not the feeling of that moment of his weakness. Kate still believed they could succeed and live to write the report. She did not want her brother to die.

Colin recognized his own cowardice in the act he contemplated. Too many lives depended on the duty his birth bound him to perform. What did one soul, even his own, matter in that balance? He shivered, realized the chill was only partly dread. Soft rain had begun falling since his mind had wandered. The weather suited his mood, he decided, letting both arms hang loosely. He walked slowly toward his sister while he pulled his thoughts together. They met a few yards from the tumulus.

From the cottage below one could not see the changes the archaeologists had wrought on the site, but now he looked about him with dismay. They'd been staying in the village, so the site itself supported only one large tent, for sorting and washing the finds. But they had cleared the bracken in a wide circle around the mound and added a narrow asphalt cart track to the site from the main track a mile away. A battered Volvo sat on the asphalt near the tent.

If you didn't know what to look for, the tumulus might have been just another rocky outcrop. The circle of beaten earth, damp with the morning drizzle, uncovered more of its substructure than Col had ever seen before, but if he didn't know better, it would still look like a tumble of stone left in an unruly heap by the last ice age. In fact, it looked like most major burial finds for this place and era, with just a few important differences. Archaeologists might puzzle over those differences, but Col knew why they existed, and their meaning chilled him.

It faced the wrong direction, for one thing. Oriented north to south, Anris' prison never received direct sunlight, never warmed, not even on the solstice. The chill was more than an effect of weather and orientation, though; a proper tomb oriented east and west so that the soul of the dead could find its way to the next world by following the path of the sun. But Anris was not going home. The cold of eternal darkness was the doom set upon the soul trapped here by a people whose blood flowed through his veins.

Trapped long ago, but the archaeologists had set him free on the people of Thorgill now. The largest stone that had sealed the entrance to the tomb lay tumbled on its side, several high-powered battery lamps propped against it. Yellow tape, stretched on stakes, surrounded the crime scene. Within the cleared perimeter, the air held the cold of the tomb, rank with decay.

A man and a woman waited just outside the yellow tape. Col recognized the iron-haired woman in the tweed jacket and trim slacks. "Beth," he said.

"Colin!" The woman ignored Gathers' hand and gave him a hug. "And Kate! How is Katy, then?" She hugged his sister.

"National Trust send you?" he asked. Of course, they must have, he knew.

"Uhuh," she mumbled over Kate's shoulder. "I was in York already, so I came up with the forensics people yesterday." She straightened, visibly paler. "I've never seen anything like it, Col. Whoever did this must be completely insane!" She swallowed convulsively and pulled herself together with an effort.

"I'm supposed to keep the police from mucking up the findings at the site, keep it viable for study. Speaking of which, this is Inspector Powell, from York."

"I'll settle for a handshake," the man said. He was taller than Col, and solid, about thirty-five, and he'd run into the wrong end of a fist somewhere, judging from the crink in the bridge of his nose. Col took the man's hand in a brief clasp and finished his own introductions: "DCI Geoffrey Leach, New Scotland Yard, seconded at request."

"We were expecting just the sergeant," Powell said. "But since you're here, you may as well take a look at these." He handed over a file folder, and Col caught a glimpse of a forensics report—no photos this time, thank God."

Col waited until Leach glanced up from the file, then continued the introduction. "Inspector Leach, this is Dr. Beth Newton. She oversees research projects in Neolithic culture for the National Trust."

Newton shook Leach's hand and turned back to Col Gathers. "I'm surprised anyone in London had the sense to send you, Col, but I'm very glad they did. Makes this job a little easier.

"His special expertise will prove invaluable to you, I'm sure," she explained to Powell.

"And what expertise is that?" Leach's tone was soft, but Col Gathers didn't trust it or the blandly expectant expression that Leach usually trotted out to convince suspects he knew more than he did.

Beth Newton frowned, her glance darting from Col to the DCI and back again. "His studies in the culture of the Neolithic period, of course. I don't know why you are here, Inspector Leach, but I had assumed your superiors assigned Sergeant Gathers because he had some experience in the field. He didn't finish his degree, of course—shifted into abnormal psychology, if I recall, didn't you, Colin?—but your father still has hopes you will return to the fold."

"The fold? Could you explain that, please?" Leach asked, patiently questioning the witness, and Newton looked decidedly uncomfortable about it. "Am I speaking out of turn, Col? I mean, why else would you be here?"

"I had thought it was his knowledge of the current residents," Leach provided with a smile that Col Gathers did not trust one bit. "But apparently there is more to our Detective Sergeant than meets the eye."

Col interrupted while he had a shred of credibility left with his superior officer. "My father, Jack Gathers, is curator of indigenous Neolithic artifacts at the British Museum," he explained, "but his special area of interest is reconstructing ancient cultural practices from vestigial folklore. My mother's people come from Thorgill. They met when he was doing field interviews here, I'm told. They married, and eventu-

lly I followed him into the field. My stay in archae-
logy was brief—the pull of the living proved more
owerful than that of the long-dead—but my father
till fosters hopes best left at rest."

He took a deep breath, giving Leach more truth
han the man would recognize: "I don't talk about it
ecause I left all that behind, just a false start and not
vorth mentioning."

"I see." Leach seemed to drop the subject for the
noment, his expression its most blandly professional.
Then you'd know how to make one of these axes the
nurderer used."

Kate smothered a short laugh, and the archaeologist
ave her a conspiratorial wink before turning back to
each. "If you want to see how it is done, I'd better
how you. Col never did get the knack. He took after
is father that way—better at collecting stories than
vorking with artifacts."

"I'll hold you to that, after we've had a look
round," Leach agreed. The DCI turned away, but Col
elt the dangerous edge of the question. If Gathers
eeded more proof, Kate's worry provided it. She took
is hand and held on tight. So, he'd become prime
uspect, had he? That did complicate things, not least
ecause his own feelings teetered on a raw edge up
ere, in the place where friends had died.

"How is Dad?" Kate asked Newton.

The archaeologist sighed, something dark behind
er eyes. "He knows the village, would have been the
etter choice to act as liaison with the police, but he's
retty torn up about the murders. And your mother is
n quite a state, but I don't have to tell you what some-
hing like this would mean to her."

Col nodded, knowing that Leach was taking in
very word and that there'd be hell to pay for it before
hey were through. Ironic: he'd spent the whole of his

new life in London trying to escape his birth and now, with the old curse rising up to snatch him back, all the things that he had done to deny its existence made him look guilty of the very murders he had been born to stop.

If only he'd been more open with Leach when they were both back in London—but he knew that had never been possible. Leach invited confidences as little as Gathers offered them, and Col couldn't think of a single time in the two years he'd known the DCI when the man would have accepted this story. And it would get worse, no matter which way things went in the next two days. Maybe Tuttle had been right—they should have locked Leach up and set him free when they were done. At least then Col wouldn't be standing in front of the one place he hated more than any in the universe, waiting for his superior officer to arrest him.

But Col believed in the right to choose—that's why he'd gone to London, after all—and he couldn't deny that right to Geoffrey Leach, no matter what it cost them. So he walked a tightrope of words. On the one side he found the worried concern of a teacher who had known him all his life and who admired his father in spite of, not because of, his eccentric views about Thorgill's legends. On the other he found the suspicion of his superior officer, who was moving him rapidly up the list of possible maniacal killers. He devoutly wished they'd both go home.

"Da and Jerry Monk were pretty close," he acknowledged, turning his attention back to Beth Newton. "He was Jerry's tutor, stood up for their oldest. He'll feel responsible for Mary and the kids at a time like this."

"Yes, I can see that." The archaeologist paused. "Joe Bartram was in the program when you were, and Janet Tyler," she said, and Col nodded.

"I didn't know them well," he added. When he'd heard about the dig, he'd contacted one or two old friends and talked them out of coming up here. Janet had responded, with her usual arrogance, that it was worth the trip just to disprove Jack Gathers' culture survival theory. Well, now Janet knew, and Joe had paid a high price for following her. Col figured he had until the squad in London contacted Leach with the results of their background interviews to get the job done, because after that he'd be in the nick, awaiting trial.

"You know he tried to stop the dig," Newton added.

"Da? I didn't know, but I would have expected him to fight it. He always said there was more to the old stories he collected than scaring the children to keep them off the moors." Each child of Thorgill carried the moor bone-deep and in his soul, Col knew, and each learned the stories as lessons and as warnings about the thing that dwelt in the tomb. But Leach was looking at him with sad wariness, and Beth Newton had never believed Jack Gathers' theories. And they were running out of time.

"Where's Tut?" He scanned the low countryside surrounding the dig but found no sign of the constable. "Last night he said he would meet us here."

"Constable Tuttle?" Inspector Powell asked. "When I spoke to him yesterday, he said the same, but I haven't seen him yet. Do you want to wait?"

Col considered for a minute. Something didn't feel right, but then, nothing ever did in this place.

Before he could answer, Leach stepped in, taking charge with a cold nod. "The constable found the bodies, so he'll need to go over his statement and the forensics reports with us, but we can get a start with what we've got."

"Yes, sir." Col let go of his sister's hand and stepped to the mouth of the tomb.

"Is there room inside for two of us?" Leach asked. He picked up a high-powered lamp from alongside the tomb. Col nodded and realized that Leach had been waiting for that; the DCI had been watching him, not the archaeologist or the inspector from York, both of whom had actually been inside yesterday.

"All right then," Leach interrupted his dark ruminations. Gathers picked up a lamp and switched it on. With a last backward glance at his sister, he bent low and entered through the narrow tunnel-like opening. Then he felt it: something cold *lived* in this place, or lingered here undying through the ages. The sense of that presence clung to his skin like cobwebs, reaching to hold him here, and he gagged, reached out to balance himself.

Inside the floor of the tomb sloped down, so the roof of the stone chamber arching overhead actually gave them room to stand. At the deepest curve of the wall the body of Anris the magician lay. Little remained but bone, a flint ax head resting at the feet, his skull facing the altar that squatted between the body and the doorway. Gathers' stomach clenched painfully, imagination painting the picture . . .

"This is where they found the first two, and then the fourth?" Leach bent on one knee and touched the stained earth at the side of the altar.

Gathers shook his head. He didn't trust himself to speak for a moment, remembering in vivid detail the forensics photographs, the familiar faces distorted in terror and pain. "Joseph Bartram, Janet Tyler. Later they found Jerry Monk in the same place."

If he'd ever held any hope, it vanished here in Anris' resting place. The magician hadn't died alone here five thousand years ago; Col's sweeping glance found the second set of Neolithic remains, untouched by the current investigators—Beth Newton would have seen to that. The Finlay. He rested, head leaning back against the wall next to the entrance to the tomb: a grim watchman through the ages.

No gifts of food or flowers had ever lain beside this body, no vessels rested beside him to light his way into the next world. For all the evil they had brought on Thorgill, Col hoped that one good had come from opening the tomb: they had freed the Finlay. Col wished his long-dead ancestor well on his long trip home.

Then past and present seemed to merge in his vision: Gathers knew it was the fate of his kind, the tie between the jailer and the jailed so deep that it was sometimes hard to remember on which side of the prison bars he stood. The Finlay had passed beyond what little difference there might have been. If things went ill tomorrow, he might be called upon to do the same.

In the stillness of the tomb, an alien presence pulled at his scalp and the back of his neck. Anris remembered, recognized what Gathers was across the murky tracks of time. Col knew the creature wanted him, could feel it testing his strength and resolve.

Even Leach shivered in this unnatural chill. He stared at the rough stone platform at the center of the tomb, and in his face Gathers saw the nightmares coming home to roost. Blood that was old when Caesar ruled colored the stone.

"This is where they did it, then?"

Col nodded. He barely suppressed his dread and loathing in the straightforward narration: "Anris tortured and killed them on this stone. They found him here, and the Finlay killed him on his own altar. He held Anris' spirit bound to the stone while the survivors built the cairn around it. We've been guarding it ever since. Until now."

"I meant the archaeologists." Leach stared at him for a long minute.

"Them too." Col took a last look around them. "Let's get out of here. I've seen enough."

He didn't wait for Geoff to answer but ducked his head and plunged through the entrance, longing for sunlight, or even the feel of the drizzle on his face.

CHAPTER 9

Leach swept the beam of his lantern around the tomb, not so much to impress the image in his mind—he expected the place to take a starring role in his nightmares for a long time to come. No, he wouldn't forget, but still he could hardly credit it as real. The altar hunched there, new stains seeping into old, mingling the blood of how many people? The entire village of Thorgill might be mad, but the stone wore its own legacy of pain and death before him. The soil around it showed a pattern of richer brown from the new blood spilled here—worms had long ago eaten all signs of the first deaths in this place.

Surrounded by the stony cold of the grave, he unconsciously tried to hold his breath. Logic reminded him that the archaeologists had opened the tomb three days ago; the air had long since mingled with the fresh breezes of the moor. But a darker place he didn't know he had insisted that he breathed the air of the dead, that death entered his body with each indraw, and life departed with each exhale.

He shone the light on the corpse lying with a flint ax at his feet. The murder weapon in Thorgill this week had looked a lot like it, except that this one was older beyond his comprehension. This body had lain here before the Romans had passed through, put to rest with religious dignity before Christianity had come to

Britain. But those beliefs, and the people who held them, had died long ago, leaving fewer remains than the body stretched out in a shallow depression on the floor of the tomb. Or so he would have said yesterday afternoon.

Too much rode on the impossible answer to an insane question. Was this Anris, magician and murderer, or a hapless soul whose tomb inspired fantasies and whose rest had been disturbed first by the archaeologists, then by the madman roaming Thorgill? The beam of his lamp caught the second corpse, the guardian at the gate to heaven, according to Col Gathers, barring the dead with his own immortality. In the shadowy light of the lantern, the body seemed to transform itself; dark stains spattered on the blue uniform of a soldier gasping out his life on the broken pavement of a Londonderry street. Nails and slivers of glass decorated the wounds, sticky red in the glow of the sunset.

Why didn't men hurt that badly lose consciousness? He'd wondered that sitting next to Colin Gathers on the grimy floor of a condemned terrace house. *Hold on. Hold on.* Dunlop hadn't, cradled in his arms on the broken pavement. A child whose name he never knew hadn't, lying in the ruins of his own Molotov cocktail, Geoffrey Leach's bullet in his heart. A year or two older than Katy Gather? Not much more than that. He'd died quickly enough on those streets, not like Dunlop, who wept as the blood leaked from a hundred wounds concentrated in his abdomen.

If Col had done these things because he truly believed this king business, if he had murdered the outsiders in a twisted attempt to save the village, his home, from the predations of the local legend, he'd get a fair trial, probably a sentence to a maximum security hospital. But what if it wasn't Gathers? Tuttle could have done it, or Barbara Finlay, for reasons like those he'd imagined for Gathers, or for their own purposes. Jack Gathers added one more name to the list of suspects. Men had killed before to protect their professional reputations, and it sounded as though the name of Col's father depended quite a bit on the legends he took, along with a wife, out of Thorgill. Perhaps the man had helped the legend along to validate his academic theories. Col would be laying his life on the altar of his father's ambition for a myth, a story. Would the man kill his own son to protect his name? Leach couldn't allow that to happen.

But the spirits of the dead seemed to whisper in Leach's ear, the wind sighing through the tunnel entrance like the wails of the dying. What if Gathers was right? The gun weighed heavily at his side, and Katy's body replaced the Irish boy on the street. What if he—but no. It was madness to pretend the old legends were true. Madness, with six dead already, to face the killer unarmed. Disgusted, he turned and ducked out of the tomb.

Kate stood alone, her arms wrapped tightly around herself, just outside the perimeter marked in yellow plastic tape. Powell had disappeared, along with the archaeologist and Col Gathers.

"They're in the tent," she explained, "checking out the place where they found Margory Halliday's body."

Leach nodded. "And there was a third site where a body was found up here, right? The report said a mine shaft?"

"Ben Halliday's body," she confirmed. "He was staying at Laura's B and B with his wife Margory until this happened. They found him after the first series of killings, but before the last, lying at the bottom of the shaft." She pointed along the new cart track to where it intersected the old road. A crumbling stone structure surrounded by a tall chain-link fence rose out of the bracken where the two tracks met.

"That fence ever left open?" he asked.

Kate shook her head. "It's closed with a lock and chain. Inspector Powell had to send to the owners in York for a key."

"So how did Mr. Halliday get down the bottom of the shaft?" he asked.

"I don't know, Inspector. I wasn't there, and neither was my brother. If you are very lucky, you will never get to ask the only one who knows."

The three others exited the tent then, and Kate went to her brother. He wrapped an arm around her shoulders, and a sudden sharp pang of jealousy shook Leach. He wanted to rip Col Gathers' arm away from his sister and place his own there in its stead, and he knew the desire made no sense. Gathers was her brother, for Christ's sake, not a rival lover, and Leach had no hold over her whatsoever. But a small voice in his head told him that no one had ever supported him like Kate Gathers supported her brother. That no one in his life had ever loved him so unconditionally and completely. It wasn't fair that Col Gathers should have so much and that his superior officer should have so little. But the four of them were coming toward him, so he schooled his features to show nothing of the strange thoughts that assailed him.

"Find anything?" he asked.

"Only what's in the report," Col replied. "We ought to check out the old mine, but I'm getting worried. Tuttle should have been here by now."

"Tuttle found the body in the mine shaft, didn't he?" A rhetorical question, Leach neither expected nor received answer to it. "All right, then. We can check on the constable and take a look at the mine shaft this afternoon, when he is with us."

"In the meantime," Kate said, "I'd better get back down the hill—Katy will be home for lunch soon." She gave her brother a quick hug, then followed by hugging Beth Newton. Leach was glad to see that she only shook Powell's hand before she cut out at an angle to intersect the edge of the moor.

"I'll be leaving for a bit myself." Inspector Powell reached out and shook Leach's hand. "Have to check in at the office. We should have reports worked up on the interviews with the locals by this afternoon—I'll bring them back with me later today." He paused a moment, then asked, "Can I offer anyone a lift?"

Beth Newton looked askance at him. "I thought you'd never ask, Inspector. I was just wondering how I was to return to York."

Powell bowed elaborately. "Your carriage awaits, milady," he said with a flourish, then opened the passenger door. "Can I take you gentlemen anywhere?" he asked.

Leach wondered if the man would like to drive them to perdition and leave them by hell's curbside, but Col Gathers answered before he could speak.

"It's just as fast on foot, as the goat travels." He turned to Leach. "Unless you'd rather ride?"

"You're the local expert," Leach demurred. The rain was starting in earnest now, but he didn't relish even a short drive in the back of the Volvo.

"Suit yourself." Powell got in behind the wheel, and Leach closed the door using the edge of the open window for leverage. He did not let go when the latch caught, but leaned over.

"Ask forensics for a comprehensive toxicology screening on the bodies, will you?"

Powell gave him a narrow-eyed stare. "Can I tell them what you're looking for?" he asked.

Leach considered his answer for a moment. "Hallucinogens, naturally occurring and pharmacological," he finally said. "Or anything else that doesn't look like it should be there."

"Hallucinogens. If you say so." Powell studied him for another minute. "If you had found anything, you would let us know?"

"We've too many bodies on this one to jockey over jurisdiction," Leach assured him. "So far it's just a hunch. If I get anything concrete, you'll be the first to know." He moved away from the car without waiting for a rejoinder, and Powell didn't bother to comment. He switched on the engine, backed and slewed the automobile around until it pointed down the track, and headed out. Leach waited until he had turned onto the main track before he spoke to Col Gathers.

"I assume you know the way into the village."

"This way." Gathers nodded and set out down the steep incline, in the direction opposite the cottage.

They walked in silence except for the occasional surprised grunt as Leach slid on the wet hillside, grasping at the stunted bushes they passed to stop his fall or catching up his footing on an outcrop of stone. Gathers seemed lost in thought, effortlessly compensating for the terrain underfoot and moving farther ahead as Leach struggled after. The rain fell harder now, and mist filled the valley so that Leach lost all sense of direction. The thought came to him suddenly, how simple it would be for Gathers to kill him out here. Alone, lost in the fog, who would question a fall that smashed a stranger's skull. He wondered briefly what the locals had told DCI Powell. Would the man suspect Col Gathers? He should have mentioned his suspicion, but he knew he never would have done it.

Gathers was his man, his problem if it should come to that. One way or another, he needed proof, and he still had suspects to question. He made a mental note to have one of the men in London check out Gathers' father, discreetly, for his movements over the last week and wished he'd mentioned that to Powell as well.

Shit. A stone turned as he put his weight on it, and Leach lost his balance.

"Watch your step." Gathers was beside him suddenly, pulling up on his elbow. "We should have taken Powell up on his offer," he said as he let go of his hold. "I've been doing this all my life, forgot you hadn't!"

Leach shrugged his jacket more comfortably on his shoulders. "Woolgathering," he said by way of apology. He knew Gathers had felt the sudden tension between them, saw it in the pinched lines around the man's eyes.

Gathers nodded acknowledgment of the explanation both spoken and unspoken. "Right. It's not far now." He stayed close then, and Leach glanced over to find Gathers studying him.

"Well?" he challenged, dividing his attention more carefully between the sergeant and the ground underfoot.

"I'm not the enemy here, sir." Gathers paid scant heed to the hazards of their path but adjusted for them by habit, Leach figured. "I don't want to see anyone else hurt, but I'll do what I must to keep him from destroying this village."

"And what does that mean, Sergeant Gathers? Justification for homicide?"

Gathers sighed and hunched his shoulders. "Anris works through people. He takes them alive, and he keeps them alive. Seems to enjoy the horror at what he makes them do.

"I think I'll be able to control him if I can touch the person he's using. If he has a gun, I may have no choice but to kill the body he's taken."

For a moment his control slipped, and Leach saw the misery behind the words. Gathers turned eyes of stone on him. "I don't want to have to kill a friend."

They were close enough to the village now that the ground had leveled out. A loud call would bring help if he needed it. Leach stopped and rested the fingertips of his right hand on Gathers' sternum, above his heart, restraining without threatening.

"You don't have to do this, Col. Talk to me. We can go back to town tonight, get you help."

Gathers laughed bitterly, his eyes on some middle ground where monsters roamed. "I didn't murder these people," he said. "But I am responsible for stopping the horror that has." He met Leach's gaze, seemed to weigh what he saw there.

"A deal, then. Send the gun back with DCI Powell. You know I didn't bring one. We'll try it our way, the Thorgill way. If we are right, the killing ends, case solved. If you are right, well, you are a trained officer and former soldier, not an archaeologist or a farmer or the owner of a tea shop. And you are forewarned. You still have the evidence you need to convict . . . me."

"You have a plan." Leach read it in the man's eyes—certainty, but no hope. Gathers expected to fill the place of Anris' gatekeeper when they were through. Leach knew it. At first he'd thought it a metaphor for dying on the job, residual depression from the close call just months ago. Now he wasn't sure. The body at the door had broken fingers, and Leach remembered bloodstains on the stone that had filled the entrance. Col Gathers didn't just expect to die; he dreaded the fate of the guardian, buried alive and beating his hands to a pulp against his dark prison. A king. He'd read somewhere that back then the tribes sacrificed their king at midwinter to ensure the return of spring.

Not on Geoffrey Leach's watch. "Jesus H. Christ, Col, what are you going to do?"

"Not now." Gathers shivered. "We need Tut."

He strode off across the green, and Leach followed.

CHAPTER 10

Col scanned both sides of the narrow high street. Truth to tell, he needed Tuttle's affable strength right then. He needed Tuttle to remind him why he was planning to walk unprotected into that tomb, knowing he could spend the last hours of his life tortured to death there in the dark. He pulled himself away from the brink of that thought with a shudder; he couldn't think about it without his nerve crumbling, didn't know where he'd find the strength to do it when the time came. Hell. Yes, hell, indeed.

They had reached the office of the constable, and Col yanked the door open. Pointless to brood, when there was no way out of it. The usually relaxed station house was a shambles. Chairs lay upended, files were strewn about the floor, and the desk drawers were scattered and broken amid their contents. Constable Tuttle was nowhere in sight.

"Looks like he had company."

Col nodded, ignoring the wary question in Leach's voice. *Not me,* he thought. *I was busy having nightmares of my own while Anris was upending the station.* But he said only, "He must have gotten in somehow—wait here until I check it out."

"Try the door for starters. It was unlocked, remember?"

"The warding was intact until you scuffed through

it—" Col pointed to the salt scattered in a thin line across the threshold, then moved to the window, checking the ward there—intact. On the desk he found the empty sachet of Tuttle's warding charm, its ties half knotted. Tuttle had taken it off, must have been adjusting it when Anris came upon him. But Tut had taken the necessary precautions with the household wards; he should have been safe in here.

In the lavatory Col found what he was looking for. The tiny window began above eye level, but he brushed his fingers delicately along the sill and felt the break in the line of salt. "Found it," he called into the other room.

"No," Leach answered, "I found it. Gathers, get in here."

He followed the shaky voice into the lockup area, impelled more by the urgency of the tone than the words. Tut. The constable lay unconscious on the floor of his locked cell, his arms curled at an unnatural angle around the bars.

"Anris." Gathers sagged against the wall behind him as a wave of nausea passed over him, leaving a knot in the pit of his stomach and a clammy sweat in its wake. "Is he breathing?"

Leach turned and scanned the room. "Where are the keys?"

"They should be on the hook." Col pointed at the empty nail pounded into a board set with coat pegs next to the door.

With a disgusted grunt, Leach squatted next to the cell and reached an arm through the bars to press two fingers to Tuttle's neck. "Pulse fast and thready, but there." He shifted the fingers to feel for exhalation beneath the constable's nostrils and nodded. "Breathing, for now," he said, "Christ, what a mess."

Tuttle's face was an unrecognizable mass of swollen

purple bruises and dried blood. The left side had been crushed, leaving a slight indentation along the length of contact with the cell bar, from forehead to cheek-bone to jaw. Both arms looked broken. Resisting the urge to vomit, Col slid past the door and searched for the phone, found it and called emergency services. That done, he returned as Leach rose from his place next to the battered constable.

"They're sending a helicopter from York," he said, "It should be here in about half an hour."

Leach nodded and began sifting through the mess around them. "Help me find the keys."

"You can't open the cell door, Geoff."

Col stood with his back to the door, his head pressed back against the sturdy wood as if it could somehow compensate for the pressure inside that threatened to explode through his eyeballs.

"Be serious, Gathers!"

Col turned on the other man, the outsider. After everything he had seen and heard, Leach still refused to accept the real danger. "I am. Deadly serious, sir." He couldn't keep the bite out of the honorific. "Anris took him, and my guess is Tuttle locked himself in the cell so that he couldn't hurt anybody else."

"Not likely to hurt anybody now, is he?"

"No, but Anris will kill him trying. We have to protect Tuttle first." Gathers hardened his voice, the terror pushed somewhere in the back of his mind until he had the time to deal with it. He'd wanted a reason. Well, he had one. Now, he had to convince Leach.

He looked around and found the keys and the scattered contents of the broken warding charm beneath some debris just out of reach of the cell.

"Lock me in." He opened the cell door and slid inside, then handed Leach the key. Leach took the key, and Gathers recognized the calculating glint in the man's eyes. Where better to put the suspect, after all. But there was still Constable Tuttle to consider, and they couldn't risk moving him. "Find Kate. Let her know what's happened to Tut, and tell her I'll need a new warding charm. Don't spare her any of the details, Geoff; she needs to know. And don't open this door until Kate tells you it's safe. No matter what you see or hear."

Leach looked at him strangely. "What are you going to do, Col?" Finish the job? Leach didn't say the words, but Col saw them written in the real question behind Leach's unflinching gaze: would they all, family, friends, and strangers, have been better off if Col Gathers had died on that landing?

No, Geoff. No. And God help us if you don't figure that out soon. Out loud he tried to answer both questions. "Protect him. That's what we're paid for, isn't it?"

"How can I be sure?" Leach asked, and Col hated the terrible indecision he heard.

"Tell me what you want to hear, Geoff. But do it quick, because Tut is running out of time."

Geoff looked at him a moment longer, as if he meant to protest. Finally he shook his head and locked the cell. "I'll be back," he said, and left.

Alone with the constable at last, Gathers took the warding charm from around his own neck and slipped it over the other man's head. Tuttle's breathing seemed to ease a little then. Col knew that on some level the charm had eased the constable's fear—not of what Anris had done or would do to him but of what he might do under the earthbound spirit's control. He took the blanket from one of the two bunks and covered the unconscious man, but he knew better than to try to move him.

When he had done as much for Tuttle as he could, Gathers sat on the bunk, his back against the cell wall, and tried to prepare himself. Kate would be there soon. He could hold out until she arrived.

A sudden chill signaled Anris' presence. Gathers felt the lick of a nonexistent breeze lifting the hair at his neck. Laughter whispered in his ear, and desire more powerful than any he had felt before—he felt the sensations in his body, bucking, plunging into a body, and saw Kate's face, held between his hands as his flesh moved in hers and then, in the moment of shock at the surge of power when he spilled into her, he felt the sudden twist of his hands, heard the crack as her neck snapped and watched the life leave her eyes while malignant laughter echoed in his head.

"No!" The image faded, replaced by the weight of a flint ax in his falling hand, then blood slick from the gushing wound at the throat—Geoffrey Leach's throat, and the betrayal choked him—slash, and the inspector's clothing fell away. Slash. Blood and flesh and yellow fat parted; Col reached into the open cavity and pulled out entrails, slippery and steaming, to hold glistening before the eyes of his victim.

Gathers reeled under the sensations, vomited until the spasms brought up nothing but flakes of bile while defense techniques learned at Granny Finlay's knee returned to shore up his flagging sanity. Slowly he fought control away from the earthbound spirit, willing his mind to empty itself, grow blank. When he had attained some measure of calm, he began to fill the void with the image of a wall. Dartmoor prison grew in his mind: high stone walls, barbed wire, iron gates. He built it all with himself at its center. This prison did not contain the evil but stood as a fortress against it. Instead of bars and ranks of cells, he filled the walls of his prison with light, blinding white light that admitted no thought, nothing but the image of high stone walls.

He felt the presence rage about him, throw itself against the fortress of gray stone while the light poured out of him like blood to feed his defenses. Anris took and took, swallowed light into darkness and blighted Gathers' courage with purposeful rage. Sweat beaded on Col's temples, across his upper lip. *Hold on, hold on.* When strength failed him, he reached out, drawing on the Earth and wind and long-forgotten lessons to reinforce his control, but Anris fed on his feeble attempts to summon the discipline he'd denied for so many years.

The walls were beginning to crumble. Memories of darkness—millennia of bitter darkness—flooded him until he wrapped his arms over his stomach and curled his body tightly around them. The cold black singularity of Anris' existence sucked him into itself, and Gathers felt himself reduced to a point suspended in a void. He fought nonexistence with light, strengthened the stone walls of his fortress with more defiance than he thought he had in him.

Terror and pain licked at his mind as Anris fed him the spirit's own death. Flint sharp at his throat, cold stone at his back, and his own face twisted with grim purpose—he saw and felt with eyes five thousand years old. The exultant fury of the spirit beat at his defenses, and he blocked with light.

One thought alone he permitted himself, not a distraction but a lifeline: Geoff was bringing Kate. They would be on time, before Col Gathers could hurt anyone.

"Col?"

Geoff's voice. He couldn't allow himself to listen, couldn't allow his relief to weaken his concentration. Kate would be there, protecting him, warning the DCI what was safe to do and what was not safe. Talking right now wasn't safe. He heard the door open, and Leach stood at the bars.

"Dear God in heaven, what's happened to him?"

"Anris. Spirit attacks aren't pretty, Inspector." Kate's voice forbade further questions. "Go outside, Geoff, and lock the door behind you."

He didn't move, and her explanation was a reprimand: "You are still carrying a gun—we can't risk him getting his hands on it. Stay with Barbara outside until it's over. She'll know when it's safe to come back in."

There was a pause, and Col knew the stubborn scowl the DCI would be turning on the woman, knew the calm immovability of his sister. He hoped Geoff knew better than to cross her in this mood. "But will you be safe?" he said.

A good question. Col wished he knew the answer when Kate passed the question on to him.

"Col?"

He nodded, slowly, once, and felt a tiny glimmer of hope when both his stomach and his head stayed where they were. "Hurry," he added for Leach's sake—Kate knew what the momentary calm was costing him.

"This is insane," Leach said.

They waited, the only sound the labored breathing of the constable on the floor. Finally, Leach set his indecision free in a long, compressed sigh. "If you need help, just call. I'll be right outside."

Col heard his departing footsteps and the door closing behind him. Only then did Kate open the cell door.

"Col. I'm here."

He looked past her bleakly, his face pinched, his eyes focused on some distant point, afraid to draw the thing's attention to her. Too late, of course. Always too late.

"Kate," he whispered, while his fists clenched and

unclenched against the lick of Anris' desire curling through his stomach. Walls crumbled in his mind.

"*Hit her*," the voice whispered in his ear. "*It will feel good. Hit her.*"

He bit his lip through, felt the blood trickle down his chin. At his calling, thoughts of London flooded his mind. Lights and traffic, but no people. No targets. Then Kate was at his side, the leather thong of the warding charm sliding over his head, down his neck. The pressure eased with an echo of harsh laughter in his ears. "*Not the end,*" the voice promised. Not even a contest: just teasing. They both knew where the real battle would be waged. Then Anris was gone, leaving an aftertaste of his own death in passing.

"Can you stand?" she asked, and he nodded, struggling to his feet. He swayed, and she slipped a shoulder under his arm.

"It was too close, Col."

"Yeah." He would never tell her how close a thing it had been. "But close doesn't count."

Kate glanced at Col, waiting for his word, but he could not think past his confusion. "I didn't kill you?"

She smiled at him. "No. You didn't even try. But you did get very sick. I want to clean up a bit for Tut."

He shook his head, almost tracking but not quite. Kate was alive, but the twisting in his gut was real. "Evidence," he said, on automatic, while he brushed uselessly at his arms, trying to clean himself of the visceral slime of the spirit's track on his soul, and his mind played back Anris' words in his head. Had it been a true test of their respective strengths, Col would be dead now, or Kate would. "*Later,*" the whisper promised. "*Later.*" Gathers had learned one thing waiting alone for help to come: if Leach fought him on this, Thorgill would lose. Col did not have the strength to fight them both.

"Sit." Kate led him to the outer office and pushed him down in Tuttle's chair. She unlocked the door and motioned for Barbara, with Leach standing at her side, to enter.

"I'll clean up—"

"Don't touch anything." He recognized Leach's voice, heard the apology in it. "You shouldn't be here as it is."

"Evidence," Kate answered. "I know. Col told me."

"I didn't hurt him," Col insisted. Suddenly it seemed more important than anything in the world that Geoffrey Leach believe him, not for later, or for Thorgill, but for now, for Gathers and his own need to know that he was not the evil that had slithered through his body, fingering his soul.

"I swear." He left his expression open, hiding nothing. Exhaustion was written there, and fear. Memory of the darkness to which he would return his enemy etched itself in the lines radiating from his eyes.

"I don't think you did. But we won't prove it by obliterating the evidence."

Col watched the grim anger set the features of his superior officer, knew that anger was for him, for the haunted pain running deep in his eyes. Evidence. *Anris doesn't leave fingerprints, Geoff.* But he didn't say it.

"Col—"

The confusion in Leach's voice scrawled a new pain across Col's heart. "I hate it that you could die here because my family—I—failed in a responsibility we've had for five thousand years. Anris will know that, will try to use it against us. That will be his mistake. He will not expect me to stand firm against you, but I will look into your eyes and know what he has done to you. And we will both do what we have to do."

Some certainty seemed to shatter deep inside the DCI. "You think I'm going to kill you."

Gathers remembered the pictures in the file, knew Geoff did the same. Anris' victims had been alive through most of it, agony and terror frozen on their dead faces for all eternity.

"I'm counting on you to try." Col wished it could be that simple. He knew beyond need of faith that Geoff would not hurt him, and he filled his words with all the trust of that one certainty, forged on a bloody stair landing in London: "It's up to you now, guv. Bring him to me, and together we can finish it." The plan would work, but he wasn't up to arguments or explanations so soon after his battle with Anris. He needed sleep and perhaps a shoulder to weep out his exhaustion on. But Tuttle needed Kate, and Barbara had no comfort to offer.

"Take him back to the house." Kate helped him out of the chair, and Barbara took his arm, guiding him out of the station house. Leach did not follow them but stood in the doorway, watching, weighing something in the shadows of the sergeant's eyes; and Col stopped for a moment, turned to meet the level consideration with the realization that he brought away from his confrontation with the earthbound spirit.

"He made a mistake, that first Finlay. Trapping a soul in eternal darkness is a terrible thing. They should have found another way. But they didn't, and I don't know what else to do."

"Do what your sister tells you, Gathers. We'll talk later."

Barbara took that as her cue to get him moving again. "I brought the car down," she assured him. "It's just a few steps, then you can rest."

She let go when he slipped into the passenger seat, and Kate stood at the door. "The rescue team should be here soon for Tut," he told her. "They were sending a helicopter from York."

"Don't worry." Kate shut the car door. "You have to rest."

"Rest." Col let his head fall back on the headrest and closed his eyes while Barbara started the motor and smoothly circled the village green.

"They've gone inside," Barbara confirmed for him, and then she turned the car away from the village and picked up speed.

CHAPTER 11

Geoffrey Leach watched from the doorway with his hands in his pockets as the Fiat turned away from the village. His head ached, and he wished that just once on this case someone would tell him the truth—for the novelty of it, if for no other reason. But he had little time to contemplate the sergeant's destination; the sound of helicopter rotor blades reached him through the thinning mist. He turned to go inside, to tell Kate Gathers that help was near, and found her at his elbow.

"I didn't touch anything," she assured him. "I had to make certain Tuttle was still alive. I've known him since I was a child, you understand, Inspector. For us, this is not a case, it is home and friends in danger."

He nodded. "Where did Ms. Finlay take your brother?" He hated being formal with her; he wished he had the right to call her Kate, to put his arm around her and feel her head rest on his shoulder. As if she knew his thoughts, she slipped a hand through the crook of his arm.

"They won't be far, Geoff. But Col needs rest, and Barbara will make sure he gets it." She gave him a wry smile, and he acknowledged that she had read all the many meanings behind the words—the policeman worried about a possible suspect and witness to whatever happened in the jail cell, and the friend who

wanted to ensure Colin Gathers' safety. He wondered
if she'd read more than he'd figured out for himself,
but he had no time to ponder the idea or even to enjoy
the feel of her hand on his sleeve. The emergency helicopter had landed on the village green; figures poured
from it, running toward him with their heads bent to
avoid the rotors. He recognized DCI Powell with a
smaller man carrying a deep briefcase at his side, their
civilian overcoats a contrast among the green-jacketed
emergency medical team members.

Kate turned to lead the medical team through the
outer room of the station, into the jail where Tuttle lay.
When Powell caught up, he stopped inside the door
and motioned the man with the briefcase to follow the
emergency medical team. "Try to get some prints off
the undersides of the drawers, the surfaces that usually stay out of reach," he said, gesturing to encom-
pass the overturned room. "That's where we're going
to find the prints we need."

The man with the briefcase raised an eyebrow in a
sardonic pantomime of surprise. "Telling me how to
do my job, guvnor?" he asked, and Leach caught the
not-so-subtle reminder in the question. In Yorkshire as
well as London, it seemed, forensics believed that the
detecting side of the house couldn't find its own backside without a full report from the labs.

Powell didn't bite. "This one is important," he said.

"Aren't they all?" The forensics examiner didn't
bother to wait for a reply but followed the medics into
the lockup.

Powell turned his attention to Leach then. "DCI
Leach."

Leach gave a slight tip of his head in acknowledgment. He'd expected the man to show up but resented
it, especially now, with the puzzle of where Col
Gathers had gone on his mind.

As if reading Leach's thoughts, Powell gave a quick glance around the room. "Is Sergeant Gathers about? I'd like to speak to him."

Something in the man's expression warned Leach against offering any information yet. "About," he said. "Why?"

Powell took a deep breath, let it out in a long sigh that tightened the bands of tension at Leach's temples. "Your team in London completed their interviews with the office of the National Trust and British Museum. They faxed us the report, with a request to pass it on to you."

"And?" Leach held out his hand, waiting for the file that did not come.

"My men left by car the same time we left in the helicopter; they should be here in fifteen, twenty minutes. They are bringing the report."

Leach did not bother to ask the obvious. He was on Powell's turf, and the man wanted to make sure he knew it.

"The interviews raise some questions about Sergeant Gathers' involvement in this case," Powell continued. "We'd like to take him back to York, where he can give us a statement. Purely a formality. I'm sure the young man will answer our suspicions, and that will be that."

The medics rescued Leach from the need to answer immediately. They swung past with Tuttle strapped to a backboard. Kate followed as far as the door.

"Will he make it?" he asked her.

"They don't know."

She stopped beside him, her voice stretched thin with the effort to maintain her calm, and Leach reached out instinctively to wrap an arm around her shoulders and pull her close. Her body pressed against his side, yielding to the comfort he offered.

"I'm going to take Ms. Gathers home and make sure someone is there to take care of her," he said. "She has had a trying day." Powell hadn't seen the lockup yet, and he wouldn't, now, as Kate Gathers had. Tuttle was gone, leaving the chaos but not the human price of Thorgill's secret, whatever that was. He shook his head, trying to break free of the image of Constable Tuttle broken on the floor, of Sergeant Gathers pale and trembling, the muscles in his arms and shoulders rigid as he fought an unseen enemy. The memory eroded his own certainty, but left no acceptable alternative in its place.

He should have known Kate Gathers would pick up on the tension between the inspectors, though. "What has happened?" she asked.

Powell answered before Leach could intervene. "We've had some reports from London. The authorities there have picked up the senior Mr. Gathers, and I'm afraid it doesn't look good for your brother, miss." He gave the woman at Leach's side a professional smile. "I'm sure it is all a misunderstanding," he finished, "and we can clear it all up with a few questions back at headquarters."

"My brother didn't do this." Kate tried to move away from him, but Leach held her firmly at his side. She surprised him by acquiescing, leaning against him as if she were supporting him instead of the other way around. "Nor did Jack."

Leach noticed that she used her father's first name, and saw that Powell had picked up on it as well. Showing his surprise would give Powell an edge, though, so Leach brought the question back to the more pressing issue: "Are your men bringing a warrant, Inspector?"

"Warrant? You are taking the reports more seriously than we are, Inspector Leach. But then, you know your own man best. I thought we could keep all this informal, off the books, so to speak. Sergeant Gathers can answer a few questions, and we'll proceed from there."

"I see." Leach nodded his head. "I really must take Ms. Gathers home, Inspector," he said. "In the meantime, Gathers is unarmed and unaware of your suspicions. He won't be going anywhere."

Hadley would make him pay for that particular lie; in fact, Leach figured, he'd be lucky to get out of this with his pension intact. But Kate rested her head on his breast, and he felt her tremble along the length of his side. If nothing else, he could give her brother time to explain. "When you have that report, drop it off at the Finlay cottage, will you? I'll take a look at it and talk to the sergeant. We'll let you know what we come up with."

"That won't be enough, you know—"

Leach interrupted the objection: "If the evidence points to London, Inspector, the case is ours. So unless you have a warrant from London, that will have to suffice."

He tipped his head in a gesture just short of dismissal, and guided Kate out past the inspector to the empty street. Barbara Finlay had his car. Powell had come in the helicopter; the DCI and his forensics specialist were stranded until the units from York arrived.

"Can you walk?" he asked Kate.

"I'll be fine, really, Inspector. It was just the shock of seeing Tut that way." She straightened then, putting just a whisper of distance between them, and began to walk slowly across the green. "Growing up, I thought he must be immortal. It's uncomfortable, having one's childhood illusions so viciously torn out by their roots."

"And what illusions have you held about your brother?" he asked.

"I meant what I said, Inspector Leach. Col didn't do this." Although the words distanced him with their formality, Leach noticed that she did not pull away.

"Where did Barbara take him?"

She looked at him, studying his face with Col's eyes and seeing more than he wanted her to see, but it satisfied her for some reason. "Somewhere safe," she assured him. "He needs rest, and Barbara knew he wouldn't get it here. You can't imagine what it cost him to sit in that cell, Tuttle dying on the floor in front of him and Anris beating at his defenses."

Leach remembered the pale face, clammy with sweat and spittle, saw again the eyes reflecting only the black pits of his horror. "I think I can," he admitted. "I saw him too." The old cliche rose up to mock him: "He looked like he'd seen a ghost." Or it could have been madness. He wondered briefly if Barbara Finlay would be safe with her half brother but found he did not believe Col Gathers could kill in cold blood. Perhaps not even to save his own life. This time, when he tried to reassure her, he realized he told the truth.

"For what it's worth, I don't think he murdered anyone, Kate." He risked her first name, and she rewarded him with a smile.

"Why now?" she asked.

The question went to his reasons and not to the truth of his words. "Like I said, I saw him in Tuttle's cell. Saw him lock himself in, saw him when we came back for him." He stopped for a minute, pondering the moor high above the fertile sides of the valley while he tried to sort the tumble of impressions. The answer came easily enough, though the questions it raised would be longer in the solving.

"Col doesn't usually show much of himself to the world. Day to day, you never get past the masks. I've known him two years now, but I feel like I've only really met him twice. Once, when he was wounded in the raid a few months ago." Blood. Leach shook his head to erase that memory. Gathers had believed he was dying and it had seemed, on that staircase landing, that death would be a gift to the young sergeant. "The second time was in your Granny's workshed. I thought that time the Col Gathers I was meeting had gone completely mad, but I knew, absolutely, that he believed every word he said. This magic thing, being a Stone Age ghostbuster, mattered more than anything else in his life. Today makes three times I've seen the real Col Gathers."

He shrugged his shoulders, unable to explain what he had felt when Col locked himself in the cell with Tuttle.

"When we came back for him, I could tell he was scared, Kate." Hell, the man had been sick all over himself; he looked as though he needed a hospital as badly as Tuttle did. "He wasn't hiding anything, and I don't think I've ever seen a human being that terrified." Not since Dunlop, but death had surprised the soldier.

Kate said nothing, waiting for him to finish, but she slipped an arm around his waist, and this time when her head rested at his shoulder, he felt the support she gave rather than took.

"Not anger," he explained, "not hatred. Just fear from the gut, but this time he was fighting it. And he made me want to fight it with him. I just wish I understood what we were up against."

"When you're ready, Inspector, we will help you all we can."

"When will that be?" he asked. He couldn't ask

what he wanted, that she call him Geoff and look past the policeman to the friend he wanted to be.

The arm around his waist shifted slightly. He felt the electric touch of her fingers on the butt of the Browning he wore at his belt, and he reached for the gun, imprisoning her hand between the steel of the weapon and the warmth of his palm. The blood rushed from his head; he would have given her the gun, offered her his own head on a platter if she'd asked for it, but he didn't think he could live with her blood on his hands.

"God, Kate!" The words erupted breathlessly. "Don't you think I want to? I hate the damned thing! But he'll kill you!"

"Who, Inspector?"

"I don't know. God's honest truth, I don't know."

They had reached the cottage, and Kate led him inside. "Laura will have a room made up for you at the B and B," she said. "Why don't you pack, and I'll make some tea."

He stared into her eyes a moment longer, but the woman who had stood by his side in the chaos of the morning had disappeared again, leaving the polite stranger behind. Then he nodded, unsure what she wanted from him, and started up the box stairway. Behind him, he heard her footsteps moving away, toward the pantry.

CHAPTER 12

Steam rose sweet and strong from the cup of York-shire Gold Kate Gathers set in front of him, and the imaginary bands around Geoffrey Leach's head seemed to loosen a bit. Just for a moment he gave in to the luxury of drifting, letting the puzzle of Thorgill work its way into the corners and crevices of his back brain, while his conscious mind hung fire.

"Do you get many tourists up here?" he asked, thinking that the place had a bleak charm even in the early spring. He could imagine its exultant beauty when the heather woke up in late summer.

"Between murder investigations," she answered.

Yes. The Yorkshire moors had more than their share of serial killings. The place seemed to breed madness, or trained up its children in a tradition of murder and vengeance with the stories parents fed them with their porridge. Until now, he'd had no part in the dementia that solitude cultivated. London murder seethed with emotions somehow hotter and more immediate—love and hate focused in the flashpan of thwarted desire, for sex or money or power. He'd come up against some bad ones in his time who killed without feeling to take what they wanted. Until now, he'd never faced a killer who did it for the pleasure as this one seemed to do.

Leach sipped from his cup, pretended to concentrate

on the tea leaves sifting gently to the bottom. His grandmother used to read the leaves, finding dragons in the patterns of their fall and reading the shapes as symbols for all the things that men murdered for. Find a love or lose one, inherit money or drop it all on the stock market, win power and position and respect, or live in obscurity and shame—all of it lay there at the bottom of his cup. He wondered what the old biddy would make of Thorgill.

"Shit," he said with feeling. "Kate, where is he?"

Of course, she did not ask who "he" was. "Safe. At least until tonight." She sounded angry, but she would not meet his gaze.

Leach set down his cup and ran both hands through his hair, head throbbing. "I've got to talk to him before DCI Powell finds him," he explained.

The door opened suddenly, and Barbara Finlay stood there with little Katy. Katy had been crying. Barbara Finlay looked, well, as though the ocean could break at her feet for millennia and never touch the ice of her composure. Leach mocked himself with an ironic twist of the lips. He never went in for poetry, except for the odd Kipling when he was a kid, didn't expect to hear himself spouting lyrical in his own head. Something about this damned place did strange things to a man. Look, after all, at what it had done to Colin Gathers.

"Is Sergeant Gathers with you?" he asked.

Barbara Finlay's glance was colder, if that was possible, before it passed on to the tea things on the table. "Go wash up for your tea, Katy," she said, and nudged the little girl toward the doorway.

When the child had passed out of sight, Kate Gathers stopped Barbara's angry retort with a gesture. "DCI Powell is back," she explained. "The London police have picked up Jack, and Inspector Powell wants to question Col about warning off the archaeologists before the dig. Inspector Leach thinks they are going to arrest Col."

"I stalled for time because he doesn't have a warrant," Leach said. For a moment he glared at Kate Gathers; she seemed to know what would be in the report London had sent, and Leach really hated being closed out of the loop like this. He couldn't believe he'd been fool enough to think he'd gotten through to her, even a little, and his anger showed itself in the impatience with which he finished his explanation.

"If Powell thinks he has cause—and he does think so, believe me—he can phone in the request for a warrant through channels. If the judge agrees with him, your brother will be under arrest, or a fugitive from justice, by tomorrow afternoon at the latest.

"If he'll come in and talk to me, I can probably pull jurisdictional rank on York and keep him out of the nick until we find the killer. If he remains a fugitive, he is subject to arrest by whoever finds him, and DCI Powell is not as inclined to accept Col's innocence as I am. He'll be better off with me."

"It sounds like you are building a murder trial out of a simple request for information, Inspector."

Barbara Finlay poured herself a cup of tea as she spoke. She didn't bother looking up to see the affect of her words, as if his response were irrelevant. "You are the one with the suppositions, the 'if's. Maybe you want my brother to be guilty, to ease your conscience about his recent injury in the line of duty. If my brother were a mass murderer, then his near brush with death would be only his due, wouldn't it."

"That's not fair," Leach objected. Barbara Finlay did look at him then, and he shivered at what he saw in her eyes.

"None of this is fair, Inspector. Ask Col, when you

see him. He will tell you how little fairness has to do
with Thorgill."

Leach nudged his saucer, pushing the tea things
away. "Thank you for your hospitality." He rose to his
feet and took Kate's hand in his. "You can reach me at
the bed and breakfast if you need me. Remember, I am
on your side."

"I'll remember, Inspector," she answered, and
released her hand.

Leach turned with a curt nod to Barbara Finlay and
saw Katy Gathers standing in the doorway, listening.
She met his look with wide, sad eyes and ran away
again, back to her room, he supposed. Then he
reached for his valise.

A knock on the door stopped him. He straightened
and went to answer.

"Sir. DCI Powell said I was to give this to you, sir."
The uniformed policeman handed Leach a thick
manila envelope. "Inspector Powell will come by
when he is finished at the station house, sir. He asks
that you all stay here until he can speak to you."

Leach nodded, but he had already dismissed the
man. Absently he closed the door, his valise and his
intention to leave forgotten. He pulled out the contents of the envelope, a file folder, and reached into his
breast pocket for his reading glasses. "Someone
should get Katy for her tea," he reminded the women
at the table. "I'll take this into the garden, to be out of
your way." He did not wait for a response but left
them to stare at his back.

In the garden he found an iron bench beside a small
garden table and sat down, spreading the report
before him, his own notebook next to it. According to
his superiors at the museum, Jack Gathers had been
on holiday when the murders began. Flipping
through the pages, Leach had to admit that Gathers'

motives seemed pretty clear-cut: the dig put his professional reputation at risk. But according to the report, his colleagues valued the senior Gathers for his detailed work in classifying Neolithic artifacts by location and influence, not for his questionable theories about the origins of local legends. The term "Jack's hobby horse" appeared in several of the interviews, including that of Beth Newton.

The report confirmed that Col's mother came from Thorgill, and Leach put as much professional distance as he could between himself as a policeman studying the background of a potential villain and as a superior officer prying into the private life of a man in his command. Mrs. Gathers, according to all reports, had "fragile nerves" and had endured more than one hospitalization for depression. She had not been seen at her home for several days, and neighbors assumed she was once again in the hospital. Prior hospital records included reports of one suicide attempt, but according to officials at the hospital, she was not at present a patient.

Clenched-jawed, Leach closed the file and stacked it under his notebook. He really didn't want to know this, didn't want confirmation that a family history of mental illness had appeared murderously in Col's generation. He needed to talk to Col, badly, and before DCI Powell got his hands on the man. When he looked up, Katy Gathers stood watching him, her eyes wide and liquid with distress.

"What's the matter, Katy?" He smoothed the frustration from his face and spoke to her as softly as he could.

"Mommy's crying," she whispered. One tear, then another, left a glistening trail down her cheek to hang a moment at her jaw and fall to the collar of her sweater.

"I'll bet she could use a hug right now," he said, and Katy nodded.

"Well, then. Why don't you go inside and give her a nice big hug. And you can ask Auntie Barbara to come out to the garden and keep me company. How does that sound?"

"Good," she whispered.

Katy turned and ran into the cottage through the potting shed door. After a moment or two, Barbara Finlay appeared in her place. Leach swept up the file and stood, waiting for her to approach.

"I thought manipulating a child's feelings was beneath your dignity as a policeman, Inspector Leach," she greeted him. "I see I was wrong."

"I didn't bring the child to the scene of a mass murder," Leach reminded her, and gestured for her to take the bench.

Barbara Finlay sat. "Someday Katy will hold responsibility for Thorgill. She needs to start learning that now."

"Insanity is a learned trait in the family, then, and not an inborn one?" Leach didn't bother to mask the sarcasm. Barbara Finlay pointed at the file in his hand.

"I assume that remark refers to Kate's and Col's mother. The woman lost her brother and his wife. They were very close, and she never quite accepted his loss. Is that why you brought me out here, Inspector? To interrogate me about my aunt? You are grasping at straws!"

Leach perched on the table in front of her. He wanted his headache to go away, he wanted the Gatherses and Finlays and Powells of his world to go away. Mostly, he wanted the murderer of half a dozen innocent people put away where he could do no more harm. At the moment, he would have settled for two aspirin and a little cooperation from anyone involved with the case at all.

"In spite of what you may think, Ms. Finlay," he began, "I had a full and satisfying life before I heard the name of your little village. Contrary to your rather self-absorbed opinion, I did not come here to ruin the lives of your family, to pry into your personal business, or to bring down the local legend. All I really want to do right now is go home. But I am not doing that until I have your murderer in custody. It seems we have the same goal—me, out of your village. Help me and I'll leave that much faster."

"I can't tell you where Col is," Barbara Finlay insisted.

"All right, let's start with something easier, then." He leaned forward, reading from his notebook. "Col introduced you as his half sister. You appear to be younger than Kate and older than Colin, but both your siblings have the name of your mother's husband, and you do not."

"I'm actually a cousin. My father was Mum Gathers' brother. When my father and mother died, the Gathers family took me in, and I was raised with Kate and Col. We've always felt closer than cousins, more like brother and sisters, so that's what we call each other."

Leach had a hard time imagining the woman in front of him as close to anyone, but he kept that thought to himself. "That does seem to explain it," he agreed. He flipped to a clean page in his notebook then and referred to the file in his hand. "According to the report my men in London filed, your aunt seems to have disappeared. Do you happen to know what's become of her?" He left his meaning open.

"Are you asking me if my cousin killed his mother?"

Leach shrugged. "Did he?"

Her frown seemed more scornful than distressed. "Did your men ask Jack? He would know where she is if anyone does."

"According to Professor Gathers, his wife is resting in the south of France. We are checking on that, but I'd like to ask a few questions in the meantime. Did she get along with her husband, or did they quarrel, do you know?"

"I was raised in their house, Inspector. They didn't have the easiest relationship in the world. As you already know, my aunt has suffered some mental illness since my parents died. Jack has had a difficult time of it, but he does love her. And he would never hurt her.

"All of this would have been terribly distressing for her, you understand. I realize you think we are acting like children who imagine monsters under the bed, but my father was to have been king when Granny Finlay died. When my father passed away before his mother, the task fell to Aunt Katherine, then to Col when he grew old enough. She's already lost her brother and her mother, and now she faces the loss of her children. If Jack sent her away, he had her best interests in mind."

"That remains to be seen," Leach temporized, scanning the file. "Do you know why your uncle wanted to stop the archaeological excavation in Thorgill?"

Barbara Finlay laughed bitterly at him. "Maybe, Inspector, he guessed that the Finlays had a good reason for guarding that tomb! But the law hasn't changed much in the last few thousand years, has it? If you can't find the cause, kill the person who warned you of the danger in the first place. Poor Jack! He's not exactly suited to prison life. Poor Mum, with Granny Finlay and her brother dead, her husband in prison, and her son about to trade his life for Thorgill's continued existence. Mentally ill too, poor woman. Must be mental illness—why else would she be depressed!"

She rose from the bench with an impatient gesture. "I've had enough of this," she objected. "Kate needs me inside."

Leach stood as quickly and snagged her wrist before she could completely turn away. "Don't mistake me, Ms. Finlay," he warned her. "Do not let your grandmother's garden lull you into thinking this is a friendly conversation—" small chance of that, but the woman didn't seem to understand the gravity of her situation—"this is an official police investigation. Right now you are hiding a material witness in a capital crimes case, and that charge may escalate to harboring a fugitive before the day is out.

"Now, I have worked with Colin Gathers for the past two years. I am inclined to give him the benefit of every doubt I can muster, but I need your help. Or, if you prefer not to cooperate, we can take this discussion back to York and let DCI Powell ask the questions. I don't think I have to tell you that the DCI is not as predisposed to assume your cousin's innocence as I am. So let's just sit back down and see what you *can* tell me that will help to clear Sergeant Gathers."

"But not Jack?" She asked it like a challenge, but Leach did not rise to the provocation.

"I do not know your uncle. I do know Col. Let's start with that and see where it takes us, shall we?"

Barbara Finlay relented enough to return to the bench, but Leach did not return to his seat on the table. Instead, he stood over her, using his presence to intimidate her. Or, at least he tried. Her expression told him she knew exactly what he was doing and thought him a fool for trying it, but he did not relent.

"Do you know where Colin Gathers went on the days of the murders, Sunday and Monday of this week?"

"Visiting his parents, perhaps?" she offered.

"That, unfortunately, is what DCI Powell suspects. Col said nothing to you about a trip?"

"No." She considered for a moment. "But if Jack took Mum to France, Col might have gone with them to help."

"*If* they went to France," Leach emphasized her words. "We have men checking on that. Did you know that Colin Gathers had warned several of the researchers scheduled for this dig that they should not come?"

"He was right, wasn't he?" she answered.

"Again, I ask you: where is Col Gathers? For his own sake, I have to know."

She stood up then but did not move away, and he remembered the fire, and his hands, burning. Instinctively he backed a step, and hated the residual fear that she inspired. "I'll tell him what you've said," she offered, and Leach realized she meant it as a compromise. "Tonight is impossible, but tomorrow morning perhaps he will see you."

She began to turn, and he stopped her with one last question. "Last night—"

"Yes, Inspector?"

"Would you have let me . . . you know . . . the fire . . ."

"Would I have allowed you to plunge your hands into the fire?" She stared at him, features frozen in a mask of judgment. "Oh, yes, Inspector. But you are asking the wrong questions. You should say, 'Would Col have permitted it?' No, he would not. And, 'Did you know that he would stop you?' Yes, I did. And that Kate would have if Col hadn't."

She smiled then, mocking him. "I'm not your murderer either."

Leach watched her walk away then, knowing it was pointless to try to stop her. Before she could reach the door to the potting shed, however, Kate Gathers appeared, leading DCI Powell.

"There's been another murder," Powell said.

CHAPTER 13

"What happened?" Leach asked the York DCI.

Powell rubbed his palms together, and for a moment Leach thought of Lady MacBeth—"Out, damned spot"—but no blood sullied the impeccable shirt cuffs showing a proper half inch below the sleeve of his jacket. "Constable Dickens has had his throat cut with a bread knife; not as picturesque as a flint ax perhaps, but it did the trick as far as Dickens was concerned."

"Where?"

"His throat." Powell hesitated, then massaged his forehead with the fingertips of one hand. Leach knew exactly how the man felt—he'd be rubbing his own weary temples if it wouldn't look redundant.

"You mean, where was he killed." Powell seemed to pull himself together with an effort. "Behind the tearoom in the village. Dickens and Pankowitz were setting up our local operations center there. Pankowitz has gone missing, and Dickens is dead."

Leach nodded, leading Powell around the cottage rather than through it. Katy was inside, and she'd already seen and heard more than a child should.

Powell's car waited at the front of the cottage; his driver saw them and leaped to open the doors. Leach gave the anonymous policeman a nod, then pressed gently on Powell's shoulder, using his other hand to push the man's head down enough to pass unscathed into the back seat of the patrol car. He went around to the other side and slid in beside Powell.

"Any witnesses?" he asked, trying to put the pieces together and calculating in his head. Where had Barbara Finlay taken Col, and how long had it been since Finlay herself returned? How long had they been talking in the garden? It didn't seem likely that Col had had time to return from wherever Finlay had left him, to commit murder, and to capture, possibly injure, another policeman. It seemed even less likely that he could have done so undetected while a full-scale search went on around him.

"Pankowitz, I should think," Powell said, and Leach heard the anger in his voice, knew its source. He'd felt it himself in Derry, in London. The men under your command were not supposed to suffer and die because of your orders.

"Dickens your first casualty?" he asked, sharing the man's loss.

Powell nodded. "Christ. He and his wife were planning to get pregnant in the spring. Now Kris will have nothing."

Kris. The wife, who would never look into her child's eyes and see her husband there.

"Why now, damn him?" Powell rubbed at his eyes, and Leach pretended not to see the hint of moisture. Damn. Leach could find nothing to say that would ease the burden of a man lost, maybe two, so he said nothing during the short drive.

It had taken him fifteen minutes to walk the distance with Kate, but the patrol car reached the center of the village in under five. Leach noticed that the activity around the station house had dropped. One

guard stood at the door, while a man in a plaid jacket
wandered out, his hands full of plastic bags of
evidence. Powell's driver did not stop until they
reached the tearoom, where the police activity had
shifted. Powell was first out of the car, and Leach followed him past the police cordon. The smell of musk
and carrion and rust hit him just inside the door of the
tearoom, where its proprietress sat giving a statement
to a plainsclothes junior, both looking rather pale from
the stench.

"Why don't you take that to the church," Powell
instructed the junior, and Leach realized they were
fast running out of places in the village that had not
been designated crime scenes.

The junior rose with a relieved, "Thank you, sir,"
but the woman stared at Powell with a kind of numb
disbelief on her face. Leach took her elbow and helped
her to her feet.

"Col didn't do this." She clutched at his arm, and
Leach recognized her then; she'd been part of the
crowd at the Finlay cottage the night before.

"Do you know where he is?" Leach asked, his voice
low and urgent.

The woman shook her head. "Don't let them take
Col away—we'll all die!"

"We need to find him," Leach said, but she shook
her head convulsively, the motion communicating
itself through her body in violent tremors.

"It will be all right." Leach bit back his frustration.
"Go with the officer," he told her. "He'll take care
of you."

This time she nodded and followed the junior out
past the cordon. Leach sighed. "It was worth a try," he
explained to Powell.

"Do you think she knows where he is?"

Leach looked out through the doorway for a long moment. "No," he said, "probably not." He didn't mention Barbara Finlay but followed the stench into the storage room in the back.

The quantity of blood on the floor shocked him into immobility, until he realized that he was already standing in it.

The man who'd arrived with Powell earlier in the day knelt on one knee in the middle of a plastic trash bag spread on the floor next to the uniformed body stretched before them. Leach lifted his foot gingerly, cringing at the ripping sound as the sole pulled out of the sticky mess, but he took a step farther into the room so that he could see over the man's shoulder.

"Malcolm, this is Inspector Leach," Powell introduced, and, "Inspector, Malcolm Waat, our forensics specialist. Did you find anything?"

Waat had turned back the corner of the tablecloth someone had thrown over the corpse, incongruous with its embroidered flowers on glowing white. Leach had seen cloths just like it in the tearoom as they passed. The open gash in the dead policeman's throat left little doubt as to the cause of death.

Waat pulled himself to his feet and leaped lightly over the worst of the blood on the floor to land next to Leach. He reached out to shake hands, and Leach hesitated, looking suspiciously at the gloved hand Waat offered. The specialist withdrew the gesture.

"Right," he said, dusting his hands off one against the other. Then he turned to Powell, who stood in the doorway, his face pale, eyes bleak. "I won't know for sure until I get him back to the lab, but we may be able to get some partials off of Dickens' clothes or skin."

Waat shrugged. "As for the rest, there's no sign of break-in, nor should you expect any at this time of day, I would think. No sign of a struggle either, until the actual knifing. We've got some scuff marks—" he pointed to a series of six or seven black marks on the concrete floor— "looks like Dickens' shoes. He realized what was happening to him, tried to regain his footing and put up some kind of defense—there's a slash on his right forearm, as if he tried to ward off the knife, but then it ended quickly. You see, nothing was knocked from the shelves, nothing overturned."

A wave of his hand took in the undisturbed supplies around them. "I'd say Dickens was standing right there when his assailant came upon him, probably from behind, and died where he stood."

Powell nodded.

"One other thing, guv," Waat added. "The lads are pretty nervous, what with the attack on the local constable and the stories about evil spirits spreading faster than the flu on a Monday. I'm surprised that someone could take Dickens that unaware."

"Unless he knew him?" Powell asked.

Waat nodded. "That would be my guess, sir."

"Did you find any trace of hallucinogens in the bodies you've examined?" Leach asked.

Waat shook his head. "So you are the reason for that request. Not a bad call from what I have seen here, but so far, nothing."

Leach stared at the body, trying to imagine Col Gathers with a knife in his hand, killing the man, but he couldn't make it fit. "None of your men met Gathers, have they?" he asked Powell.

"You know that doesn't mean anything. He could have identified himself as a policeman to Dickens and put him off his guard."

"With your men out looking for him? Doesn't seem likely." Leach scanned the storage room as if something on the shelves or floor might tell him who had done this, but the boxes and sacks remained pre- dictably mute. "Can you take water samples, soil and air samples back with you?" he asked Waat.

"What do you expect to find, Inspector?"

Leach shrugged. "Maybe nothing. Anything strange, that shouldn't be there." He glanced up then at the sound of a helicopter, the second to descend on the village in less than twelve hours. Waat heard it too.

"Well, I hear my ride—I'd best show them where to bring the stretcher." The forensics specialist gave Powell's shoulder a pat as he passed the man in the doorway. "I'll see what I can do about those samples," he promised, then disappeared into the tearoom, leaving Leach alone with his opposite number from York and the man's dead officer.

Powell finally came into the room, stepping care- fully over the trails of blood where he could, until he reached the plastic bag Waat had left next to the body. He fell to one knee, studying the face of the dead man. "He was too young, you know?"

"They always are," Leach acknowledged.

Powell nodded without turning. He replaced the cloth over the body, grimacing at the gaping wound in the man's throat. "We'll find your man Gathers," he said, but the words seemed to come from some far place that Leach couldn't reach. "And he'll pay for what he's done here."

"I expect he will," Leach agreed. Guilty or not, Gathers was in for a rough time with this lot, mourning one of their own and wanting someone to blame, to send into the desert with their own guilt added to his burden. Good officers didn't let their men die. But the whereabouts of Officer Pankowitz troubled him more, at the moment, than the location of his own man. If Gathers' story was true, then what would happen to Pankowitz? He turned around and walked away, leaving the DCI alone with his thoughts in the bloody storage room, and headed for the church.

CHAPTER 14

The bare church held a scattering of worshipers reading prayer books or otherwise holding vigil, but no junior detective or witness. Leach found the woman on the second try, at the parsonage next door. He followed the parson, who had a slight family resemblance to Constable Tuttle, into the parlor where the woman sat fighting back tears with a trembling chin.

"Has there been any news of my uncle?" The parson asked.

"You're related to ..." Leach almost asked if the parson had been related to Pankowitz, but then he remembered that resemblance.

"Constable Tuttle," the parson confirmed. "My uncle."

"Nothing yet. I'm sorry."

The parson nodded. He did not leave them in privacy as Leach expected, but returned his attention to the woman on the sofa.

"I'm sorry to disturb you," Leach began, but the woman waved away his apology with a sweep of her embroidered handkerchief. Sitting on the parson's Victorian sofa, she looked younger than her manner indicated, and her valiant struggle to pull herself together in front of him made her look younger still.

"You are not disturbing me, Inspector." She managed an ironic little laugh. "I'm already about as disturbed as I can be. But you must want the key to your room. I'll get it for you." She rose from the sofa and fussed at the top of the spinet, where her purse lay amid sheaves of music, the post, and sections of the *Sunday Times*. When she fished out a key on a plastic ring, he realized who she must be.

"I should have known. You are Laura—I'm sorry, I didn't catch your surname, but Kate Gathers said you had a bed and breakfast in town."

"Laura Simms." The woman gave him her name and handed him the key. "But if you didn't come looking for your key . . ." Fear crossed her face again, and her fingers rose to cover her mouth, as if she could somehow hide her reaction.

"Exactly. I've come to ask you a few questions about what happened in the tea shop."

Simms shook her head, but Leach could see she denied what she had witnessed, not his request. "It was horrible," she said, "but I already told the detective all I could."

"I'm sure you did," Leach assured her. "I'd just like to hear it from you myself. I might think of something the detective forgot."

She did not resist when the parson took her arm and guided her back to the sofa. "Thank you," she said. "I'll be all right now."

Leach drew out his notebook and pen and nodded to the parson. "Is there somewhere I can speak with Ms. Simms privately?" he asked.

"I know when I am not wanted," the parson smiled, taking the sting out of the words. "Feel free to stay as long as you need—I'll be in my study." He turned to Laura Simms and patted her on the shoulder. "If you need me, just call." With that, he left them, closing the parlor door behind him.

"So, Inspector Leach, what can I tell you?"

It disconcerted him that the woman knew his name and his purpose in the town, more about him than he knew about her; it felt too much like giving up the high ground he preferred in any investigation. It did, however, save time on explanations.

"I'd like to know what you saw in the storage room of the tea shop, Ms. Simms."

"Nothing," she answered. "Or, more precisely, I saw the body of a dead policeman on my floor. If I had seen more, you can be sure I would have died as well."

"I see." Leach gave her a moment to relax, then asked, "Where were you at the time the attack occurred?"

"I was in the shop, preparing afternoon tea. The tourists are gone, but I thought the policemen would need a break, and a nice tea would set them right up."

"And offset the loss from the departed tourists, no doubt." Leach observed dryly.

"I *am* a businesswoman, Inspector. And as such, one thing I know is that dead men don't drink a lot of tea, nor does having the body of one littering up the storage room enhance the reputation of an establishment such as mine. So if you are hinting that I may have killed the officer in a disagreement about the biscuits, please think again!"

"I thought no such thing, Ms. Simms, as I am sure you well know." He stopped when the parlor door opened to admit the parson with a large tray. It held, not surprisingly, a teapot, two cups with saucers, and a sugar bowl and creamer.

"I am trying to conduct a murder investigation here, not a French farce!" Leach bit back the sharp retort in the face of the parson's shocked chagrin.

"I didn't mean to pry!" he protested, then belied the

words when he turned to Laura Simms. "Are you all right, dear?"

"Yes, Henry," she answered, "but we will finish here sooner, I think, if we are left alone."

"Of course, my dear."

The parson left empty-handed, and Laura Simms poured the tea. "Sugar, Inspector?"

"No," he sighed. "Let's try to finish this up before Henry finds another excuse to defend your honor, shall we."

He took the milky brew she held out expectantly. With a quick, somewhat desperate look around him, Leach spied a curio table next to an overstuffed armchair that clashed with the sofa. Setting the tea on the table, he sank into the armchair, not quite suppressing a sigh. "Let's start at the beginning, shall we?"

Her expectant attention encouraged him to continue. "The two officers entered your establishment at what time?"

"Four o'clock," she answered promptly. "I remember because I was a bit rushed, adding a few extra luncheon things to the usual tea. I thought the officers might be hungrier than the usual tourist."

Astute, Leach agreed, but he kept the thought to himself. "And—" he encouraged with a blandly attentive expression, his pen poised to take down her words.

"The officers came into the shop. They asked if they could use a bit of the shop for a command center, and they were looking for Col. They asked if they could search the back room. Of course I said yes."

"How did they seem to be getting on, did you notice?" The last was scarcely necessary; Leach had a feeling that Laura Simms didn't miss much that happened in Thorgill. Nor was he disappointed.

"They seemed on good terms," she said. "They

introduced themselves very politely, of course, and commented on the display, and how they'd got the best of the deal setting up for their guv in a tea shop. The one officer, Dickens, called the other Panky. It seemed a regular thing between them. Dickens made a joke about Panky's appetite, and the other officer, Pankowitz, I think was his full name, referred to Constable Dickens as 'his lordship,' but it seemed to be all in fun, if you see what I mean."

"Yes, Ms. Simms." There may have been a bit of hostility buried in the joking between the men, but not more than you'd find in any group working together day in and day out. Not enough to kill for, at least. "Then what did the officers do?"

"Officer Dickens said they would be back. He used a funny accent, and Officer Pankowitz laughed and called him Arnie—Schwarzenegger, I assumed, and I laughed too. Then they went into the storage room." Laura Simms grew very pale then, and tears filled her eyes.

"Then what happened?" Leach asked softly. "I know this is hard, but if I am to save Col out of this, I need all the help I can get. You were there—who killed that man?"

"I didn't see," she objected, but she seemed torn. "You really want to help Col?"

Leach nodded his head. "For what it is worth, I know Barbara drove him out of town. He didn't have time to kill that man, kidnap his partner, and disappear again—so at least on this one, he is in the clear with me. I can't tell DCI Powell that, however, or he will start arresting people for conspiracy." He gave a short bark of laughter. "Including me. And then we'll never clear Col, or get to the bottom of Thorgill's murders, will we?"

She shook her head, then made her decision. "Anris

killed Officer Dickens, but you must have known I would tell you that. I saw the look on your face when you remembered that you'd seen me at Granny Finlay's cottage last night. You are a very suspicious man, DCI Leach."

"That's what they pay me for," he observed, then brought the questions back to the point. "Last night Kate explained that this Anris uses the bodies of living people to do his murders. Whose body did he use this time?"

"I heard them in the back room while I was setting the tables," she said. "They seemed a little nervous. Dickens mentioned that the suspect they were hunting was a policeman, and Pankowitz said that there were still the two of them together and a village full of uniforms, that the fugitive didn't have a chance.

"Then Officer Pankowitz began to laugh, but it didn't sound like his voice, of course. Dickens told him to stop messing about and to get back to work. I heard a scuffle, and a noise like someone trying to call out, but gagged midway. I went to the door, and Anris stared at me for a moment out of Officer Pankowitz's eyes. I was protected, you see." She touched the charm that hung at her breast, and Leach felt the leather thong around his own neck; he'd forgotten that he wore it.

"The officer turned and ran out of the delivery entrance in the back, and I ran to the station house looking for you. You weren't there, but one of the officers noticed I was crying and took me to DCI Powell. I told him about the dead officer, but none of the rest."

"Thank you for trusting me," he said.

"Col trusts you," she corrected him, "and we will follow his lead because he is our king. But we'll be watching you as well."

Leach closed his notebook. "I'd find that more

encouraging if you weren't planning to make him the star of a human sacrifice," he pointed out.

She had no time to reply, however; there was another soft knock at the door and the parson entered, hesitantly. "I am sorry to interrupt when I promised not to," the parson explained, "but DCI Powell is here and he'd like to speak with you, Inspector Leach."

"We are done for now. Would you tell the Inspector that I'll come out? We've monopolized your parlor enough for one day."

When the parson had once more disappeared down his own hallway, Leach turned to Laura Simms. "If you need me, you will know where to find me," he said.

"Of course." She offered her hand and he took it in a firm parting clasp. "You'll be in 2C, second door on the right, loo is at the end of the hall. Until later, then."

Leach followed her as far as the front entry hall and watched her walk across the green.

"My man said she didn't know much." Powell sounded exhausted.

It was more than the long hours; Leach knew it would get worse as the investigation lengthened. He wondered if they would find Pankowitz alive or dead. But Powell was still talking, so he tried to focus on the man's words. ". . . must have come upon the scene within minutes of the murder. Lucky woman, she could have been the next."

Almost of its own will Leach's hand went to the charm at his neck. Luck. Maybe. He shivered, almost couldn't meet the other man's eyes. How had he gotten so entangled in Thorgill's insane secrets?

"It's late," he finally said, "and you haven't eaten since you got here." He looked at his watch: eight o'clock. "Find your driver. We'll stop at the White Rose for a bite, then call it a day."

"Yeah." Powell turned and left the parsonage as if he were on automatic pilot. Leach followed and gave the man waiting for them at the wheel of Powell's car directions to the pub on the road out of town.

CHAPTER 15

Col woke to a sense of safety he hadn't experienced since childhood. The feeling made no sense, given what Thorgill expected of him, but he accepted it in this, the only place where neither his real nor imagined demons could reach him. Above him, dust motes hung suspended in the sunlight. Evening, then; the sun had dropped low enough to pass under the swept thatch and in through the dormer windows facing west, the path to heaven.

Col lay in Granny Finlay's bed, his feet pointing toward the windows, and smiled. The old lady had taken no chances on the path her soul would take. One evening she'd just slipped away, following the sun over the moors, to greet those among her ancestors resting between turns of the wheel.

He let his eyes close softly, then, refusing the memories and dread that rose with the acid in this throat. He denied the images of the night, of tomorrow and the eternity that stretched before him trapped in the dark with the insanity of Anris beating at his defenses. For now, he rested in a holy place. Unreachable. Untouchable. He slept.

CHAPTER 16

The driver turned their car at the swinging sign with the White Rose in full bloom upon its surface and parked on the empty tarmac in front of the pub. The building itself looked like any of the stone cottages that clustered along the gill that gave the village its name, but the door opened easily when Leach turned the handle. Inside, the pub stood nearly as empty as the parking area. A lone table of locals stopped in their leave-taking to glare at the policemen, then passed out the door with a low rumbling of conversation.

"What I like best about being an officer of the law," Leach commented, "is the appreciation we receive from the people we serve."

Powell turned from the departing locals to face Geoffrey Leach. "It doesn't usually bother me the way it has this time."

"Didn't lose a man trying to protect them before, though, did you?"

Powell flinched as if he'd been struck, and Leach shook his head, remembering something Col had said on the way into the village. Needed their kings, but didn't love them. Killed them when the need arose. Not what he'd call a loving people, but he didn't inflict that morose thought on Powell.

"Sit down before you fall down," he ordered the man instead. "And call me Geoff."

The driver sat at the bar, facing the door. Leach felt some of the tension ease out of his shoulders then. He'd forgotten how much he missed someone guarding his back.

"George." Powell sat.

In better times Leach would have enjoyed the pub with its dark wood everywhere, its trestle tables and small but well-stocked bar, bottles gleaming in mirrored rows. Now, he let the policeman from York slide into the corner seat with his back to the wall and took a place opposite, glad for the driver at the bar. He looked around for service and found the lone waitress, a middle-aged woman with the bleached remnants of a bouffant hairdo, leaning against a pass-through window to the kitchens.

"Could we order, here?" Leach called to her, and she turned her head but otherwise didn't move.

"What do you want?" she called back.

Leach glanced at Powell and realized he'd get no help from that corner; the man stared at the scars in the table as if they could give up the secrets of life. Menus, or even a recitation of the items available in the kitchen, held no sway over the man's desires.

"Two chicken pies," he hazarded, "and two whiskeys while we wait."

The waitress turned back to the pass-through window and spoke to someone on the other side. After a few minutes had passed, however, Leach realized she had either forgotten or dismissed his order for drinks.

"Can we have those whiskeys?" he asked again.

"Right, guv." She did move this time, and Leach figured he'd got the trick of it now. One request at a time she could handle, but her attention span didn't stretch to include two.

"Single malt or blended?"

Powell's driver intervened softly, then. Leach didn't hear what the man said, but the waitress reached for a bottle and filled two shot glasses. She only spilled a little when she put them on the table.

"Drink," Leach ordered.

Powell did, wincing at the bite of the liquor.

"Do you want to talk about it?"

Powell shook his head, but the words came anyway. "They were good lads. Dickens was taking classes at the Open University, wanted to make Inspector grade. He said a man who wanted a family had to plan for the future."

Leach nodded, a policeman's trick, to show interest but not stop the flow of words. He had every intention of getting Powell drunk and sending him home talked-out. But their pies rested on the sill of the pass-through while the waitress returned to her chat with the cook and gave no sign of delivering the food. Finally, Powell's driver walked over and muttered something in her ear. She bustled away while the driver brought over the pies.

"Welcome to Fawlty Towers," he said. "She's gone to get the silver. I'll make sure she doesn't forget where it's going."

"Thanks," Leach said, and meant for more than the pie. The driver seemed to read his intentions in the word.

"No problem. My name is Toby, by the way." He gestured with a tilt of the head and added, "Take care of the guv, and we'll be even."

The waitress finally approached their table with the silver, and Toby returned to his own pie at the bar. The door opened then, and two policemen in plain clothes hesitated on the threshold. With a silent exchange, Toby's empathic shake of the head followed on their part by one brief nod of understanding, the two men left the pub. Leach figured their hostess might object to the turning away of her custom, but she had returned to the pass-through window without a glance at the door.

Leach let the silence carry them through dinner, but when they were nearly done, Toby appeared again at Leach's elbow to place a bottle of blended whiskey on the table with the comment, "I put it on your tab."

"While you're playing publican, have a lemon fizz, on me."

Toby shook his head. "Black coffee," he said. "I think it's going to be a long night." The sun had gone down sometime during supper. Leach figured this night had already been too long, but he took the man's meaning. The only thing he hated more than being on this side of the bottle was being on Powell's side of it. Toby read something in Leach's expression that he took for dismissal. Nodding, the sergeant wandered over to the pass-through window and slung an arm around the waist of the hostess. Whatever he said in her ear made her laugh, but the coffee appeared in record time.

Leach left him to it. He filled both shot glasses and sat for a minute staring into the clear amber liquor. "I lost a man in Derry," he began. "Two, really, but it's Dunlop I still dream about. I was a lieutenant, first in an army family to make it out of the noncom ranks, which didn't sit well with the old man. Nor did my assignment in Londonderry. Said I was a glorified policeman, nothing like his days in Burma during the war and then in India putting down the riots before independence.

"Burma I could understand, but I didn't see the difference between what he did in India and my orders for Ireland. Told him so, too." Leach sighed, almost forgetting why he was telling the story to this stranger. "It set a rift between us that just got wider as time went on. We haven't spoken since I joined the force."

Powell said nothing, just turned his glass; his attention seem focused on the glint of lamplight on the whiskey. Suddenly he picked up the glass and drank it off in one clean gulp. Leach filled it again and waited until Powell drained the next one, glaring at him over the top of the glass. Leach shrugged and poured more whiskey. When Powell made no comment, Leach went on:

"Anyway, we were called out to control a fight between some laid-off factory workers and the hired muscle the owner had brought in to protect his interests. Or, at least that's what we thought it was. We didn't even make it to the location. Kids attacked us with Molotov cocktails and someone threw a pipe bomb under the car.

"That was early on, you understand; we hadn't brought the armored cars in yet. The car went over. We were scrambling for cover when I heard a shout to duck, and Sergeant Dunlop dropped on top of me. When I rolled out from under, I saw that he'd been hit, had a gut full of glass fragments and rusty nails. The kid who'd gotten him stood watching in the street. When he saw me moving, he lit another bottle. I shot him."

"Am I supposed to feel better, DCI Leach?" Powell asked him. "Is this some sort of induction ceremony into the order of men with lurid stories to tell?"

"When I'm awake," Leach said, ignoring Powell's questions for the moment, "I see Sergeant Dunlop crying in my arms with a gut full of scrap. But when I'm asleep, I see the shock on that kid's face when my bullet dug a crater in his heart.

"He was a kid, but he was trying to kill me, already

had killed my sergeant, bar the shouting. I wanted to get out of there alive. But I'll tell you what I've never told a soul: in that moment, I wanted to see that kid die. And he did."

Leach drank off the whiskey in his glass and poured another. "In the split second between the firing of the gun and the bullet hitting him in the heart, I'd realized I was wrong. But you can't call the bullet back once you've pulled the trigger."

"I assume I am to take some lesson from that story, Inspector—Geoff—but I've had a long day, and the part of my brain I use to solve riddles is down for maintenance. So just spit it out, will you?"

"The point is this, George. You've lost a man today. I hope we find the lad who's gone missing, but given the track record of the killer, we've got to assume that we've got another man down—alive, if we're lucky— but he'd have reported in if he could."

"Tell me something I don't know."

"You will never forget the look of death on your man Dickens' face. You'll never stop wondering if you could have given some other order that would have kept him alive. Oh, it won't be true. Nothing short of a crystal ball and the talent for it would have stopped what happened in Thorgill today, but you'll never really believe that. And telling his wife that Dickens won't be coming home is just about the hardest thing you'll ever do. Easier, maybe, to be the one with his throat cut."

Powell drank off his whiskey, and Leach refilled his glass yet again. Then, he changed direction.

"Do you have a wife, George?"

That stopped the man for a moment. "Yes," he said. "What has that to do with Dickens lying dead on a slab in York?"

Leach leaned across the table, his face as close to the

other man's as he could get it. "Just some advice. Go home tonight and take your wife to bed. You climb right up inside her and stay there until morning. Let your prick do your talking for you—it never lies—and listen when it tells you that you are a human being like the rest of us. A direct line to the angels doesn't come with the title DCI, nor does it confer godhood. For tonight, let it go."

"Leave my wife out of this."

"Fine," Leach agreed. "Just, don't you leave her out of it, or you'll be spending your nights alone in a pub drinking back the memories for the rest of your life."

"Spoken like a man who knows?" Powell asked. He didn't sound quite so hostile this time.

Leach nodded, more deliberately than usual. The whiskey was beginning to work on his reflexes, but he still had one thing more to say. "You're angry now, at yourself and at the man who did this. Your lads won't be blaming you, but they'll be mad as fire at the perp. Now, Colin Gathers may or may not be guilty, but killing him won't make you feel better, nor will looking into the eyes of one of your officers and seeing the memory of another policeman's death on his hands."

Powell put both palms down on the table, bracketing the whiskey bottle. In spite of the drink, he spoke clearly. "When the call came in about the beating of the local constable, I authorized guns for any man who wanted to carry one for the duration of this operation. Few chose to do so, believing our numbers here protected us. I think you will see that change tomorrow.

"If you know where this man Gathers is hiding, I'd suggest you get word to him and urge him to surrender. Too many people have died here to waste my time on pity for their murderer."

Powell rose from his seat then, and moved carefully to the door. His driver fell in behind him, grabbing open the door to let the DCI pass. "Need a ride?" he asked Leach.

Leach shook his head. "I could use the walk to clear my head."

"You're sure now?" Toby peered out into the darkness. "It's no problem to take you back into town."

"Don't worry, Officer. I'll be fine." Leach's hand crept to the charm he wore. In spite of himself, he found that it gave him a sense of safety. Hell, the place was rubbing off on him. But he did carry a charm that would stop a flesh and blood specter—and it carried a thirteen-round clip. "Go ahead; take him home."

The driver nodded and followed Powell out the door. Moments later, Leach heard the sound of the engine turning over and the car moved away, leaving behind just the shuffle of the waitress' feet and the clatter of the dishes as she cleared up the table.

"It's past closing time," she hinted with the subtlety that had marked the rest of her service. "Are you planning to stay long?"

Leach shook his head but continued to sit, staring at the label of the whiskey bottle without quite seeing it. In the morning, he knew, the dale would be crawling with armed men who did not know Col Gathers but were hurting from the loss of one of their own. With the senior Gathers already in the nick, they'd elected Col as most likely suspect, but they had no proof, no solid circumstantial evidence. If you took the motive—Thorgill's legendary murderous ghost—at face value, as a warning, not a threat, they had nothing but a knot of coincidences made up mostly of where Col hadn't been at the times of the murders. Not at work, when the archaeologists were murdered, not in custody when someone beat Tuttle and sliced Dickens' throat.

He tipped the empty bottle onto its side, imagining a three-masted schooner in full sail riding on the dregs. If you turned the problem on its side, what did you get? Think warning, not threat. Col had grown up here, knew these people intimately. And he'd grown up under the shadow of the tomb itself. So he would have known if a local had a fixation on the legend. But why keep it a secret? Not just another villager, then, but family? Barbara Finlay had driven Col out of town and returned without him, but she'd been with Leach, answering questions when Dickens was killed. And Kate had been in the cottage as well. Common sense left him Col, or a stranger, but he didn't believe it was the latter—everything in the village pointed to the Gathers. That left Col, or . . .

"Do you have a public telephone?" he asked the waitress.

"In the back, there," she answered, and added, "closing in five."

Leach nodded. Making his way to the back of the pub, he fished a pile of change out of his pocket and fed it into the telephone. He dialed Pickering and waited, giving the officer on the line his identification. "Patch me through to London, major crimes," he asked.

When a familiar voice came on the line, the tension eased a bit at his temples. "Jack," he said, "I need some information from public records, I need it tomorrow morning, and I need it kept quiet."

"Is this about Col?" the man on the other end of the line asked. He'd been in on the London connection with the museum and the National Trust, Leach remembered.

"What do the lads think?" Leach asked, and waited

out the pause on the line. Jack thought before he spoke, always.

"Col's a strange duck, no question about that," he said. "But the lads trust him. What's up, boss?"

"York has him in their sights as the killer. And I mean that literally. They've lost one of their own, and the DCI in charge is taking it very personally."

"Just tell me what you want, DCI Leach. We'll handle it."

God, it felt good, like talking to a voice of sanity after a day and a half in an asylum. "Get to public records," he said. "I want birth records on Col and his sister Kate, and their cousin Barbara Finlay. Check for other relatives they may have in Yorkshire. And find his damned mother."

"We've been looking for Mrs. Gathers, but she seems to have disappeared. We've put an inquiry through Interpol, but so far nothing." Leach sensed the disappointment in the man's voice. While there was no proof that her disappearance had any connection with the Thorgill murders, finding her would go a long way toward unraveling the case they were building against Col.

"Anything else, sir?"

"I don't want the information faxed or telephoned through York. Send Jacobs and Spencer with it in the morning. And make reservations for them in Pickering, for the duration."

"Armed?" Jack asked.

This time, it was Leach's turn to hesitate. "Armed," he finally said, and rung off. He'd done all he could for one night. Passing back through the pub to the front door, he dropped a few bills on the table. "If I owe you any more, send the tab to Laura Simms' B and B in the morning."

CHAPTER 17

This time when Col awoke he found himself in silent darkness. His head felt heavy, his thoughts moved sluggishly, and for a moment fear almost tore the veil of fog from his mind. His good neighbors, uncertain of his cooperation, had drugged him.

But he knew that wasn't true; they needed his willing cooperation as much as they needed his body. As the pounding of his heart settled, he remembered the first time. He'd understood only vaguely what they'd expected of him, except that he had to go clear-headed to his duty because the offering of his selfhood had to be freely given. His father had walked with him and reassured him, and Granny Finlay had been there, standing next to Kate. The old woman who was the Finlay, Thorgill's king, had wrapped her fragile fingers around his neck and kissed him on the forehead when he approached her. Raging with embarrassment and fear of what he would do, he'd resisted her until he'd seen the tears in her eyes. Then he'd known there would be no escape.

Slowly Col grew aware of a change in the quality of the darkness. Red light glittered in the stairwell, rising with the sound of shuffling feet and the rustle of leaves and branches. Henry Tuttle reached the head of the stairs, his torch held low to protect the thatch. "Time, Col." he said.

Gathers closed his eyes. "This isn't real."

This isn't real; he repeated the words silently, like a mantra, as five or six of the townsmen crowded into the room. Charlie White stood candles on Granny Finlay's dresser and on the bedside table. He lit the first from Henry's torch, then moved from one to the next, tongues of fire springing to life in his wake. Col watched, mesmerized, while some distant part of him moved deep, deep, curled in the pit of his belly. His vision closed down around a reality narrowed to a dark tunnel that ended in the languorous writhing of a candle flame. *I am dead, I am dead, and they cannot touch me—*

Work-roughened hands lifted him at the shoulders. He helped them that much, turning to sit on the side of the bed while they stripped off his shirt and socks and unfastened his belt and his jeans. He would tell them later it was pointless; he had died there, lying in Granny Finlay's bed, and waited only for the candle flame to become a path of light to follow.

"Come on, Col. Up with you—"

He stood at their urging, let them strip the clothes from him until he was naked, and then the sponge, warm with herb-scented water from the gill, passed over his chest, his thighs, his genitals. He shuddered at the touch but said nothing as he continued his silent mantra: *It isn't real.*

Pressed against the gable end of the room, Henry held his torch high enough to read from the Psalms, though it wasn't green pastures they planned for Col to lie down in that night. Closer, the voices of Charlie and Dick Morgan and the others murmured old chants in his ears as they brushed his flesh with boughs of laurel. The deeper Col drew himself inside his body, trying to escape their ministrations, the more acutely aware he became of what the men were doing, but he would not show the pain that each gentle touch became.

I am dead, he repeated to himself, *I am stone*. He let them move his arms, his legs, incapable of lifting even his eyelids without instructions. His father should be here to whisper that he was doing the right thing and to hold him when it was done. No Finlay had ever gone to the tomb so alone before, at least not in village memory.

Dick Morgan seemed to read some of Col's dread. His hand lay warm on Col's shoulder. "I'm so sorry about this, Col, but I'll be with you tonight. We won't let your da down." Morgan dropped his head to rest for a moment on his own hand at Col's shoulder, and Col remembered that the man had loved his mother once. If not for fate and a passing archaeologist with a passion for old legends and an infatuation with the girl who lived halfway up the valley, Col's last name would be Morgan; even now, most of the villagers seemed to think she had betrayed Dick Morgan for the stranger.

But Henry had finished his prayers with a sign of the cross traced in the air, and the others had finished their chants to god and goddess, to earth and air and the place below where spring waited out the winter to burst forth again into life. They wrapped Col in a tunic of fine linen, embroidered with an explosion of spring flowers and tied at his waist with a silk cord, and they put soft boots on his feet. Then they snuffed the candles, one by one, and filed down the stairs again, Henry in the lead and Morgan last, with Col before him. They would leave the house through the potting shed, he knew, but he was unprepared for the smell of evergreen and laurel that filled Granny

Finlay's parlor. The scent threw him back in time, and he was suddenly fifteen again and terrified.

"I can't," he said.

Dick Morgan held tight to his shoulder. "You'll do just fine," he whispered. "Your father would be proud of you."

They were in the garden then, joined by about ten others who murmured softly in the dark.

The dark. Col looked up, but he found no stars, no moon, only an unrelenting drizzle that misted his face and chilled him under the light tunic. But torches had been lit and passed around. Silent but for the hiss of the mist dying against the torch flames, the group moved up the slope at a gentle angle that would put them on the moor a short distance from the tomb.

From the direction of the village another torchlit procession already moved higher up the slope toward the tomb. Col knew that his own party's start had been timed to reach the meeting place shortly after the other, but he could not let his mind take him beyond the awareness of the torchlight moving in the dark. The boots he wore had no soles to speak of, but he seemed to move above the ground somehow—no stone or branch disturbed his footsteps. His father had said that the earth bowed to honor the Finlay in the moments of high ceremony. Older now, Col knew he was just numb.

They reached the break in the stone fence that marked the beginning of the moor and passed through. Already the party ahead of them had come to a stop at the tomb. The dreadful irony struck Col that the archaeologists had done them a favor when they'd cleared a wide circle around the site. He hoped the dead appreciated their contribution. But Henry gave him no time to reflect on the tragedy. The parson reached the first party, the women's escort, and began to sort the band into a circle, alternating man and woman, as Col's escort party entered the clearing around the tomb. Finally, Dick Morgan stepped into the circle, his hand at Col's back pressing him forward. Morgan took Henry Tuttle's torch and stepped back to close the circle again, leaving Col to face Henry alone.

"Do you come before the good people of Thorgill as their anointed king, their protector in all things above the earth and below?" Henry asked him, and Col replied, "I do."

"Do you come before your people prepared to perform the duties of their king, in the giving of life and the taking, in bounty and famine?"

Col hesitated. Here was the crux of the matter. If he answered yes, he would belong to the people of Thorgill thereafter. If he answered no, the circle around him would thin, inexorably, as Anris tolled his dreadful revenge. Henry waited.

"I do," Col said.

Henry Tuttle nodded the village's acceptance of Col's vow and asked the last question: "Should there arise a time of need or despair, of famine or disease and pain, do you pledge your life to the earth and the winter gods below, to treat with them for the lives of your village?"

It was easier to promise to die for the village than to live for them; Col did not hesitate in his pledge: "I do."

"Now is the Spring, the time of giving life, of plowing fields and planting seeds. Your people rejoice in you; they rejoice that their king, husband of his people, plants the seed of his successor in the belly of the land."

Henry reached for him then and held Col close for a moment. "Have courage," he whispered. "Do what you must, and God will forgive you." Weeping, the parson freed the silk cord from Col's waist and unwrapped the tunic. Behind him, hands lifted the tunic from his shoulders and he was free, drifting over the gathering like a spirit. He saw his own body, naked but for the soft boots on his feet, and heard Henry speak to the flesh he had been: "Behold the Earth, your bride," he said, and stepped away.

Over the heads of the circle he saw Barbara standing guard next to the tomb. Her face showed no emotion, a state he'd only seen when she was in the deepest distress. Finally, he let himself see the grassy roof of the tomb. Kate lay there, naked except for her own boots and the tunic that lay open on the grass. Their mother sat cradling Kate's head, holding Kate's hands to her heart.

"It will be all right, Col," Katherine Gathers said, but the tears ran unheeded down her face, as they ran down Kate's. Then, drawn back to flesh by duty and the honor he owed Kate to be there with her, soul to soul, Col felt the dampness of his own tears. He did not reach to brush them away; they were his gift to Kate, recognition that he shared her sorrow.

Hands urged Colin Gathers forward, and he climbed to the roof of the tomb and stood over his mother and his sister. "I'm sorry," he whispered, and heard Kate's low, "I know." Then he fell to his knees and swept her into his arms, crying, "I'm sorry, I'm sorry," while she stroked his back and his arms and whispered, "I know, I know," and the chant of the villagers mixed with the smoke of burning torches and the smell of young grass broken beneath them. And the woman in his arms became all women to him and the Earth that was their mother. His body moved in the rhythm of the chant, and she accepted him and drank his tears, and the chanting masked their weeping.

CHAPTER 18

Leach glared into the impenetrable darkness beyond the pub, angry at himself for refusing the ride to his bed and breakfast. He'd let his need to remove himself from the anger and guilt of the Yorkshire DCI blind him to the facts of the Thorgill landscape, had forgotten that dark fell like a stone here. And the drizzle had started again. Behind him the lights of the pub went out, changing the quality of the darkness but not his ability to navigate it.

With a sigh that admitted defeat, he turned back to the pub and beat on the locked door. A man wearing a light coat and a hat opened it and frowned when he saw Leach.

"Forget something?" he asked.

"I'll need to use your telephone," Leach said. "See if I can call for a pickup." He felt stupid standing in the dark, trying to avoid explaining to this man that he couldn't find his way back to the village on the only road leading in that direction.

The man looked over Leach's shoulder, into the night, and nodded. "Give me a minute to tell the Mrs.," he said, and closed the door again, leaving the inspector to the dark.

No, not all dark. There, on the side of the valley, he noticed a flicker of red. Fire. He heard an engine kick over then, and the publican drove around the corner of the White Rose in a battered Ford. The waitress sat at his side; she reached behind her and unlocked the back door.

"Just put those box lids out of your way," she instructed him when he ducked into the back seat. "You staying at Laura Simms' place?"

"Yes. But first, we need to report that fire—" Leach pointed to the angry red smudge and realized that it had moved.

"No need," the waitress said. "It's taken care of."

Leach settled back for the ride. When no alarm seemed to raise the lights in the village, though, he wondered whether the publican had in fact reported the blaze.

After a short trip in silence, the Ford drifted to a halt in front of a lightless cottage not much larger than the two or three that marked the stone-chip road between the village and the Finlay cottage on the side of the dale. Leach got out with a thank-you aborted on his lips. The publican had begun to roll the car before Leach had closed the door, and he had to run to make sure the latch caught. He watched, but the old Ford headed farther up the road, not turning. Nothing up there but the Finlay place, as far as Leach could tell, and the fire, of course. He cursed softly under his breath; he couldn't follow them on foot through the darkness, and the liquor had left him rather the worse for police work anyway. He felt unaccountably embarrassed about facing Col's neighbors in that condition, so he tried the door to the B and B, before rousing someone inside.

The door opened at his touch. He tried to enter quietly, but the dark was even thicker indoors. He only noticed the hooked rug at the entrance when he tripped over it. He stumbled, caught his balance with an arm around a lamp, and managed to save himself before he brought the lamp down as well. So much for unobtrusive entrances. He snapped on the light in a Victorian wonder of a parlor, all cut-velvet upholstery and embroidered antimacassars that reminded him of the bloodstained tablecloth that had covered Constable Dickens. The lamp stood on one of several heavily pedestaled mahogany tables, for which Leach felt heartily grateful; had it been one of those fragile little things that Margaret used to keep scattered about the house, it would have gone over, lamp and all, in a mess of shattered china and broken wood. Once he'd gotten it righted, though, he realized that no one had come looking for the cause of the disturbance.

"Ms. Simms!" he called, wanting to reassure her that the noise was a clumsy boarder, not a thief or the Thorgill murderer, but she gave no answer. Finally, Leach stopped and really listened to the house. Empty. He was sure of it, but he wandered through the ground floor turning on lights and looking for signs of life.

Laura Simms' bed and breakfast had a dining room across the hall from the parlor and a kitchen with a back door onto the garden behind it. Staring into the night from the back door, he could see the fire he'd reported to the publican, and he realized why the man had shown neither surprise nor alarm. The flames were moving all right, but in a straggling, deliberate line up the side of the valley. Leach went back into the kitchen and rummaged through the drawers until he found the flashlights. Choosing one with a strong, steady glow, he turned off the house lights and stepped out into the night.

The garden backed onto the slope a few hundred yards down the valley from the Finlay cottage. Here most of the stones had been cleared, and the grass underfoot was newly mown. Locating the flames again, Leach realized that they had stopped on the moor above the dale; he couldn't be sure, but it seemed that whoever was moving about up there had come to rest overlooking the Finlay cottage. Not surprising, he supposed; the village seemed to take this king business seriously, and Gathers had gone missing. Or maybe not. Barbara Finlay'd had time to bring him home, though he'd given her credit for being smarter than that.

Leach had just one sure way to find out. He focused the beam of light on the ground at his feet, watching for rocks or vines that occasionally reached out to trip him, and moved off at an angle that would take him to the moor just short of the archaeological excavation.

As he approached the rise on the moor, Leach heard the sound of chanting, the words obscured by distance or the rain or by the alien quality of the sound. Just ahead he saw the undressed stone fence that marked the boundary between the valley and civilization, and beyond it flames danced on torches that circled the tomb where the archaeologists had died. Leach snapped off his own light and crept closer, unwilling to disturb the villagers until he understood better what was happening. By the torchlight he could see clearly now. He watched, frozen, just outside the circle, as two entwined bodies, naked except for their suede boots, moved in the frenzied rhythms of sexual orgasm on the roof of the old tomb.

The chant itself gained speed to match the pair on the tomb, and a roar went up from the torchbearers as the man threw back his head in blind experience of his own sensations at the moment of completion and Leach saw his face. "Col!"

Leach broke through the circle as it began to break up, figures moving in the flickering light to lift the detective and support him. Leach remembered the face of Dick Morgan, the grocer who'd been waiting for Col with a sack of rock salt and the clutter of a handyman's drawer when they'd arrived in Thorgill. And Henry, Laura Simms' nervous parson, stood next to Gathers, reading from his Bible while men with stolid faces he did not recognize lifted the sergeant's naked arms and covered him with some kind of vest that did the minimum for decency.

For a moment Leach stared into Colin Gathers' eyes and thought that he'd been mistaken. The man he'd worked with for two years had never shown him that face, tracked with tears and lined with a terrible knowledge. The eyes of this man held a depth of horror that could swallow a soul whole, and Leach broke contact before those eyes could suck him empty. Then lids shuttered the darkness, and Colin Gathers stood in front of him, or nearly stood, held up by the men who supported him on either side.

Barbara Finlay pushed forward then. "Take him home," she ordered the men, and added, "don't let him fall!" when Col would have done so. When he had moved out of the light, she turned on Leach.

"What the *hell* are you doing here?" she demanded.

Leach caught a breath to answer and lost it when he glanced at the tomb where Col had been. "Kate!" he said, and his stomach knotted. Not Kate, who saw too much and knew too much and recognized him as more than the memories that haunted his sleep. He could have loved her, accepted her child as his own.

Leach doubled over, trying to hide his face while his dinner and half a bottle of blended whiskey emptied themselves on the bracken surrounding the clearing. A woman's hand touched the back of his neck and he wrenched away.

"Leave me alone!"

"You've had a shock, Inspector." The parson held out a linen handkerchief. "Take it slowly; get your breath back." Henry stood there with his Bible tucked under his arm and an expression of understanding on a face that no longer seemed laughable.

Leach took the handkerchief and wiped his face with it, but he was left with the taste of bile and stale whiskey in his mouth and a question about his own sanity in his mind. Laura Simms watched him solemnly from beside the parson until Barbara Finlay took her place; then she slipped away.

"I'm going to kill him," Leach decided, and didn't realize he'd spoken out loud until Barbara Finlay answered him.

"No, you won't, Inspector." She paused, thoughtful for a moment, then shook her head. "Not my decision. Do you think you can get him home, Henry?"

"Laura's?"

Leach heard a hopeful note in the parson's question, but Barbara Finlay dashed his hopes.

"The cottage. Col will have to deal with him. In the meantime—" she stopped, looking at him with a degree of contempt he hadn't seen since Derry, and turned away. "I don't have time for this. Kate needs me."

The parson waited until she was out of earshot and shrugged. "Sorry. I had hoped . . . but she's right, Col will know what to do. But, well, the boy could use some help himself right now."

"Looked like he was doing fine on his own," Leach pointed out, sarcasm heavy, partly from outrage and partly to mask his own shaky control. He'd never had children of his own, but he knew that you sorted this sort of thing out when they were young, before it got to . . . this. You didn't sell tickets.

The parson shook his head and sighed. "Don't condemn what you don't understand, Inspector Leach.

Thorgill has its own troubles and its own way of dealing with them."

Leach gave that the credence it was due and looked around at the villagers beginning to drift down the side of the dale.

"Where's Kate?" Then, with a realization that raised a blind rage boiling behind his eyes, "Where's Katy?"

"Asleep in her bed," Tuttle assured him. "And if you are here, Jean and Frank must have gotten the pub closed, so they'll be with her."

Well, it explained their hurry to be rid of him. Leach let some of the anger go—they hadn't corrupted the child with their abominations, at least. But he resisted when the parson put a hand on his sleeve and urged him toward the break in the stone fence.

"I'm sorry, Inspector, but Col will be judging tonight, and you've got a pretty heavy charge against you, coming up here like this."

Somehow the notion of answering to a man wanted for questioning on mass murder for the charge of observing same in the act of fornicating with his sister in a public place pushed the whole night into the realm of the absurd. Leach began to laugh. "This is a hallucination," he explained to the parson. "And tomorrow I shall swear off liquor."

But the laughter was gone, slipping inexorably into tears, and Leach fought them back. For the job, for the dead, and most especially for George Powell's young constable, whose wife would never hold their child, Geoffrey Leach would stop Colin Gathers.

CHAPTER 19

Leach stumbled in the dark and cursed. He found some twisted solace in the words and in Parson Henry's discomfort, but he couldn't have stopped the stream of vilification if he'd wanted to. The words poured damnation on Colin Gathers and his mad relations, on the village of Thorgill and the moors that crouched above it. By the time they reached the cottage, Henry was staring at him with blind compassion, and Leach cursed the parson for realizing he was out of control.

"Thorgill is a little different," Henry cautioned as they neared the potting shed, "and the next hour or so will be a bit uncomfortable for everyone. But if you try to understand, if you can convince Col you are not a threat, I'm sure it will all work out."

"I'm sorry, Parson, but things are not working out in your little village." Leach had regained a bit of control, but the anger still simmered, fueled by fear and by pure Christian indignation, if he'd admit it, which he wouldn't because he only went to church to please Margaret—Leach took a deep breath to pull his skittering thoughts together. "When DCI Powell returns tomorrow, he will have a warrant for Gathers' arrest on multiple counts of murder. While the evidence is circumstantial on the murders, I saw him rape his sister. I can't ignore that."

Henry stopped him in the doorway. "What exactly did you see, Inspector?"

Shocked, Leach pulled away from the man. "I saw it all. I'll describe it in court if I have to, but I'm not about to repeat it for you!"

"Remember Col, Inspector," Henry urged him. "Did he look to you like a man who was indulging lustful passions with an inappropriate partner?"

Leach worked his way through the parson's indirection. "The crime of rape does not require that the perpetrator enjoy the act," he explained. "Commission of the act suffices in the eyes of the law and in the eyes of the victim. I'd suggest you spend a little of that Christian charity on her."

"You might do the same," Henry cautioned.

Kate. God. The warmth of her smile flickered through his awareness, swallowed by the memory of her naked legs entwined with Col's, her arms wrapped tight around his shoulders. She had wept when her brother left her body—no! Shaken, he let the parson guide him through the potting shed and into the parlor.

Col sat in the rocking chair in front of the fireplace. Flames crackled on the hearth, but their warmth did not relieve the fine tremors that shook the sergeant's hands where he gripped the arms of the chair. He'd added a pair of soft brown trousers to the gaudy vest and suede boots he had worn on the moor; Gathers should have looked as though he had just walked off the stage of a costume play somewhere, but his face still carried the mark of this night's work, the reflection of some horror that Leach could not see flickering in his eyes. Leach felt the presence of time in the room, as if all the Finlay kings that had gone before him were resurrected in Colin Gathers' terrible, unseeing eyes.

Leach wrenched his gaze from Col—no king of his,

but a policeman gone too big for his britches—to scan the room. He recognized most of the people standing at respectful attention there, but a brief catalog of the newcomers and the absent seemed more note-worthy to him. Neither Kate nor her daughter were anywhere to be seen. Constable Tuttle, who had called Gathers to Thorgill, lay in a hospital bed in York; he would not be home for a long time. And an older, grayer version of Kate stood just behind and to the side of the rocking chair, one hand on its back. He would have spoken then, but two villagers moved forward to face Gathers.

"What brings you to the Finlay?" Col asked.

The taller of the two men twisted a cap between his hands. Leach remembered the man on the moor, lifting Gathers from the roof of the tomb, and could not reconcile the image of that grim watchman with the servile cotter who stood in Colin Gathers' parlor.

"Begging your pardon, your Lordship, but Tucker and I have property abutting on the other side of the dale. Since the time of my grandfather, both families have honored the oak tree he planted there to mark the boundary line."

"And?" Col turned to the other man, who pushed more defiance into his tone but still did not lift his head to meet Col's gaze head-on.

"Lightning struck the oak tree last summer, your Lordship, and Finch here claimed the tree, and the land it stood upon, as rightly his."

"Was my grandfather planted the oak—his tree, our tree." Finch interrupted his neighbor, who gave him a dirty look before continuing his explanation.

"My boy, come home from Leeds for a visit, said, 'Get a survey done right from the county engineer and find out who actually owns that piece of ground.' I've got the results right here, showed 'em to Finch, but he would have none of it." The man pulled a thick sheaf of paper from his breast pocket and handed it over.

Col looked from one man to the other, the packet unopened in his hand. "Who has cared for the tree since its planting?" he asked.

"Both families, for three generations," Tucker answered.

"It's a shame the Tuckers and the Finches have fertilized the soil with their good sense, leaving none left for themselves when the tree had died," Col observed. "Very well. This is my judgment, as well you knew it would be, scoundrels both of you: the boundary stays where the good faith of your families put it. The death of the oak tree in no way breaks the agreement sealed with its planting. You will, both Tuckers and Finches, share in the cutting of the tree, and equally share in the cord wood derived from it. What say you?"

Tucker ducked his head. "The law is just, My Lord."

"Thank you, My Lord," Finch agreed.

"And Tucker—" Col flipped the packet of paper that represented the land survey into the fire. "Get that boy of yours down from Leeds to help with the cutting. He needs a reminder that Thorgill still lives by its old laws.

"Does anyone else among you ask for judgement?" Gathers asked, and Morgan, the grocer, nudged Leach forward.

"Last," Gathers admonished, and Leach felt the tension in his shoulders relax a bit when the sergeant's attention had moved on. The realization annoyed him; Leach was too old, too practiced in the ways of the world to give himself over to superstitious fear of the mad.

Laura Simms stepped forward then, her head bowed. Henry gave Leach a reassuring pat and then followed her onto the braided rug that marked the judging area before Col's chair.

"Yes, Daughter?" Col asked, although Leach figured the woman had six years on him at least.

Laura Simms did not seem surprised at the form of address, however; she smiled and held out her hand. Henry moved to her side, and clasped the offered hand in his own.

"I wish to take this man for my own, dear Lord" she said, "and he wishes to be mine."

"Is that so, Henry Tuttle?" Colin asked. Though the words carried due solemnity, Leach saw humor glinting in the eyes of both men.

"Pardon that I call no man my Lord but God himself in heaven, Mr. Gathers, but it is so. I do wish to be the man of Miss Simms' heart, as she wishes to be the woman of mine."

Gathers smiled and reached to Laura Simms, who went to him and bent low to accept his kiss on her forehead. "Then take him, Daughter, to your home and heart. Be happy with him all your days, and greet him when he joins you for the next turning of the wheel."

Releasing her, he turned to Henry Tuttle. "I suppose you'll want a proper Christian wedding, Henry?"

"As you say, Col. But we both want you to say a few words, to make it official in the eyes of the village as well."

"If your God and mine grant me life, I will. And thank you, Henry." Col's glance rested just a moment on Leach.

Henry Tuttle seemed to read his meaning; he glanced in the same direction, then nodded. Laura took him by the hand then, and led him from the circle.

"And now, Morgan? You had a petition?"

"As you well know, Col."

This one didn't bother with the amenities, and Leach saw in the confrontation the living reality of Col's earliest words to him about Thorgill's history. To Morgan, a king was a king only as long as he served his purpose—to judge the villagers and to die for the village. Leach figured he was the sort of man who would chuck the local Judas goat off a cliff first and ask questions later. He had company there; hands, neither as friendly nor as comforting as Henry Tuttle's had been, took hold of Leach by the arms and drew him forward to stand on the braided rug in front of the fireplace. Ludicrous, but he didn't laugh.

Morgan stood behind him—to keep him from running or from attacking?—and Leach reviewed the fifteen ways he knew to subdue the man, lingering over the deadly ones a moment longer than was absolutely necessary. He knew better than to think he could take on the whole roomful of people, though; best to let the farce play itself out.

"Mrs. Jack Gathers, I presume?" Leach tilted his head in a tight nod of acknowledgment at the woman who stood at Colin Gathers' back. "Your husband has been arrested for your murder, among others," he informed her.

"Jack didn't kill anyone," the woman answered. "But he will do what he must. He understands the danger Anris threatens, not only to Thorgill but to the world."

"Isn't 'the world' reaching a bit, even for a family as megalomaniacal as this one?" Leach asked.

"The last time, Anris didn't have jet planes or railroads," Col's mother explained. "If we don't stop him here, now, he will make Hitler look like a dime-store villain."

Morgan spoke up then, but he did not move from his place guarding the "prisoner."

"Save your breath, mum," he said. "This one don't believe and never will. Tut tried, Barbara tried. Very good at not seeing what he should, this London high muckamuck, but bloody awful at not seeing what he shouldn't."

The grocer then shifted his attention to address Col: "I know he's yours boss, but if he reports what he's seen, they'll take Kate's children away. Granny Finlay had the raising of you for most of your young life, but who will guard the tomb when you are gone and Kate is alone if the children never learn the duty they were born to?"

Children. Katy too? Leach shuddered. He had thought her a cute little thing, a bit solemn, but—did she know who had fathered her?

"I won't let anything happen to Katy or the boy. You have my vow. All of you." Col glared them down, the very image of the outraged father.

"Deny it, Col, please." Leach slid the plea between the words of a prayer, but whatever God he spoke to wasn't listening.

"They are my children, too."

And Col's mother had the same gray eyes, the same hair, as Col and his sister and as Col's daughter. How long . . . ? *At least it would bolster support for a plea of insanity,* Leach thought. Inbreeding did strange things to the psychological profile—it wouldn't be the first time it turned murderous. If a man were innocent of anything, it was his own genetic makeup.

"He's seen, for Christ's sake, Colin!" the grocer said.

"Christ had nothing to do with this evening, Dick," Colin reminded them, his voice more bitter than Leach had ever heard it. "What are you suggesting?"

In spite of himself, Leach held his breath.

"You know the price for seeing what this one's seen tonight."

Colin Gathers closed his eyes. "Do you want his blood on your hands?"

"Now wait—" Leach took a single step forward.

Col opened his eyes again, pinning him with a raptor's gaze that paralyzed him. "Stay out of this, Leach," he said, "you are in more danger than you know." The sergeant looked past him, then, at the grocer who stood at Leach's shoulder. "I'll decide what's to become of him when I'm ready, Dick."

Not likely. Leach wasn't about to stand quietly by while a perverted cult of loonies decided his fate.

"If you plan to kill me, Sergeant, do it now. Or surrender yourself for arrest."

Col leaned forward in his chair, exhaustion burned away suddenly in the swift burst of anger. "You sell your life cheaply, Inspector."

"Not cheaply." Leach's voice dropped, bravado gone. His fault. "I should have stopped you in London."

The twist of a knowing smile told Leach that Gathers understood more than either would say, that he shared Leach's vision of the bloody stair landing. But this time, when Gathers bled and gasped for breath, Leach did not call for help or demand that Gathers hang on to life but wept and said, "I'm sorry, Col, I'm sorry," while Gathers gripped his hand and then embraced his death. Easier for all concerned, perhaps, that smile seemed to say, and Leach denied it, though they both knew it was true.

"I should have put it on record that you weren't fit yet. I didn't, and now young Constable Dickens is dead, his partner missing. It has to stop, Col!"

"I haven't killed anyone." Gathers paused, his attention leaving Leach to drift over the solemn villagers. Leach would not give them the satisfaction of looking over his shoulder, though the skin prickled down his back as visions of bloody bread knives danced in his head.

"Yet." Gathers finished the disavowal. "But you have, Inspector."

Leach met Col's gaze and followed it into darkness.

"If you die here, tonight, know that you throw your life away for Thorgill's reasons, because your continued existence endangers its future, not to placate some bitter god of your own conscience. Your past means nothing to us." Gathers beat at him with words while the man's bleak eyes burned Leach to the soul. "You mean nothing."

Leach gave a bitter, reflective laugh then. "I'm a policeman, Col. I'm accustomed to meaning nothing to the people I serve, but I owe them no less because of it. Where's Pankowitz? His family hasn't done a thing to this town—they deserve at least the right to bury their dead son."

"I don't know where he is, DCI Leach." Col seemed to be listening to something no one else could hear; then his attention returned to Leach. "But I doubt that he's dead yet in any event. May wish he were, if Anris used his hands to kill a friend, but it was none of my doing.

"Give us tomorrow, DCI Leach. Help us put Anris away." Col smiled at him, and Leach shuddered to see the cold, mad sanity of the man. "I don't guarantee that you will live through it, but you can at least give some meaning to your dying."

"I can't. I'm just a cop, like you, Sergeant. I do what the law tells me. Let me take you in, before Powell comes looking for you tomorrow morning. His men will be armed. They're frightened and they're grieving.

At least let me get you home in one piece for the docs to take a look at."

"You're a fool, Inspector." Gathers rose from his chair and paced the distance of the hearth and back, coming to rest so close that Leach could smell the musk of sex still clinging to him. "What would it take to convince you that you are wrong?"

"Think about what you are asking me to believe, Col. It isn't rational."

"Rational? No."

Gathers beat his fist against the mantlepiece, and Leach heard the snap of breaking bone. Sick, he remembered the body that Gathers called the Finlay lying in the entrance to the tomb above the cottage. The sound of bones breaking against the stone that sealed Gathers' long-ago ancestor to his fate echoed in the crack of Col's hand against the mantle. Leach tried to imagine what it had been like, to die in the darkness with only madness for company.

Col remembered too. He sank into his chair, the fear suddenly so stark upon his face that Leach could not bear to look at it.

"What would it take?" The fear was gone as fast as it had come, smoldering anger regaining its place. They'd talked about that problem in Colin Gathers' nature before: the man never coped well with stupidity.

Suddenly the roof overhead burst into flames, the snap and sputter of the fireplace magnified a thousand fold as the thatch caught and burned. Leach coughed; the heat overhead raising a sweat and burning it off again. He fought the urge to run, and the memory of his first night in his house kept the terror out of his voice, if not out of his gut.

"How did you drug me this time, Col? Something I touched? Something in the air?"

"Col!" Morgan, his voice hoarse, called Gathers' name through his own coughing, and Leach saw the hand that Col's mother lay on his shoulder tighten until her knuckles showed white. Someone at the back of the crowd fainted.

"That's enough, Col," she said quietly.

Col's eyelids fell slowly, and as they did, the intensity of the fire above them dropped, too late to stop a shower of cinders that fell on Leach and burned their pinpoints into his skin.

Hallucinations. He'd been drugged, Leach told himself, but the smudges of ash felt real on his face, and the burns they left stung his cheeks.

Barbara Finlay, whom Leach had come to suspect more than her cousin, simply looked exasperated. "How far does the damage go, Col?" she asked with long-suffering patience in her voice.

"Hit the moor pretty badly," Col admitted without opening his eyes, "but I think the valley stayed out of it."

Leach followed Barbara Finlay's gaze to the ceiling, but her next words made him slightly ill: "It was time we had a slate roof on this place anyway."

People didn't share the same hallucination. Suggestion required some clue—a word, a gesture—but Col had said nothing, nor had he looked at the thatched roof overhead. Of their own accord, it seemed, the muttered words spilled from Geoff's lips, and he realized he was praying and that the parson was doing the same beside him. But Dick Morgan was shaking his head.

"Enough." Col barely voiced the word; his hand lifted in a warding gesture. "I need to speak with the DCI, alone," he said. "Then I need to prepare for tomorrow. Any man or woman with a case to bring will gather in the garden at midday. For the rest, we will meet here tomorrow night. One way or the other, we'll finish it then."

The parson tightened a hand on Leach's arm for a moment of reassurance. "Col will know what to do," he said. "Try to listen with an open mind, Inspector."

"We'll see you back at the house," Laura Simms assured him. She took Henry's hand, and Leach watched the couple follow the others from the cottage.

When they were alone, Col's mother pushed the hair back from her son's forehead and lightly brushed a kiss where it had lain. In the flicker of that moment her face played out all the love and pain and regret she had not shown to the villagers. Col had learned his masks from a master; Leach wondered which image of the woman was true—the flash of feeling or the emotionless monster who let her husband lie in prison for her murder while she urged her children to a frenzy of unnatural passion? Then she left them, and Leach faced Colin Gathers alone.

CHAPTER 20

The fire, sunken to coals in the fireplace, mesmerized Col. He felt the pain in his hand grow distant as awareness sank more deeply into the steady glow of the embers, until his body almost ceased to exist. That this too solid flesh . . . but he dared not think of defeat, with Katy sleeping in the next room and Kate with her, carrying his son now.

His son. The thought floated, radiant in his mind, and he gave himself to the sacred awe of life, unchanging and infinitely new. If he did his job tomorrow—no, tonight, midnight had come and gone—his son and daughter would know peace, and their children after them. But he refused to think of Katy in the arms of her yet unborn brother. If he could find a way to end it here, now, forever, he could free his children from the terrible prison that duty made of Thorgill.

"The sun is up."

Leach's voice, shocked, as if the DCI had only just realized that time had passed since they'd come down from Rose Moor. The sound of it more than the words drew him back to duty and the pain in his hand. He'd have to deal with Leach soon, but the man's presence had grown too familiar over the years in London; Col found himself thinking of Morgan and Tucker and

Finch as the outsiders and looking to the DCI for understanding the man couldn't give him.

"I know." Weary, Col would have melted right through the floor if he could and let himself be absorbed, exhaustion and all, into the earth. But he had a job to do and Leach to deal with before he could rest.

Leach said nothing for a moment, then, "You should let me splint that hand."

Col tried to ignore Leach, denying the pain. He'd been stupid to let his temper overcome good sense, and he'd pay for it in the struggle with Anris. He heard the man's measured footsteps pass out of the parlor, down the hall. The phone rang once, followed by the deep rumble of Leach's voice, then a long silence, an abrupt "Thanks." The footsteps returned, more slowly, and Leach dragged a chair over to the fire.

"Let me see that."

Col held out his hand, wincing as Leach palpated the finger.

"Broken, all right. I can tape it, but we'll need to get it looked at in London." Leach accompanied the words with the actions, shifting the finger slightly until the ends of the bones met cleanly, "That was Jack Bannister on the phone, from London. Spencer and Jacobs are on their way. They'll be coming in from York with Powell's men, so at the least, there'll be lads you can trust to take you in."

Leach slipped the words in without looking up from his work, but Col started, the pull on his broken hand shooting pain up his arm.

"Keep still if you don't want this to heal crooked." The DCI looked up long enough to glare disapprovingly at him, then returned his attention to wrapping Col's finger in gauze before he began to tape it.

"If you take me in, more people will die here. Anris will wipe out the village. And if he can escape the village itself, there is no limit to the destruction he can cause."

"No 'if' about it; they've got a warrant. It's your choice to go in with us or with Powell."

Col forced himself to confront Leach's level gaze, letting the man see the depth of his fear: of Anris and of Leach himself. If he saw the accusation in Geoffrey Leach's eyes, the knowledge of just how alone he was would go heart deep.

"Do you think I killed those people?"

Leach frowned, as if he were seriously considering the question for the first time. "You had the opportunity, and Powell seems to think you have a motive. As for means, could you have murdered all these people?"

Leach shrugged, a gesture of uncertainty that Gathers clung to. "Maybe the archaeologists; they weren't expecting trouble in spite of your threats—"

"Warnings, not threats," Gathers corrected.

Leach just sighed and shook his head, not convinced that the distinction made a difference there.

"Tuttle wouldn't have suspected you. But could you have taken Constable Dickens unawares? Are you strong enough to overpower a trained officer without a struggle? I seem to be the only one who thinks you are not recovered enough to be on active duty, but I wouldn't have given much for your chances against a nervous policeman and his partner."

The answer puzzled Col. "But you left me alone with Tut."

"Ah. Well, that was another question entirely." Leach explained. "Could you have done it? Maybe. Would you have done it? I didn't think so."

Gathers held his breath while Leach studied his face

with thoughtful calculation. "After last night, I just don't know."

Leach threw the roll of tape and the box of gauze on the floor next to the hearth. "It's time you told me what is going on here."

"I've been telling you since we arrived, Leach."

"Ghost stories don't tell me what sex with your sister has to do with the body count this town is racking up. Or," Leach paused, and Col looked up, waiting. "Who your father is."

Col just stared. He'd never faced it, really, never in his entire life said it out loud, even to himself. Over time he'd learned how to skitter past the question in his own mind—he could almost answer Jack Gathers' name without his throat tightening around the fear that someone would discover the lie.

"Last night, before I came upon your little party on the moors, I called Jack Bannister, asked him to check the public records. Your birth certificate, and Kate's, lists father as 'unknown.' Your mother's marriage certificate is dated a week after your second birthday, and there is no record of Jack Gathers visiting this part of Yorkshire until six months prior to issuance of the marriage certificate."

Leach had firm control over his expression. The man wanted answers, but how ready he was to accept them, Col just didn't know.

"Katy's birth certificate also lists the father as 'unknown,'" Leach continued, "but we both know that's untrue. I'm guessing it's no secret in Thorgill who your mother was messing about with either."

"Not here." Not in Granny Finlay's parlor, where his mother had wept when the old woman explained to a frightened boy what the village expected of him. Not where he'd lain in bed and listened while the old witch chastised his mother for taking him to the city where he'd picked up outsider ways that considered Thorgill's sacred trust a matter of snicker and dirt. But getting out of the damned chair took more effort than he expected. He tried to push off the arms of the chair and winced as fire shot through his injured hand.

Leach grabbed his elbow and hauled him upright. "Are you sure this is wise?"

Wise would see Geoffrey Leach dead and Colin Gathers well-hidden before Powell and his men arrived, but Col didn't mention that. He led the way slowly through the potting shed into the garden, concentrating on escaping the weight of his oppressive memories.

Reaching the comparative freedom of the garden, Col shivered in the morning chill, thinking about the question, innocently asked to mean was he strong enough to go wandering the Thorgill dawn. In his mind he reviewed everything he had done since he'd gotten the call from Jack telling him the museum had won, the National Trust would let them open the tomb.

Nothing that followed had been wise, least of all his unreasoning certainty that Leach was the key.

"Holy Jesus, what happened up there?"

Col looked up at Rose Moor looming above them, though he knew already what he would see. Smoke tangled with the morning mist drifting in tatters over the charred landscape.

"I lost my temper," he said.

"You don't. You aren't . . ." Leach pulled his gaze off the blackened moor, and Gathers flinched at what he saw there.

"What kind of a monster are you?"

Col hesitated. He wanted to deny the charge, but couldn't, in conscience, do it. "The kind my people made me: monster enough to do the job they created me for." *Different enough to send out to die with little regret,* he added to himself. Didn't expect Leach would take well to a maudlin magician-king, though, so he kept that one to himself. Kept the pleading out of his voice too.

Leach stared at him, accusation clear in his expression; Col had never seen a man so disappointed to hear the truth.

"I knew you were there." A darted look told him what he needed to know without words. Leach understood he meant the ritual on the tomb and had figured that out for himself already.

"Why?"

Just one word, the question aching with a disappointment Col recognized as a reflection of his own soul.

"I didn't want to come back here," he reminded the DCI. "And I certainly didn't want you involved." Whether he meant Leach, personally, or anyone from his life in London, Col didn't exactly know himself. He didn't want to think about how much he was risking on a feeling, a memory of Geoffrey Leach holding his hand and swearing at him to stay alive, damn it, or the twisted logic that told him it was Leach's fault they were here, now. He'd done as he was told and stayed alive, and Leach owed him for it.

Leach gave him a look that said it was long past time for recriminations about how they had come to be here. That was done, and Col had just one chance left to explain a dead policeman and a midnight orgy.

"Anris and the Finlay were brothers." Gathers leaned against an elderberry tree, his face turned away from the moor, and let his gaze rest on the shadows that still lay deeply over the dale spread out below them. Leach wore his warding charm, a good sign, though the break in the line of the man's jacket told Col the DCI still carried the gun.

"Maybe, when he still lived, there might have been another way. Reason. I don't know." Col spoke softly, but his vision remained fixed on that distant past playing out against the shadows that Leach would never understand. "If they'd released his spirit, given him a proper burial, he might have passed on, wiser from his mistakes in the life he had lived.

"When the expedition won permission from the National Trust to open the tomb, Kate and I still hoped that with his own bloodline scattered, the spirit would pass on and leave the village in peace. Jack had studied everything he could find on spirit captivity, though; he didn't think Anris would be able to escape even if he wanted to.

"You have to understand, Geoff, that he'd nearly wiped out the population from here to Pickering. Partly, as I said at the beginning of this thing, because he could raise power that way, killing people. Partly, it was a fight over the succession.

"According to the history passed down through the family, Anris was the older brother, rejected in the succession after his mother because his brother carried the Finlay magic—innate control of the forces of nature—more strongly. What the people would not give him, he tried to take. And he might have succeeded, except that at the end, the Finlay trapped him up there, sacrificed him on his own altar, and held his spirit while the people built the tomb around them."

"One of them was alive when they sealed that tomb," Leach said, as if Col needed reminding.

"I know." Gathers shivered, remembering the body that rested at the entrance to the tomb. He imagined what it must have been for his long-dead ancestor, his spirit entombed with that of his mad brother for all the long millenia. He prayed, silently, that the Finlay had found peace at last, and he wondered if some child of his children a thousand years from now would pray for him.

"We always knew this could happen. 'King' is an honorary title here in all but one respect. And for that, they need the blood of Anris and the natural magic of the Finlay. Fortunately, both breed true." He met Leach's curiosity with the dignity of the Finlay kings—it was time, now, to accept what he could not put aside. "My father died when I was a year old. In an automobile accident. I called him my uncle all my life. But he was my father, and my mother loved him both as the brother he was and as the lover he should never have been." He laughed, bitter irony—

"It's supposed to be a sacrifice, you see. The man gives his seed to the earth, his sister, and the gods reward them with fertile soil for crops and mild weather for growing. Progeny are the signature of the gods on the dotted line of the contract. Sacrifice accepted, covenant made. The children carry the magic forward, and their seed and fertile soil make the covenant anew each generation."

"Maybe it's time you people got out of the farming business," Leach suggested.

Gathers heard the incredulity in his voice. "I'm not insane, Geoff."

"Well, for God's sake, don't tell the judge that."

"It's not that simple." Gathers gestured out across the dale and regretted it; he'd almost forgotten his broken hand until the motion set it throbbing again. "Thorgill doesn't do any serious farming, hasn't since before Granny sacrificed her virginity on Anris' tomb. The whole practice would have died out centuries ago, except that Thorgill held the key to Anris' prison.

"It started as a fertility ritual and served that purpose side by side with its darker meaning for Thorgill. When the one died, the darker covenant remained.

"It's the little death, you see. In the ritual, the king plants his seed and ritually dies. The symbolic death seals the contract that the Finlay began when the village sealed him in the tomb. The death is acted in the ritual, but the Finlay is the eternal offering, reborn in the pure blood of the line, sacrificed again to redeem his people. As long as the sacrifice was made, the tomb would remained sealed.

"My mother and her brother made the ultimate mistake, for a Finlay. They gave themselves to each other, not to the gods, for love and for sacrifice. Well, they have paid for that mistake since. The gods took my father, and now they've set Anris loose. He's been trapped in the darkness for five thousand years. His goal might once have been simple power; now, he hates everything that lives, everything that has known the light while he lay chained to the bones of the earth. And most particularly, he hates the Finlay, who put him there. Contract void, time to renegotiate."

He couldn't hide the anger, though he wasn't sure of its direction. How could he hate his mother, who had made the best of a warped situation, and had suffered all her life for it? How hate gods he didn't believe in for a string of coincidences that led him to his death whichever way he looked. Geoff Leach deserved it least of all, but he was present, and he had forced the telling of a story Colin had hidden from himself all his life.

"I suppose I should be grateful for the way things turned out. By any logic, Kate and I should both be so riddled with genetic defects that we would never have seen the outside of an institution. Instead, I'll be dead tomorrow, and Kate will raise alone the children I could never acknowledge."

Gathers studied the gray distance, waiting. He didn't have the courage to look at Leach, afraid he would see the disgust he knew would destroy any remaining respect his senior officer might hold for him. Most of all, he did not want to see proof that Leach would not keep the secret of Thorgill. If they died together, fighting a common enemy, so be it. But to face Anris with coldblooded murder on his hands, the murder of a friend—he shuddered.

"Does Jack Gathers know?" Geoffrey Leach sank to the low stone wall, and Gathers followed his gaze, searching the horizon overhead. Smoke still hung in the air over the moors, with an occasional fountain of ash spiraling against gravity in a thermal eddy.

"Jack knows all of it now. He didn't, really, until Granny Finlay died and the university started nosing around Anris' grave, but it turned out he'd guessed most of it anyway."

Gathers turned to face him then. Leach shied away from the contact, and Col didn't force the issue. Everywhere he looked, Leach confronted some truth to the story. Col saw the moment when the roof of the cottage riveted the DCI's attention, when the question, how had they gotten out alive at all, sent a superstitious shiver through the man.

"The whole story turns my stomach." Leach fairly spat the words. "But you don't have to die for it. If you didn't commit these murders, come back with me and we'll prove it. Your incestuous little cesspit will keep the papers busy for the duration of the trial, but you'll be alive, you can start over."

Gathers leaned over and touched him then, just fingertips on his jaw, but Leach jumped, held still with a control clenched rigid. "Are you going to kill me now?"

"I should." Gathers shook his head. "No. But if you do not help me tonight, you will die here. Not my doing, but I won't be able to stop it, either. Look around you today. I know it's hard, but examine the evidence. And when you do, remember that you are not investigating a serious of murders, you are trying to stop a war."

"Powell will take you in," Leach pointed out, but Gathers just smiled. "He won't find me."

"I'll have to tell him, Col. He's got a warrant!"

"You won't know." Gathers stood up then and walked into the cottage.

CHAPTER 21

"You'll have to do a better job than that if you expect to hide from Powell's men," Leach muttered to himself, but Col had disappeared, and he couldn't remember where the sergeant had gone, nor, a moment later, could he remember why he was standing in Granny Finlay's garden. Col's words remained, however; threat or warning, he had to stop him. But the cottage roof still smoked in places, easily enough explained by a careless candle flame, but this time Leach didn't think so.

More tired than he could ever remember, Leach set off down the slope toward Laura Simms' bed and breakfast. In that order, he promised himself. He needed a few hours sleep before he faced Powell, but the sun was fully risen now—he'd have to settle for a lot less.

Laura Simms was waiting for him in the front parlor, a pot of tea steaming on a silver tray that rested on one of those heavy tables he'd stumbled over the night before.

"Inspector," she greeted him with a hesitant smile. "Would you like a cup of tea?"

Leach shook his head, almost too tired to answer, but he managed to summon some basic courtesy. "If you don't mind, I'd just like to rest for a while. Could you knock on the door when DCI Powell arrives?"

"Of course." Laura Simms answered with an understanding smile. "I talked to Barbara; she said Katy would bring your bag down after breakfast. In the meantime, Henry left a pair of his pajamas for you."

"Tell him thank you for me."

Leach shambled up the staircase to the bath, then found his room, second door on the right. The furniture was heavy and surprisingly masculine considering the decor of Laura Simms' living room. The Reverend Henry Tuttle's striped pajamas lay folded on a comforter the shade of fine claret. Leach threw them on the desk, next to the tobacco jar, and followed them with his own clothes on the chair. Finally, it seemed, he pulled down the cover to expose crisp white sheets that called to him with the promise of blessed rest. He slid between them, promise kept, and the world went away—until a rhythmic thud entirely too close to his head brought him back to the living. He opened bleary eyes and, with a quick glance at his covered lower torso, clutched the sheet and coverlet to his throat.

"I brought your bag from the house." Katy Gathers watched him solemnly from the desk chair while her right foot swung—kick, kick, kick—at the bedpost. Leach noticed that his clothes had been deposed to the floor next to her chair.

"That was very nice of you," Leach answered politely. "Now would you go downstairs and tell Ms. Simms that I will be down shortly and that I would like some of that tea if it is still available?"

"Aunt Barbara said to tell you she'll bring a tray up." Kick, kick, kick. Katy did not move.

"That won't be necessary."

"Yes it will. She said to tell you DCI Powell will be here in about fifteen minutes, and you won't want him to see you in your present condition." She considered him thoughtfully for a moment. "Are you sick?"

"Not physically." Leach came to the conclusion that he'd have figured out the Thorgill secret for himself much sooner if he'd had this discussion yesterday. He could hear the deliberate cadence of Col Gathers' voice in her words, and he surely knew that persistent interrogation technique. Hadn't realized it was part of the package, though. "See here, nice little girls don't invade gentlemen's bedrooms while they sleep. And they don't sit and observe them as they wake up. Or dress."

She ignored his pointed rebuke. "I'm supposed to go right home," she admitted. "But Mummy's been sick this morning, and she's been crying again, and Grandmama Gathers is snapping at everybody, so I came here. I'll bet that's why Aunt Barbara came to visit Ms. Laura this morning too. Did you really arrest my grandpapa?"

"Not me. But don't worry about your grandpapa. For the moment the police are keeping him safe, but he'll be home soon."

He couldn't guarantee that a court would agree with what Leach had come to believe, that Jack Gathers was no more than an innocent bystander. At the most, the man was probably guilty only of keeping the Thorgill legend alive in his work, giving the local nutter ideas. But out the bedroom window he could see stray tendrils of smoke still rising on the moor.

"What's penance?" The question must have been important to the child—she stopped kicking the bed to ask it.

"When someone does something that is wrong, they must do something to make up for it. Like, if you stole a piece of candy from Mr. Morgan's grocery store, you would have to pay him for the candy, and ask his pardon, and promise not to do it again. That would be kind of a penance."

Leach didn't know why he'd ended up cowering stark naked under his covers answering the theological questions of his sergeant's bastard child, but he didn't much like it. Nor did he like the look she gave him, though he was sure she hadn't guessed at his state of undress, or given any thought to him at all other than as an excuse to escape her grandmother.

Katy frowned at him, clearly unhappy with that answer.

"My daddy doesn't steal," she told him, as if the definition of the word 'penance' were his fault. "He's a policeman."

"I didn't know you had a daddy," he answered with a caution that was wasted on the child, who met this lie with the scorn it deserved.

"Uncle Col's my daddy!" She dropped her voice then, as if sharing a secret. "I'm not supposed to tell, but I heard Aunt Barbara and Grandmama talking about how you already knew. Aunt Barbara thinks Daddy was stupid to tell you, but Grandmama said that Daddy was the Finlay, and it was his decision. I'm going to be the Finlay some day, and then I can tell whoever I want to!"

A familiar, unwelcome voice interrupted from the doorway. "You won't be the Finlay until you are old enough to know better than to tell everyone you meet about it." Barbara Finlay stood there, a small silver tray with a light breakfast and pot of tea on it in her hands. She put the tray on the bedside table and poured the tea into a matching cup, then added milk.

"Send the brat down to us when she's worn out her welcome," the woman said, but she mussed the child's hair playfully, with the first smile Leach had seen on her face since he'd met her. In the moment it took him to recover from the surprise, she was gone, and he'd missed his opportunity to point out to someone with authority over the child that she'd worn out her welcome with the first kick she'd applied to his bedpost.

"You said my daddy steals," she persisted when they were alone again, "but he would never do anything like that."

"I know he wouldn't. Stealing was just an example." Leach grabbed for his teacup and his toast before it could leave the tray on its own power. He didn't want to think that the child had anything to do with the cup suddenly leaving its saucer, but the memory of clay pots crashing on the potting shed floor returned, sending a chill up his spine.

"If you want some tea, ask for it, don't sneak it off my tray," he commented with some asperity. "*Do* you want some tea?"

He knew the defense strategy as soon as the words were out of his mouth—normalization. Common in cult situations and dysfunctional families: acceptance of the clearly aberrant as the norm protected those who by necessity lived day to day with the aberration. It explained why the IRA kneecapped its own kids who stepped out of line and why Kate Gathers had given herself to her brother while the whole village watched. And, when Katy shook her head to reject the offer of tea but asked politely for a piece of toast, normalization helped him to watch the toast fly over his head and land in the child's hand without more than a reflexive duck for cover.

"My daddy wouldn't do anything bad!"

"Not if he could help it, or if he knew it was bad," he conceded.

Leach could not look the living proof of Colin Gathers' actions in the face and tell her that her father could do no wrong, even if she did need to hear it. But he could say, and believe, that Gathers was not an evil man.

"But sometimes we think we are doing the right thing, and we hurt people because we were wrong."

"Is that why you are going to kill my daddy?"

"Who told you that?"

The child looked at him queerly. "Mummy. Like I said."

Somehow, Leach decided, he'd missed that part of the conversation. "What did Mummy say?"

"About the penance, and telling you about the Finlay." She gave him an exasperated sigh and licked her fingers. "Daddy told you because he wants you to kill him tonight. It's his penance, she says, or he thinks it is, I don't remember. But it doesn't make sense, because Mummy says that Daddy is good and brave and we must help him all we can because he is going to die for us. And Grandmama says that it is *her* fault, and Grandpapa's, but not Grandpapa Jack, only I don't have any other grandpapa.

"And neither of them said anything about stealing," she finished in a rush.

Leach stared at the child with a growing knot in the pit of his stomach. Clearly, the full import of the story had not made it past her immature understanding. Equally clearly, Colin Gathers was still determined to die rather than surrender to Powell or Leach, and he'd chosen Leach to do the honors. If he could find the man before Powell, talk to him, maybe Leach could work out some plan; but in spite of the uneasy feeling that he should know this, he could not imagine where Gathers had gone after the ceremony on the moor. Nonetheless, he found himself repeating, *Not on my watch*, with little to back it but the certainty that he would not take the man's life, even if it cost him his own.

Barbara Finlay chose that moment to knock and then open the door. "Powell is here, and Inspectors Spencer and Jacobs from London. They are waiting in the parlor.

"Katy, come with me. Your mother is looking for you; it's time you went home."

When the child left with her aunt, Leach relaxed back into the bed for one precious moment, then rose to face the day.

CHAPTER 22

Col entered the parlor, still lost in the spell that would hide him from the police this day. Leach complicated things. The man knew him too well and would see past simple suggestion. He'd have to obliterate all trace of his own identifiable gestures, glances, even smells from the area that surrounded him to make the illusion complete. He succeeded better than he had hoped. Kate moved about making tea at the dresser, oblivious to his presence. She cut a thin slice of bread and took a bite of it dry, then started as she realized he was in the room.

"Don't *do* that to me, Colly!"

"At least we know it's working." With a bit more effort he even managed a sympathetic smile and a glance at the bread in her hand. "Sick already?"

She nodded. "Not as bad as last time, but I don't know how much help I'll be tonight."

"You've done enough for this town," he told her. "Sit this one out." He illustrated the suggestion by throwing himself into the rocking chair by the fire.

"Fool!" She wandered over and placed a hand on his shoulder and he reached up, held it in place with his own. "Tea?"

He nodded, and she withdrew her hand and moved away.

"I assume you have a plan." While she spoke, she

poured the tea; Col could not see her face to read her judgment there. "And since DCI Leach left under his own power this morning, I assume he is part of it."

"Yes." Col took his cup, used the ritual of sipping and experiencing the sudden rush of caffeine to postpone the conversation. Even face to face Kate wasn't showing much more than a queasy stomach.

"He's still carrying a gun."

"He's wearing his warding charm, though. Hasn't taken it off since I put it around his neck."

"So tell me." Kate drew a ladder-back chair up to the fire and watched him over her teacup.

"Tonight Anris will possess him, and he will try to murder me. I'll be waiting for him inside the tomb. If I'm lucky, I'll convince him that I plan to execute him there, and Anris will leave his body. I don't want to kill him, but either way, Anris won't get out."

"Will you?"

"You know that was never a part of the Finlay bargain." Colin Gathers shook his head. "I don't know. Nothing about this feels right. Geoffrey Leach is an outsider. Even if he lives, he will have to give up something to Thorgill—his belief in the truth of his own reality or whatever trust we have built out of hard work the past two years. Either way, he could die."

A new but all-too-familiar voice added its own hard judgment to the debate: "If you know you are being unfair to him, why don't you keep him out of it?" Katherine Gathers carried a teacup over to her children. "Will they release Jack?"

"Probably." His mother was the last person Col wanted to see this morning. He didn't know why he blamed her for all his misery, but there it was. "He was already in custody in London when Anris killed the policeman yesterday, and they haven't any concrete evidence to support the indictment anyway. Since your disappearance was the final nail in Jack's coffin, and you have reappeared undamaged if not in a mentally healthy condition, I should think Leach would have him released this morning."

"Who do they plan to arrest next?" Kate asked, but her expression made it clear that she already knew the answer.

"Colin," his mother guessed. "They know Jack is innocent of the policemen's death, but Col was here, in Thorgill, when it happened. Our Inspector Powell will doubtless assume that Jack was trying to protect the archaeologists from his stepson, perhaps because he could not be part of the project himself."

"But Col never wanted to go into archaeology in the first place! That was Jack's influence, and it didn't last long."

Kate reached a hand to comfort him, and Colin flinched away. He could not afford her pity, could not bear to accept her touch in front of his mother after last night.

"The police will likely not see it that way," Katherine Gathers argued. "Everyone knew how proud Jack was when Col entered the university in his own field and how disappointed he was when Col left it. Some, the less charitably inclined, are likely to see that departure as a failure, of determination if not of intellect."

"Mother is correct, as usual." Col inclined his head in a tight nod of acknowledgment between combatants. "But they have to find me first."

"And you will be. . . ?"

"About." He handed the teacup to his mother and hoisted himself upright without using his hands on the arms of the rocking chair. "If you don't mind, I need to be alone for a while."

The sunlight bathing the garden sparked rainbows in the dew at his feet, and Col breathed in the cool morning air. A cloudless sky at dawn always filled him with expectations of wonder, as if the gods were gifting him with an advance glimpse of heaven. Today, looking into that hard blue distance, he didn't know whether to curse the gods for reminding him of what he would lose forever at midnight or to thank them for the offering of one last day of sunshine before he entered the darkness forever.

He tried to imagine what that eternity would be, walled up with madness in the dark, and almost of their own volition his feet started moving, up the slope, toward the tomb. Long after his body died, he knew, his spirit would rage at its captivity; Anris' tomb would be Colin Gathers' final resting place as well, but he anticipated no rest. He did not have the Finlay's crushing faith in the necessity of the sacrifice, nor did he face the inevitable with the certain courage that faith would have given him.

At the crest he stopped, breath knocked out of him by the sight that spread itself before him. Far off in the distance the bright young green of blueberry bushes thrust living fingers into the rolling brown of the bracken that waited dormant for late summer. But here, close to the dale, all life had gone to smoke and fire.

He moved out into the sooty remains and felt the dying fear of the small creatures burned at his feet. No sacrifice to the gods, this, but a willful seizing of the world's power.

What have I done? What have I done? Death followed his touch, death to the land, death to what else before he walked into that tomb and stopped not only Anris but himself? He could not bear the knowledge that he carried Anris within him more strongly than he carried the lifeblood of the Finlay. Brothers, two sides of a coin that was the curse of Thorgill; the village hadn't made that mistake again: only two children of the full blood and no males of the cut blood. They hadn't anticipated Colin Gathers, though, who took the life of the moor to satisfy his own petty anger.

But the Finlay had murdered his own brother and held him captive in darkness for five thousand years. Duty, yes, but the Finlay went to his final rest no innocent, but a king with blood on his hands. Suddenly, urgently, Colin needed to know if they were right, the good citizens of Thorgill and their kind, to lock their secret away in the dark again. And only Anris could tell him what that captivity would be. He struck out for the tomb, knowing that what he decided here would see the end of it tonight.

The fire had stopped at the clearing around the tumulus. The heat had dried the grass that matted the roof of the tomb, but he could still make out the patterns of flattening in the growth that his body had made with Kate's. Had it been for nothing? Staring into the stone depths of the tomb, the cold assailed him again. He shuddered, the image of Tut broken in his jail cell kaleidoscoping behind his eyes with the forensics pictures, eviscerated offerings to Anris' lust for power, and a man broken at the bottom of a mine shaft to escape the memories he could not survive. But Col had to know.

Slowly he took the warding charm from around his neck and stepped into the burial chamber. A thin light filtered through the narrow opening, and he found his way carefully. He stopped first at the body of the Finlay, let fingertips drift over the arm bones covered by disintegrating cloth, and stroked the broken fingers with his unbroken hand.

"Help me!" he insisted, but his long-dead ancestor

did not answer. Gone, at last, that spirit, or shattered into so many fragments that it had lost all awareness in the long dark.

"There has to be another way." Lives would end in this place tonight. His own he had promised to the villagers and it was theirs to spend, but Geoffrey Leach was no part of Thorgill. Col knew the villagers expected him to pick one of their own to act as Judas goat and carry Anris to his captivity, but he could not ask it of them.

Somehow, it seemed natural to expect it of Leach, who knew about death in battle, faced it in the place his nightmares came from, recognized it in the empty eyes of the dead they worked to avenge every day. How would Morgan face that knowledge, or Charlie White, or Henry Tuttle, who fought the contradictions in his soul. Old Tut might have been able to do it, but he was out of it now, would be until well after tonight's work was done.

Deeper in the shadows Anris lay, his weapon at his feet, and Col went to him, knelt beside him and dropped the warding charm on the breast of the skeleton.

"Well, you bastard, I'm here. Talk to me!"

Nothing. Col waited, kneeling on one knee before the magician who wanted to be king. Then, slowly, the sensation of someone looking at him began to grow. Col looked over his shoulder at the shadows drifting over the entrance to the tomb. The damp whisper of decay reached for him, gently at first, then growing stronger, until he choked on the smell and rubbed his hands on his arms, his face, trying to wipe away the sensation of running putrefaction that covered him. He lurched backward, grasped for a handhold and found it behind him. Pulling himself upright, he leaned for support on the altar—Anris' altar.

Laughter drifted on the decay, as pressure on his chest pushed him down, down, onto that stone slab, and he lay there, perfectly still, while the memory of Anris overwhelmed his mind with that last night five thousand years ago.

He felt the magician's rage and looked up into his own face, hard with judgment, heard his own words spoken by the first Finlay to die in this place. The words burned the soul that inhabited him.

"*Brother,*" that terrible voice said, "*know that power is for the sharing, not the taking. Do you recant and give yourself over to the judgment of your gods and your people? Do you, in front of all those gathered here, consent to the breaking of your power and the stripping of your clan rights? Do you agree to wander the earth for the rest of your days, to beg forgiveness of the land and the peoples you have harmed and the gods you have defied?*"

Col heard laughter from his own throat and felt a dreadful pain. Lost, he had lost it all, and he wept through his laughter, defying his brother to command him and mourning the empty places that grew and grew as his brother stripped from him the connections he had built into nerve and cell with the land and the sky and the stars. Col's mind became that of the killer, and he saw the dreadful sorrow that he would no longer soar and felt the dreadful hunger for sensation, for the pulsing of earth-power through his body and the blood that fed the land to pay for it. His, damn it! His by right! But the terrible face above him spoke again in Colin Gathers' voice, nothing changed in the bloodline or, perhaps, the need of the time called upon that likeness.

"*Then know, brother, that you die for your crimes against our people, for your terrible crimes against the mother that bore us and the father that sleeps under the earth until Spring.*"

He saw his own hand slashing down then and felt the flint sharp at his throat, and he screamed and screamed until the ax silenced him, leaving only the gurgle of his blood and the hiss of the air that mingled with it as he struggled to breath and drank his own blood instead. *My god, my god.* He thought he would die of the memory, that he would go mad and roam the moors mindlessly until he found a path steep enough to leap to his death in the dale below just to obliterate the heart-stopping awareness of dying, dying, with no wound, and no end to the memory. The light faded from his eyes and he lay there, spread upon Anris' altar, and gasped for life, for some hold on reality that did not come.

CHAPTER 23

Laura Simms' bed and breakfast had a big, old-fashioned tub but no shower. The basin had neither a shelf for Leach's shaving gear nor a recognizable outlet for his electric razor. The combination left him in a sour mood before he made it down the stairs. The uneasy, watchful glances of Spencer and Jacobs, lurking in the parlor, didn't help; they'd worked with Gathers for two years but didn't know the sergeant well enough to reject the possibility of his guilt out of hand. Still, they looked as though they'd ask questions first and shoot later, which was more than he could hope for from Powell's men.

Powell had two men with him, Malcolm Waat and a stranger with the mix of authority and deference that Leach recognized as the well-practiced stance of a sergeant. He couldn't help but tally the ranks with some satisfaction that they were equally matched— three against three. The same side, not opposing forces, he reminded himself, but he couldn't quite bring himself to believe it. Today Powell carried a gun, and Leach figured the sergeant did too. So did Spencer and Jacobs . . .

The parlor disappeared with a sickening drop in the pit of his stomach, and suddenly Leach was holding Colin Gathers' limp hand, searching for a pulse that vibrated weakly through his fingertips, and faded, died. Blood seeped into the knees of his trousers, the smell of it mingling with the mold and dust from ancient, peeling, wallpaper and with the sharp tang of cordite from the gun in his hand. . . .

Then it was gone, and he stood in Laura Simms' parlor, fresh flowers and sunlight and a tea tray on the table. Powell looked at him strangely, but Leach said nothing. He hadn't had a flashback in a long time and never one this powerful with Col in it—always before it had been Derry and the child. And he'd never had one that ended differently from the reality.

Leach shivered and covered with a shift of his shoulders in his jacket. It didn't pay to get too superstitious, but a good soldier didn't stay alive by ignoring signs, either. Col's life was in danger, not just from whatever suicidal fate Thorgill had planned for him, but from Leach himself, maybe from all the policemen searching the village for the killer. He had to talk to Spencer and Jacobs, alone. Powell wouldn't listen without better evidence than a flashback that ended wrongly, but he could order his own men: the guns had to go. And they would listen, even if they thought he was mad for ordering it.

"DCI." Powell inclined his head a fraction of an inch in greeting and filled a cup for himself. Waat followed his example, but the officers of lesser rank stared each other down across the faded Turkish carpet.

Powell took a sip of tea, a polite ritual, and set the cup and saucer down. "Did you learn anything last night?"

Leach shrugged. "I still think it's drugs, deliberate or perhaps a toxin that has leaked into the water."

Waat held onto his teacup. The man clearly held himself apart from the code of minimal civility between the officers and answered Leach without waiting to be asked. "We've had no sign of anything, except that two of the archaeologists had traces of THC in the bloodstream. They were victims, though, not perpetrators, and marijuana isn't implicated in cases of violence anyway."

"It could have reduced the victim's awareness of their danger and inhibited their response to attack," Leach pointed out. "Which could mean that our killer would not have to be well known to his victims, nor as strong as we thought." It didn't have to be Col.

Waat looked doubtful. "At least, for two of the victims. There hasn't been much of anything else to hang onto with the others. Dickens had taken an antihistamine, which could have slowed his reaction time, and the doctors at the hospital said that Constable Tuttle had taken a couple of aspirin during the night. Maybe a headache slowed his reflexes, but the rest were clean."

"I'm still betting on a drug," Leach insisted. "They just haven't found it yet."

Powell gave him a long, hard look that Leach met with his own bland investigator's mask that gave nothing away, he hoped. But Powell was making him nervous. Did he know about the hallucinations? Had he experienced them himself? No way to know.

"No line on Gathers' whereabouts, then?" Powell asked.

Leach shook his head. "Nothing," he said, though he could not look Powell in the eye. Somehow, his answer left him with a sense of guilt he couldn't quite explain. He didn't know where Colin Gathers was, but he felt that he should.

"DCI!"

Leach turned to the door, where a young man in a cheap suit gasped for breath.

"Bernard? What's happened?" Powell raised an eyebrow that seemed to indicate permission to proceed, and the young man slowed his breathing with an effort.

"They've found him!"

"Gathers?" Powell took a step toward the door, but Inspector Bernard shook his head.

"Panky, sir. They have him at the White Rose."

"He wasn't there last night. Someone must have moved him after the pub closed."

"The lads who found him brought him down, sir. They thought it would be best."

"Why the hell did they think it a good idea to move the body?" Powell asked, already on the move. "If he's a friend, all the more reason to leave the evidence intact for forensics!"

"Um, he's not dead," the inspector explained. "But it's not good, sir, not good at all."

The man's voice shook, and Powell stared at him for a moment before he nodded dismissal. "Sorry, Inspector. I never thought . . ."

Leach figured they were both wondering the same thing. If Pankowitz were alive but seriously injured, they would have left him in place for an emergency trauma evacuation. So what could have shaken Bernard so badly that didn't include death or physical trauma?

"Where did they find him?" Leach asked.

"On the moor, sir," Bernard answered. "He was lying up against the fence around that old engine house, the abandoned mine where we found the local all broken up at the bottom of the shaft."

"Gentlemen?" Powell nodded and led the way to his car. He and Waat piled into the back seat, and the as-yet-unidentified sergeant joined the driver in the front. Spencer and Jacobs followed with Bernard, and Leach waited until he had their attention.

"Spence, wait here in case something else should

turn up. Ben, follow with Inspector Bernard." He squeezed himself into the back seat next to Waat, and the driver pulled away without waiting for the other car.

Leach checked his watch—ten in the morning—but police and rescue vehicles filled the tarmac around the White Rose and overflowed onto the road. Leach waited for Ben Jacobs to catch up with them and followed DCI Powell into the pub. He stopped in the doorway, overcome by queasy dread.

Pankowitz carried a good bit of muscle and no little bit of excess weight on his tall, big-boned frame, which somehow made even more obscene the sight of the constable curled in a ball in the corner of the taproom. The man smelled of feces and urine and the vomit that plastered his hair. His uniform jacket was open and torn, his trousers pulled low on his thighs, and both showed some charring. Superficial burns blistered his hands and the backs of his legs. Leach figured the man had gotten himself caught up in Gathers' burning last night. Hallucinations didn't leave real burns, though, and he felt his hold on the only sane answer he had starting to slip. Then the breath whooshed out of him as if he'd been hit in the chest . . .

Leach clamped his teeth together, tight against their chattering, while the pub faded out at the edges, became another place. The sound of his own heart tripping into double time obscured the footsteps of the perp on the floor above running to make his escape through the crawl space in the attic that extended the length of the terrace. They'd get him, but first Col Gathers needed help, a hospital. Leach blocked out the yelling and the pounding of feet on the stairs until someone took the gun from his hand and helped him to stand. Accident. He'd aimed for the perp; Col got in the way. Accident. But Gathers was dead . . .

When the White Rose had grown solid around him again, George Powell had moved to Pankowitz's side in the corner, where he murmured words of comfort and safety that the injured policeman did not seem to hear. Pankowitz rocked and rocked in that curled up fetal position, his hands clenched into bloodstained fists and tucked in tight around his head, and wept.

"I killed him, I killed him, I killed him, I killed him . . ." Pankowitz repeated the single phrase over and over while Powell cleaned the man's face with a soft cloth. Waat pulled a penknife from his pocket and used the blade to lift samples of twigs and burned material and smeared blood and vomit from Pankowitz's body, placing each sample carefully in a plastic bag that he sealed and returned to his pocket. When Powell had finished with the cloth he used to wipe Pankowitz's face, Waat took that as well and sealed it into a bag.

"What did you see? Did you follow the murderer?" Powell spoke softly to the man, and Leach admired the approach. If he was too demanding, the man would withdraw even further, perhaps panic, and they could lose him altogether. "It will be all right, you did nothing wrong. He would have gone on killing until one of us took him out. We just need to know where he is—"

Unfortunately, it didn't seem to be working. The litany continued. "I killed him, I killed him," until Powell rested a hand on his shoulder. Then, still caught in whatever hell he inhabited, Pankowitz screamed and struck out.

"No! He's in my head! Oh, God, Dickens, Oh God, get away, he's in my head. Knife, oh, Dick, get away! Get out of my head! Get out of my head! Oh, God, I killed him, I killed him!"

Eleven policemen in the room and every one of them froze, Leach realized with disgust. He moved forward and took Powell's arm, pulling him away from the hysterical Pankowitz. "You'll get nothing out of him," he pointed out, "and the physical contact is just making him more agitated. He needs a hospital. When he's clean and settled, maybe you can get something out of him."

Powell nodded and stood up, and Leach guided him out of the way so that the medics could do their job. The DCI rubbed at his temples, and Leach, remembering Col Gathers down and bleeding, gave him the time he needed to pull himself together.

"Panky isn't the brightest man on the force," Powell said, "but he is one of the most solid. Unimaginative. This doesn't make sense. Even if he'd seen the killer, somehow caught up with him, I'd have thought he was the last man on the squad to fall to pieces like this."

"If Pankowitz hasn't got the personality for imagining things, then maybe his ramblings make more sense than they seem," Leach suggested. Col Gather's story of ghostly possession seemed a lot less far-fetched when he listened to the terrified insanity of the policeman who begged the medics to make the thing in his head go away and wept and screamed for the partner who had died.

"You think Pankowitz killed his own partner?" Powell asked with a dangerous drop in his voice.

"We'll know more when we find the knife that killed Dickens." Leach shrugged, knowing that wasn't enough of an answer. "Pankowitz is no more likely a suspect than Colin Gathers, but Pankowitz is confessing, and Gathers said he didn't do it."

The moaning behind them stopped, and Leach let out a breath he hadn't realized he was holding. Drug interaction or not, somebody finally had the good sense to sedate the man.

"Then you did see Gathers?"

"He knew he was a suspect before he disappeared last night, and he'd already said he didn't kill anyone. As for Pankowitz, do I think he intentionally killed his partner? No. Nor, for that matter, do I think he killed anyone else in Thorgill."

Waat joined them as the medics carried Pankowitz from the White Rose and loaded him into one of the rescue wagons. "I checked Constable Pankowitz as thoroughly as possible under the circumstances, and he's got no cuts that would account for the amount of blood on his hands. I won't know until the lab has run some tests on the samples I sent back with the emergency team, but if I were a betting man, I'd put money on the blood being Dickens'."

Powell nodded, taking it in, but, Leach figured, not accepting it. He couldn't blame the York DCI; after all, he felt the same about Colin Gathers' innocence, at least where it came to murder.

"I'm taking your man Bernard to show me where they found Constable Pankowitz," Waat continued.

"We'll be along in a moment." Powell dismissed the forensic pathologist and turned to Leach. "You expected that, so let's hear it, DCI Leach. If the question is not who, then explain to me how."

"It's what I have been telling you all along." Leach infused his voice with a long-suffering tolerance, although he no longer quite believed the explanation himself. "Someone is using a drug on this town. Once a victim is sufficiently drugged to be receptive, the killer uses suggestion to somehow convince his victim that he ought to kill. He's 'in their heads' as your man Pankowitz said. With the victim under the influence of the drug, the real brains behind this thing can tell them anything, apparently, and the victims believe they have no choice.

"There doesn't even have to be a mastermind if it's a toxin that induces paranoia on it's own. Then, when the drug wears off, the man is left with the memory." Col's words, he remembered again.

"At least one of the deaths since the killing spree started was a suicide, not murder, and Tuttle could have been an attempt at suicide when he couldn't resist the killer's commands any other way." Leach found himself believing that some part of Thorgill's legend could be true. To become like Pankowitz, or like Tuttle: the thought chilled him to the bone.

"It seems pretty far-fetched," Powell objected, but he rubbed his forehead with a weary sigh. "What would you suggest?"

"Get rid of the guns," Leach said, and he realized that Gathers had been saying the same thing to him since they'd first reached Thorgill. "We don't know who will be affected next or what the 'voice in his head' will make him do. Better if he didn't have a chance at killing a dozen people in twenty seconds."

Powell hesitated, and Leach recognized his own unwillingness to capitulate in the face of something he could not see or fight.

"Not just your men and mine," Leach added. "The sergeant here should organize a house-to-house search for weapons in the community as well." Not that he thought they'd find anything. From Constable Tuttle's comments the night they arrived, Leach figured the locals had removed their guns from temptation when the tomb was first opened. And, he realized, something in the sachets they wore around their necks seemed to afford some protection as well, even if only through the power of suggestion.

He remembered the little sack of salt and oddments

that Col had hung around his neck then, and absently his hand went to it under his shirt. He'd meant to get rid of it when he washed that morning, but hadn't, for some reason. Maybe because Col had put it there, and it represented a tangible promise that Gathers hadn't committed the murders. Or maybe the racial memory of centuries of yeomanry stayed his hand. The favors of kings of old often had power of their own, at least to trade for a boon when need required. But that was foolishness, like believing in the predictive quality of flashbacks that didn't go as they had in real life, and he dismissed the fancy with a mental shake.

"First, we'll find the knife that killed Dickens," Leach bargained. "Check the fingerprints, the physical evidence at the engine house where they found Pankowitz. If it looks like your man did it, I don't see that you have any choice left."

"You're wrong about Pankowitz." Powell turned on his heel and left the pub. His driver, anticipating the move, reached the door two steps ahead and held the door for the DCI, then followed him out.

"D'you reckon Col did it, and this Panky saw?" Ben Jacobs, at Leach's elbow, muttered the question under his breath, and Leach shook his head to refute the suggestion.

"But we can't prove it without evidence." He pulled himself up to his full height and tried to look more rested than he felt on two hours sleep. "We've a murder weapon to find, Inspector."

He led Jacobs out of the pub and commandeered a car. "There's a service road to the left that should take us to the engine house." He sank back into the passenger seat and gave a good imitation of thought while his exhausted mind danced from image to haunting image until settling on the last, which would not be dismissed. With a quickening of his own blood that sickened him, he saw played out again Kate Gathers' weeping as the village men tore her brother from her body on the roof of the ancient tomb.

Thorgill was slowly tearing Geoffrey Leach to pieces, the decency and rightness and reality that anchored him all turned upside down in this village. He sensed Kate Gathers at the root of it, calling to him like no woman in his life before. She saw to the center of him and did not find him lacking—Leach didn't know how he knew that, but it was one certainty more real than all the ways the world worked outside of Thorgill. But the one thing he had to understand for any of this to make sense was the answer to a question he could not ask: on that old and forbidding bed of stone, why had she wept?

Not bloody murder, but Leach had committed a different crime entirely by stepping over the line into personal involvement. A policeman was dead, he reminded himself, another driven mad. Leach knew, as he could not have done before last night, that Pankowitz had told the truth. The constable had killed his partner. But did he believe Pankowitz because of the evidence, or because he didn't want to prove that Kate Gathers' brother, his own sergeant, had committed mass murder?

All Leach knew for sure was that Powell hadn't been up on that moor last night: Kate Gathers hadn't looked into his soul, nor had Powell seen the way Colin Gathers' death lay waiting in the man's eyes. The DCI would be difficult to convince. Leach himself wasn't quite sure why he'd told Powell to get rid of the guns. Cop logic told him they'd find a drug at the end of the investigation, and that was reason enough. Dead magicians, after all, did not carry grudges. Until last night, though, he hadn't believed in dead magicians.

"There, sir," Jacobs pulled up between Powell's car and a marked vehicle.

Leached stepped out. "Is there a local map in there?" he asked.

Jacobs' head dipped for a moment, and the inspector came back up with an ordnance survey map in his hand. He opened it against the steering wheel and examined it with one hand balancing the map and the other poised to strike.

"There we are, sir." Jacobs poked his index finger at a spot on the map. "Spaunton Moor this bit is called." He folded the map a bit to leave the area exposed and handed it through the window.

"Thanks."

Leach studied the map for a moment, located the disused mine on it, the tumulus where—his mind skittered away from that thought—and a place called Thorgill House that he figured must be the place the locals called Granny Finlay's. When he had himself oriented to the map, he folded it away and slipped it into the inside pocket of his jacket.

"Stay by the radio," he said, and headed off to join Powell and Waat at the fence.

CHAPTER 24

Gradually the darkness faded into blacker shadows against the gray that filtered through the narrow entrance to the tomb. Col rolled to his side and sat for a moment on the altar, wiping the tears from his face and trying to still the shaking in his hands. He could not remember weeping, but the evidence lay damp on his fingertips. A small thing, but it led him to wonder if he could trust his memory. Anris still hovered, filling the tomb with his torment, but he had not driven Gathers to kill. Or so Col believed. But that lurking question—would he remember if he had killed?—unsettled him.

"*Not yet.*" The words fell on his mind with an oily aftertang of threat.

"Not ever!" Col answered it, but silent laughter mocked the lingering uncertainty.

Gathers slid to his feet and would have fallen if he had not leaned back against the stone slab for support. How long had he lain on Anris' altar? He pushed himself upright and moved deeper into the shadows, groping for the warding charm that he had dropped on the breast of Anris' corpse. The skin at his temples and the back of his neck prickled—he felt the rib cage, the breastbone of the skeleton, but the sachet was no longer where he had left it. It occurred to him then that he might be dead, the charm gone for evidence in

a little plastic baggie, but that would not explain why
they had not removed his body as well. The slab was
empty, though. If he were dead, would his spirit self
feel less solid to his own hand? Would the altar?

Col found that the idea of his own death stirred no
real fear and little regret in his mind. The conse-
quences to those around him, however, raised cold
sweat on his brow. If he were dead, who would bind
Anris to his tomb this night? Kate had to protect their
child, and Barbara did not carry the pure blood. Could
either of the women convince Leach that he had to
help? Leach would take his sergeant's death hard, he
figured, more so because this time the inspector
would doubtless feel some relief. It seemed to Leach
that fate had resolved his questions of guilt and innocence, of protecting his command or protecting the
people he had sworn to serve. The killing would go
on, of course; police procedure, even the best,
wouldn't solve this one.

Gather's imagination played out the repercussions
of his own death as they rippled through the short life
remaining to Thorgill, to his family, and to his com-
rades in the force. So much blood on his hands! That
blood would bind him here as effectively as the long-
dead Finlay had held Anris. Unthinkable! Col turned
from the shadows and made for the light. Pain starred
through his shoulder as he brushed against the stone
close around him—Did the dead feel pain? Then he
was out, in the light, with the breeze on his face and
the curlews wheeling overhead. Blood seeped through
his sleeve, and he laughed because he knew the dead
did not bleed. Foolish with the joy of being alive, he
raised his arms high and whooped a pagan cry to the
earth and sky. Then he ran, putting distance between
himself and the tomb.

When he had passed the line where fire had cleared the bracken, he slowed only enough to leap the sturdiest of the bushes in his path. He kept moving, deeper onto the moor, until he felt the slow warmth seeping into his bones that signaled the comforting presence of covert life that thrived under cover of the rolling heather bracken—quail, hare, adder. Once, hugh old hardwood trees had covered this land, but millennia ago his own ancestors came fleeing the darkness of their own woodlands. Here, blocked once again by an ocean colder than any they remembered, his people had taken their stand and unmade Creation. Now only the heather and blueberries remained, dropped onto the earth in an unfinished tangle like an untidy ball of Granny Finlay's yarn.

Col felt the ancient fear of the lurking evil in the forest and their patient triumph as his ancestors cleared the land finally and forever. In their contest against the gods, man had won, and Col shared their savage triumph in the swelling under his breastbone.

"I am king!" he said to the land, and meant, "I am your conqueror. Even the forests are lowered to their knees at my passing." And memory, like a flashback to the moment when the impact of a bullet threw him onto his back on the stair landing, struck him with an anger made more terrible by the terror that ignited it.

Col saw the forest that once stood here, mile after mile of fearful dark with only here and there a broken ray of light to remind him that a sun rode in the sky. And always the whispering overhead, the movement of those towering monsters as they bent their heads to rattle their limbs against one another and whisper, whisper behind their leaves in the tongues of trees.

He fell to his knees, ignoring the quarrelsome magpie that scuttled from underfoot. The memories were not those of Anris, though he felt the spirit of the magician feeding the fear and the anger in him. The images rose out of an earlier time by thousands of years, and Gathers cowered before their truth, as Anris did within him. This was the tie that held him tight to Thorgill. Racial memory was a myth, except that it had exploded from the depths of his cells like a secret kept too long. Men had created this wasteland, and Colin Gathers was their king.

Col felt Anris depart then, leaving behind a lingering question. Had the Finlay known? Anris had. The magician brought Col here to experience for himself the terrible knowledge that kingship brought with it. However necessary it may have been, the Finlay had taken the kingship by force and not by right of birth. As the second son, had the Finlay himself really known? Or was this a truth that only those born king shared?

Col shook his head to clear it. Pointless to question something gone to the worms when Rome was no more than a cluster of mud huts. He'd had his courses in cultural geography at the university. They'd been boring as dirt, nothing but maps dotted with irregular circles to show where the trees once grew. He'd never felt anything like this before, never cared what the land was like before he'd walked it as a boy.

He thought that maybe he should feel guilty for the changes his ancestors had wrought on the landscape. But his own childhood memories, watching the lambs fall under the twisted branches of the heather bracken and chasing rabbits while the bumble bees chased him, filled him with a quiet joy. For better or worse, the moor, wide open to sun and rain as it now was, made him more surely than that past of endless whispering forests, and he would not love it less or regret a moment of it because his ancestors had made it so.

The images shadowed him as he rose to his feet and

turned toward home. In the distance, near the engine house of the old mine, Col saw two police cars and a small knot of men. He wondered if Leach was with them, but he could not tell at this distance. They paid no attention to Col, so he figured the spell he had cast about himself was working. The possibility still remained that he was dead, of course, but he was pretty sure that had not been the intent of the exercise.

Anris knew his enemy well. Tonight, when they met, Col would know what it meant to lie on that slab and die at a hand so like his own it could be a brother's. He would know what it meant to be king and to lose that kingship. Perhaps even more, Anris wanted Col to value his freedom and the moors that created them before he lost them forever in the darkness of the tomb.

Col figured that Anris would have one more thing to teach him before tonight, and he ran until he reached the tomb, barely slowing until he was inside, on his knees beside the body of the dead magician. There it was—his warding charm. How could he have missed it before? But he slipped it over his head and sighed as the weight lifted from his heart and the darkness faded a bit from his sight. Anris would not use his body to kill to raise power. In that one thing Gathers would come to the altar free of blame.

CHAPTER 25

Leach took a good look around, imprinting the scene
for future reference. The track—actually a strip of
tarmac marked on the ordnance survey map as a foot-
path—wound quickly out of sight beneath the brush
that covered the moor for as far as he could see. Overhead a curlew mocked him, crying out as it circled
beneath the thin cloud cover that hid the sun.

Not even the police scavenging for clues a few steps
away could ease his superstitious dread of the barren
landscape. He felt unreasonably as if he'd stumbled
onto the edge of the universe, and he feared what he
might see just beyond the pearled glow of the horizon.
Not the ghost of Col Gathers' people but something
more primal than man seemed to weight the very air
with brooding watchfulness. Nothing in London or
Derry had shaken him as this place did: Leach remembered Colin Gathers moving over his sister under this
sky, giving his seed in more than just a symbol of creation. To what gods did they sacrifice their sexual
energy then? Not the God of his church and choir. But
suddenly he was with Col Gathers in that moment,
sharing the feel of the woman under him. Arousal
pulsed through him, and Leach flushed, glancing
furtively around, as if the policemen gleaning clues
from the engine house could somehow have sensed

where his thoughts had taken him. For a moment, out of the corner of his eye, he glimpsed a figure dressed in leather and a sleeveless linen tunic moving in the distance, and it seemed that the very memory of the night conjured the man at its center. When he turned to follow the motion, however, Leach realized it was just another of the sheep that roamed above the dale. This one had a streak of red paint on its side: which farm claimed the color he did not know. He watched a moment longer, but nothing moved except the sheep on the moor and the cuckoo wheeling overhead.

The case was getting to him. If Col Gathers had been on the moor, Powell's men would be after him, not combing the heather bracken for clues. If Gathers couldn't be out in plain sight, then he wasn't—q.e.d. Leach shook off the uneasy feeling that someone was watching and tried not to think about the last time he had ignored a warning just as vague. Col had almost died that time. The appearance of the man here, like an avatar of disaster, shook his faith to the ground. Coincidence was the logic of the fool, but more than the logic of the day and the city were at work in Thorgill.

"Sir?" Jacobs' voice, concern, confused, drew him from his fruitless revery.

"I'll be with Powell," he said, and moved off to join the DCI, who stood in close conversation with Malcolm Waat, the forensics specialist. Leach focused a critical eye on the object of their inquiry, the chain-link fence, about two meters high and anchored to posts placed close enough together to strengthen the overall effect of the chain. The posts, set in concrete sunk into the earth, weren't going anywhere without industrial equipment.

"Anything?" he asked.

"Not enough," Powell told him. "A good set of bolt cutters would make short work of this chain, but the fence shows no breaches or recent patches,"

Leach nodded. He wondered, not for the first time, how the archaeologist had managed to get past it and land at the bottom of a mine shaft on the other side, and made a mental note to check on the owners of the mine.

Snapping on a pair of surgical gloves, Leach squatted next to the forensics expert. Someone had cut the brush back from around the fence recently, but it had grown up enough to show some broken and bent branches where the new growth came nearest the fence. Leach pushed on the branches, testing for resilience. It would have taken a considerable weight, falling with more force than a man usually exerted to lie down, to cause the damage he saw.

Waat was ahead of him. "The uniforms found Pankowitz lying here, curled up and whimpering. Given the breaks in the surrounding bracken, I'd say that he fell, probably trying to climb the fence, and more than once before he gave up and stayed down." Waat pointed with the blunt end of his pen at several stains marking the chain links above their heads. "Pankowitz had blood on his hands and his shoes when he tried to get over the fence. Maybe he accosted the perpetrator here, wounded him, but the man escaped him somehow—possibly over the fence, but I don't see any traces of blood or scuff marks on the higher links. So, maybe there is still a murderer out there, Inspector Leach, or maybe you are correct, and officer Pankowitz murdered his partner. We won't know until we compare the blood found on Pankowitz's hands with that on these links and then cross match it against Dickens'. The weapon would help, of course."

"He held the knife, all right. The question is, who pulled his strings?"

"Your drug theory, DCI?" Powell's question carried the edge of challenge in it.

"If Pankowitz were the sort who would choose to kill the way somebody murdered Dickens and the others, he wouldn't be on his way to hospital now," Leach pointed out. "It makes sense to assume that he did not have control of his faculties when he committed the crime."

"On the other hand," Powell suggested, "if your man Gathers was not the sort to commit murder, why is he hiding?"

"When I find him, I'll ask," Leach retorted, covering his own unease with indignation. He knew why Col stayed hidden—that didn't mean he accepted it.

He pondered the tumbled building on the other side of the fence for a moment, trying to imagine it empty of the policemen prowling through it. Part of the answer lay inside, at least for Pankowitz. The location seemed to draw the ones the murderer forced to do things they couldn't live with. Leach realized they were Colin Gathers' words, and shook off the sense of doom that hung thick in the air. "I need to get inside."

"That's the shortest route." Powell did not leave his position behind Malcolm Waat, but he pointed east. Leach followed the perimeter of the fence to the gate. The lock stood open, but the officers inside had pushed the gate closed as a precaution, and Leach had to throw his weight against it to force the bracken back to let him through. Nearer the engine house the growth turned to softer grasses, and Leach moved toward the ruin.

"Watch you don't fall down the shaft," one of the

juniors warned, and Leach realized he had, in fact, come perilously close to doing just that. While the fence protected those outside it, nothing marked the shaft from the inside. So, the archaeologist might have fallen by accident, except that he still had to have climbed the fence. Even if the gate had stood open he could not have passed through it without noticing—with the growth along the inside of the fence, the gate simply didn't open wide enough to let a man through without brushing the sides or turning sideways. He may not have wanted to die, but the archaeologist had wanted to be here. And so had Pankowitz.

The owners had long ago removed the machinery and anything else useful or portable from the abandoned engine house; nothing but village memory and its location near the shaft gave away the former purpose of the ruin. This was where Gathers' own logic fell apart for Leach. The mine had played out less than a century ago and had worked for only a century before that. Why would a Neolithic ghost with a bad attitude fixate on a place that hadn't existed, even as a possibility, when he lived?

Leach figured it could be some wacko with a grudge against the government for the decline of industrial Britain in the late twentieth century. But that didn't explain the flint ax or the other site of the murders— the open tomb. Leach shook his head to clear it of useless speculation and prowled the grounds, second-guessing the juniors searching for evidence.

"Mr. Powell, sir!" One of the nameless young men hunkered down next to the open shaft, the light of his torch pointed downward. "I see a knife down there, sir. Shall I collect it?"

"No!" Waat ran the circuit of the fence and joined Leach beside the young inspector. "There's a ladder bolted to the side. I'm going down," Waat said, and followed the words with the action. Leach rolled his eyes, asking pity of a merciless deity, but followed Waat down the ladder.

The shaft cut into the earth for fifty feet or so before bottoming out in a small chamber with boarded-up entrances to three horizontal tunnels leading from it. Leach tested the boards that blocked the entrances, but they seemed untouched since they'd been put in place God-knew-how-many decades ago.

"Where does that one lead?" Leach called up to the inspector waiting at the top of the shaft. He pointed to one tunnel that seemed to lead north.

"Don't know, sir, but I can call in for a map of the old workings if you want."

"Do that."

Waat squatted on the floor of the mine shaft, measuring distances to the knife with a tape measure. "He probably threw it over the fence—it definitely fell, and wasn't placed here; you can tell by the amount of dust that covers the top of the blade. That's probably why the lads missed it on first inspection." Waat picked the knife up at mid-blade. Even wearing gloves they could contaminate the evidence, Leach knew, and he kept his own hands carefully tucked into his pockets. With suspicion already trained on Gathers, Leach had no intention of being the man who smudged the fingerprints on Dickens' murder weapon.

"That's the knife that killed Constable Dickens?" he asked, although he felt sure it was. After all, how many blood-drenched bread knives could be floating around this poor excuse for a village?

"It fits the description," Waat answered, equally cautiously. "I won't know for sure until I get it back in the lab, match it to the wound and test for fingerprints and blood type." Waat dropped the knife into a large plastic bag, snapped the seal, and gave a last look around. "I don't think we can get anything more down here, Inspector." He started up the ladder and, after a moment more for thought, Leach followed.

"DCI!"

Jacobs' pounding run shook dust loose from the mine shaft and into Leach's face. When he reached ground level, Leach was ready to rip into the junior inspector, but Jacobs' expression stopped the reprimand dead.

"Spit it out, man!" Geoff said instead, and hauled himself out of the pit while Jacobs caught his breath, explaining between gasps, "Spence called, sir. Says there's been shooting at the B and B. Powell's lads are pinned down, can't get in. They think it's Col, sir."

"Did anyone see Gathers?" Leach asked, and Jacobs shook his head. Powell was heading for his own car, responding, Leach figured, to the same news.

"Far as Spence knows, it's just speculation, sir."

"Anyone hurt yet?" Leach asked. He reached his car and slid into the passenger seat just as Powell's driver made a sluing turn off the tarmac track and pulled away.

"Spence didn't know, sir." Jacobs started the car before he had properly closed the door, and Leach held on tight as the inspector backed the car at full speed down the track. At the crossroads he righted their direction and finished his answer. "Ms. Simms and Ms. Finlay are inside, but as far as Spence could tell, the only shots fired have been at the lads surrounding the B and B. He may or may not know the women are in the house."

Or he may have used a knife, as Pankowitz had. Leach kept that thought to himself, along with the only order that immediately came to mind—to slow down. Jacobs wouldn't kill them getting there. Or, he never had before. Still, Leach had to wonder how the man had ever gotten a license to drive. The sound of semiautomatic gunfire ended that train of thought. He hadn't liked Barbara Finlay from the start, didn't trust her as far as he could throw a house, but he didn't want her dead. And Laura Simms had hurt no one. Another burst of gunfire, and another thought almost froze him with the shock of it—

"Has anyone seen Katy?"

"The kid?" Jacobs shook his head. "Don't know, sir."

He brought the car to a skidding halt on the lawn of the bed and breakfast, and Leach would have jumped out into the line of fire if Jacobs hadn't grabbed his coattails. "Take cover, sir."

The man sounded truly unnerved, and Leach took a deep breath, waiting for his training to catch up with him. Powell was good; Leach gave him that much. The DCI had pulled his men back, using the police vehicles for cover. Leach bent low and slipped around the vehicle.

"Sorry, Ben," he said. "But we have to find Spence. Somebody has to know what has happened to the kid."

"I'm here, sir." Spence appeared at Leach's right hand, Powell right behind him.

"Katy?"

Spence shook his head. "Don't know, sir."

"We're going to need you to talk your man out, DCI."

Leach stared at Powell a moment, trying to figure out what the man wanted of him. The penny dropped. "You still think Col Gathers is responsible for this?" He gave a bitter laugh. "A bit of a stretch, don't you think, George? Your own men found

Pankowitz covered in blood not his own, and you still suspect Sergeant Gathers of trying to murder his own half sister? We haven't located the girl yet—do you think he'd risk his niece to save his father's reputation?"

He choked on the words—not Col's father, who'd died young, leaving Jack Gathers to give Katherine Finlay's children a name. Nor, for that matter, Col's niece. If nothing else convinced Leach of Gather's innocence, the growing likelihood that Katy was in that house did. Gathers would die before he let any harm come to his daughter.

A scream, high and thin, from the bed and breakfast broke into the thought; behind it came the cracking of glass—the windscreen of the vehicle behind him. He was already on his way to the ground when the windows of the bed and breakfast blew out in an explosion of shattered glass.

"Jesus!" he muttered into the dirt under his face. He should have heard gunfire before the windows went, but they'd had no warning. Leach thought about Katy, curled in a rocking chair with potted plants crashing to the floor around her. Oh, yes, he had a good idea what had done the damage, didn't want to think about what had scared the girl that badly. He staggered to his feet wiping blood out of his eyes and checked around for the injured. Thankfully, the townsfolk were beyond the range of flying splinters. Most of the police had taken cover at the beginning of the siege, but that wouldn't protect them from their own exploding windscreens. Leach hoped they'd have the sense to ride it out, but suddenly, a uniformed constable broke cover to escape the fragments.

"Stop!" Leach called out to him. "He'll—"

Too late. A single shot rang out, and the man

crumpled amid the glittering shards of glass on the lawn. He moaned, tried to crawl back under cover, and another shot snapped through the morning air and struck him. The man lay still, blood turning the blue of his uniform dark.

But the flow of blood was slow, and it still came—so the man was still alive and might stay that way if they could get to him fast enough.

For a moment Leach thought he saw Col at the fringes of the onlookers, then the man was gone. Leach shook his head to clear it of the unwelcome visions and of the ringing in his ears. He jumped when someone took his arm.

"Inspector!"

"Kate!" He brought his heartbeat under control with an effort. He hadn't seen her in the crowd, and the fact had bothered him. With her sudden appearance at his side, Thorgill-sense started to click into place, which should have worried him more. "Do you know who he's holding inside?"

"It's not Col!" she answered, and he followed the direction she indicated. So it hadn't been the effect of the blast on his already-rattled brain; Gathers stood a little apart from the crowd of policemen and towns-folk, his arms crossed over his chest, his expression grim to the point of despair. No one else seemed to notice Col was there.

"I knew that," he assured her, and was glad that he could say it as truth.

"Who . . ." he began.

"One of Inspector Powell's men. Don't know his name, and he's plainclothes, so I couldn't tell the rank. He's got Katy in there. Barbara's shielding her, but she's been hit—"

"Katy?"

"No, Barbara. But Katy's frightened, and she's losing control."

Down the slope a bit, the windows of the next cottage blew with a sound like cannonfire, showering the lawn with shattered glass.

"How much damage can she do?" With glass exploding up and down the valley, it seemed pointless to argue root causes.

Kate shook her head. "I don't know. Her talent is at least as strong as Col's, and she's frightened."

Leach remembered the ash-strewn moor overlooking Granny Finlay's cottage and shuddered. Col had been annoyed, not scared out of his wits; Leach didn't want to know what that conflagration would have been like if the man had really lost control, and he sure didn't want to see the effect of a talent like that in the hands of a frightened child.

"Is she strong enough to kill with that talent?" he asked.

"We think so," Kate answered. "Col will kill the man himself if he must to get Katy out before that happens."

Leach nodded. Before he could answer, a voice he did not recognize called out from the cottage.

"Bring me the Finlay or you will all die like that one. And I'll start with the girl."

Leach didn't recognize the voice coming from the house, but he could see that Powell did; the DCI closed his eyes, slowly, as if he could blot out the grief behind his lashes. No, Leach thought, you'll carry this one forever. When Powell opened his eyes again, the pain was well under control.

"Come to the door, Sergeant. We can talk about this, get you out of here alive." Powell called to the man inside with a fatherly tone, stripped of command or threat.

A tall figure moved out of the shadows in the doorway then. In one hand he carried a standard issue Browning nine millimeter. In the other arm, tucked up close as a shield, he held Katy Gathers.

CHAPTER 26

Col pushed off from his place by the tree. Leach had seen him, maybe before Kate had broken the spell for that moment. At any rate, Leach didn't show much surprise when Gathers caught his eye. Then the stranger was standing in the doorway with Katy in his arms, and Col moved.

"I'll kill her, I swear it!" the stranger sweated and wept, tears running unnoticed down his contorted face. Col would have felt sorry for the man, who had to be confused, and who doubtless cowered in some corner of that body's mind while Anris held a gun on a child's head and threatened. "I'll kill you all!"

But Col saw just three outcomes: the man would kill Katy—Col hoped he could control his reaction in that worst of all cases, but he wouldn't bet money on Thorgill's chances. At the least, the policeman would lose what mind Anris had left him; or Katy would kill her captor, doing the-gods-knew-what to her after years of work to raise her as normal and unafraid as Kate could make her; or Colin could get to the man first and put him down before Katy discovered she could do it herself and all hell broke loose. Of the three, he found only the last acceptable.

Powell was talking then, moving forward. Col would have warned the man that Anris didn't, actually, take prisoners, but that would mean revealing himself to a squad of nervous policemen with guns in their hands and a warrant for his arrest in Powell's pocket.

"That's not you talking, Mike." Powell held his hands out to his side, the gun pointed down. "It's the drug, the toxin. Think of Marie and the boys. How would you explain hurting a child to your boys, Mike?"

The gunman seemed to hesitate for a moment, but Col saw when the gun left Katy's head, and he ran. He heard the gunshot, ignored it, put his hand out to stop the gunhand from taking up its former position at Katy's head. "Go, Katy."

Anris saw him then; he felt the eyes on him, the malevolence, but Katy had winked out, heading for her mother, Col hoped, while Anris pinned him with that twisted grimace of a smile. Anris used the policeman's body to aim the gun at Col's head, fired.

Dodging bullets wasn't his favorite thing in the world, but Col kept the presence of mind to deflect the ball's trajectory just enough. The heat of the passing bullet seared above his left temple, and the shock threw him back a step. Someone swore behind him and Col felt the eyes of the crowd, the murmur of their surprise. He'd thought he could handle Anris without breaking the spell, but he hadn't counted on a bullet coming that close. He tensed, waiting for for the punch of a nine-millimeter slug in the back while remembered pain sent fear crawling up his spine. Not again. Not now, please the gods, when he had a job to do. But Leach called, "Hold!" and Col focused again on the policeman in the doorway.

Anris looked out of the man's eyes at him, shared knowledge in his smile. Not now. Not yet. Then the policeman dropped his gun and followed it to the ground. Col closed his eyes, still alive, praying for one blessed moment of peace before he had to start fighting again with Powell for his life and the life of the town. But fate wasn't playing his game today. He felt hands on him and knew he did not know them. Not Leach. Not friendly. Then Leach *was* there, insinuating himself between the Yorkshire officers and their prisoner.

"Take care of the inspector," Leach told them, and stared them down until they moved away.

Col gave his own DCI a fleeting glance that came just short of asking what had happened. Leach was reading with all senses today, though.

"Got Powell in the leg," Leach said. "Doesn't look serious. They've already taken the foolish young man who took a nap on the lawn. Didn't need the helicopter, so I should think he will be all right as well. What happened to Katy?"

"Don't know." Col waved in what could have been any direction. "She just went. I wasn't sure she could do it, but I could at her age, thought she might. Get's harder the more mass the body puts on. . . ." He realized that he was rambling and that Leach wasn't taking any of this well.

"Daddy!" Katy was there, as suddenly as she had disappeared. But no, Kate stood next to her, relief and fear mixed. Katy—well, he wouldn't know until she dragged her face out of his stomach, but he didn't want to let go of her now that he had her in reach. He lifted her into his arms, felt the warm tears on his neck when she buried her head there, and held on tight. "Katy, Katy, Katy," he crooned. "It's all right. He won't hurt you, love. It's over now."

She lifted her head then, looked deep into his soul with eyes big and liquid with her tears. "I wanted to hurt him, Daddy," she whispered, and he almost didn't hear, but he caught the meaning at the limit of his awareness and nodded.

"So did I," he said. "But it would have been wrong."

"I know," she agreed, again in that soft whisper. "You're bleeding."

"I know," he echoed with a reassuring smile. "But it's only a little bit, a scratch. I'm not hurt, really. You did just the right thing, heart of my heart. I'm proud of you." And he wondered what had possessed him to take such a chance when the fate of Thorgill depended on him. But he held the answer to that in his arms. If Anris had taken his child, he'd have damned ritual for a fool's precautions and taken out the enemy if it meant laying the village in ruins to do it. Fortunately for them all, Powell's young sergeant was less tractable than Constable Pankowitz.

Medics and policemen converged on the unconscious sergeant lying on Laura Simms' doorstep, and Col found himself in the unlikely position of defending the body that had almost killed his daughter.

"Go easy, there," he said, and explained, "Wasn't his fault, any more than Dickens was Pankowitz's fault."

He felt a hand on his shoulder, Leach, and Col knew it for reassurance. "The man needs a hospital, not a jail cell," Col grumbled.

Leach nodded. "He'll get it. Right now, we've got some major mayhem to clean up here."

"And you don't need us in your way. I'm taking Katy home."

Kate reached out, and Col handed the child to her mother. Better to get the worst over with. "Barbara?" he asked, when Kate had gone, and "Laura?" not ready to give in to his own dilemma until he had the injured and the frightened sorted out. Laura was there with Henry Tuttle, he saw. Apparently unhurt, she wept quietly on the minister's shoulder,

"Barbara took a bullet, but she's not as bad off as the DCI." Leach's glance passed over the cleanup operation, then he added, "I suppose we should be grateful the young man was a bad shot."

"Or that a gunhand is harder to control than a knife," Gathers reminded him. "Still, if he hadn't fought the influence as hard as he did, we'd have dead bodies on our hands, not wounded."

Leach seemed about to answer, then the tension left his eyes and he shrugged. "The medics don't think it's serious, but they'd rather she went to the hospital for observation tonight."

"And Barbara wants?" Col asked, letting whatever Leach had to say wait until they didn't have quite so interested an audience. He knew without being told that nothing would keep Barbara Finlay from this night's work.

The object of their discussion stepped out of the cottage, leaning heavily on the arm of a uniformed officer. Her blouse had a bloodstained tear that corresponded to the bandage along her ribcage, and she walked with slow, painful steps. She grabbed Col's arm when the officer would have led her past him.

"I've compromised on the infirmary in Pickering, provided DCI Leach brings me back when the wound's been seen to," she answered for herself.

"I knew you would say that," he agreed. Col figured from Leach's expression that the DCI didn't much like the task. "You'll need your rest," he reminded her, and wasn't best pleased when Barbara waved that consideration away.

He watched her progress toward the waiting emergency vehicle for a moment, then turned back to Leach.

"Are you going to let them arrest me?" Low; he didn't want to give any of the Yorkshire police working cleanup any ideas. He ignored the ambiguous nature of his own question. Leach might still fight him on the real cause of the Thorgill disaster, but Col knew that the DCI never thought him guilty of the murders.

"Time we found out," Leach said, and turned him toward the cluster of official vehicles.

Powell hadn't been shipped out yet; he still sat heavily in the open ambulance, grimacing against the pain as the medic bound the wound for transport. "It seems you are in the clear on this one, Sergeant."

"Yes, sir," Col agreed, and waited.

"Where's your mother?" Leach asked him out of left field, and Col answered without thinking, "She's here somewhere, probably with Barbara, or maybe Kate."

"She's alive?" Powell asked.

Col stared at Powell, trying to make sense of the question. Gods, how could he have forgotten? Powell thought he and Jack had done away with his mum.

"Quite alive," he answered, and turned to Leach. "She'd really appreciate it if someone would get the paperwork moving to release her husband from prison." Col paused a moment. Jack was one more variable he didn't want on his plate tonight. "Tomorrow morning will do—" which seemed to shake DCI Powell, but Leach just sighed.

"It doesn't leave much case against my sergeant," Leach pointed out to Powell. Col appreciated Leach's timing; the medic was doing something to Powell's leg, which worked like a twitch in a horse's nose. Took the man's attention right off the question of Jack Gathers and why his stepson wasn't screaming for his immediate release. Powell just waved the question away.

"There's still the matter of six dead at the dig," Powell pointed out, "and a seventh at the bottom of a mine shaft."

"Respectfully, DCI Powell, you can't have it both ways," Col argued. "If it's a serial killer, the only suspect you've got evidence on is Sergeant Mike. At least twenty sworn officers and more townsfolk watched him shoot up Laura Simms' front yard and no few of the people in it. In about an hour they'll be pulling evidence out of your own leg."

Leach added his own common sense with, "You've got nothing on the sergeant, Powell. There's no evidence that Gathers was in Thorgill at the time of the murders, no motive that makes sense, and all the evidence you do have points to a case of multiple murder followed by the suicide of the perpetrator. A suicide, incidentally, which your own forensics specialist feels Constable Pankowitz may have tried to copy."

Powell stared long and hard, but Col stood unmoving, letting the man look as deep as he wanted. He knew the moment when what he saw frightened the DCI, but he didn't pull back. Finally, Powell sighed.

"There's something," the DCI said. "I can feel it. Killed them, maybe not, but you know more than you're telling."

"Just some old, old stories, DCI. If you thought I believed them, you'd reserve me a room next to Panky and the sergeant."

"Maybe," Powell conceded after another pause. "I don't have enough to hold you. You are not in my command, so I can't suspend you. But God help you both—" a wave of his hand included Leach in the statement—"if you hold out on me and it costs another life."

"God help us, indeed," Leach agreed, ambiguously.

"Now, if you don't mind, I have a date with a surgeon." Powell waved them away. Col took the gesture as a blanket dismissal of charges and put himself back on the job. He would have waited until he'd gotten Leach away from the Yorkshire contingent otherwise, but it had to be said.

"The guns," Col reminded Leach. Now they knew the answer to the question that had plagued them since Leach brought a weapon into town. Anris could penetrate the protections from a distance—bullets didn't recognize the wards the way the spirit was bound to do. "We have to get the guns out of town before we have a massacre on our hands."

Leach nodded. "He's right, DCI Powell. It's pretty obvious now that we aren't working with just one killer, and at least in the last two instances, the attackers were driven to their actions under the influence of some drug or toxin, as Gathers has said all along. Unless you have come up with another motive we haven't heard yet, we have to assume that the real killer in this town is the toxin.

"Pull your men out, send in a chemical disaster team in the morning, full environmental hazard suits and full toxicological testing protocols."

Powell nodded, and Col didn't need the powers of the Finlay to see that the sight of his officer holding a gun to a child's head already haunted the DCI.

"The lads will take your orders if you plan to set up roadblocks," Powell assured him. "You don't want to risk infecting innocent motorists."

"I'll have Col take it in hand," Leach said.

Gathers frowned at the DCI. He didn't want to give orders to the strangers who had tried to arrest him just minutes ago, and he didn't like the expression on

Powell's face, which said if he could stand on his own power, Powell would tell the medics to go to hell and do the job himself. But he kept his objections to himself, asking only, "How long should I tell them you want the road blocked, sir?"

"Until we get at least a preliminary report from the environmentalists on the safety of the area," Powell said, then asked of Leach, "Do you need transport?"

Leach shook his head. "I'll send Jacobs and Spencer as far as Pickering with your lads, if that's is all right with you. Someone has to take Laura Simms' statement, and I seem to be immune to whatever is affecting your lads, so I'll stay."

Immune indeed. Col saw the DCI's hand drift to the warding charm that lay flat under his shirt. But Tuttle had shown them that nothing was certain.

"Your gun?" Col reminded him.

This time, Leach pulled the Browning from his belt and handed it to Powell. "Leave this with the lads at Pickering," he said. "I'll need to sign it in when we're finished here."

Powell took the gun, uncertainty drawing his brows together.

"I'll do that, DCI, if you are sure?"

Powell asked it, but Col found the same uncertainty in Leach's questioning frown. He gave one tight nod, and Leach turned away.

"I'm sure," he said.

The medic interrupted then, murmuring something about the hospital, and Powell added, "They want to move me out now. Would you give the orders, DCI Leach?"

"Right away, sir. Take care."

For the first time since Leach had forced his way into the case, Col felt a stirring of confidence. Maybe, with Leach believing him, they could finish this thing once and for all. He didn't dare consider the thought growing in his mind that what they had planned for that night was wrong.

CHAPTER 27

Leach stood in the shattered parlor of Laura Simms' bed and breakfast establishment, a broken fragment of pink china in his hand. Part of a lamp, he figured, and remembered a mad grab to save the china monstrosity from falling in the dark. Wasted effort, and as distant as if it had been years ago and not days. He shuffled through the debris, wincing at the chink of shard upon shard. Shock, he recognized, and wondered when the silence would catch up with him. Powell's men had cleared out hours ago, the plainclothes back to York, uniforms not happy to take orders from the man they'd lately come to take into custody but grudgingly accepting Gathers's role as local expert for setting up roadblocks.

Leach knew why Col wanted those roadblocks: they'd keep Powell's men occupied and away from the tumulus. He wished he were out there himself or in Pickering with Jacobs and Spencer, pretending he believed his own story to George Powell. Col expected more of him, though. Kate did.

And damn it, so did Katy Gathers. Standing in the midst of the destruction, Leach started to shake while images so real he lost himself in time and place cracked like lightning in his head. Katy, gun to her head, but Leach held the gun, fired, and a boy dropped to the broken sidewalk with half his head blown away. But he'd killed in Derry with a heart shot, and then Katy lay dead in his arms on the ruined pavement, a hole in her chest where her heart used to be.

"Let it go, Geoff."

Reflexes spasmed and the bit of china fell from his hand as he turned, reaching for the Browning he no longer carried. He recognized it as Gathers' voice, so soft that for a moment Leach thought that he heard it in his head, a second before he saw the man staring at him from inside the doorway. How had Col gotten that close without Leach hearing him? More importantly, why had Gathers appeared now, when the flashbacks were twisting memory into something he could not trust. Only the sharp bite of the broken bit of china in his hand had kept him from disappearing into that place where dreams and reality merge, until Colin Gathers' voice dragged him back.

"I wasn't planning to loot the place, Gathers." Leach pretended not to understand Gathers' comment. He didn't want to know how much the man saw through his own shock.

"Did Katy really do this?" He gestured a sweep of the room, where no breakable object remained intact.

"Yeah." Gathers ran a hand through his hair and winced; Leach saw the bullet burn across his forehead and realized that Col had tugged at a knot thick with clotted blood.

"Granny was working with her to learn control; she had worked with all the children with the Finlay talents hereabout. Kate took up her training after Granny died, but there's no way you can prepare a kid for someone taking her hostage and putting a gun to her head."

"Fucking hell," Leach answered with no particular force of feeling at all. He felt . . . as if he'd been carried beyond the reach of describable emotion and dropped there, with nothing left to feel or know. "You don't half ask for much, do you Gathers?"

He *knew* the kid had the power to break things—he'd seen her do it on a lesser scale, or had come to accept that explanation for the crashing pots in Granny Finlay's potting shed. But how that translated into the mess of broken glass and pottery all over Thorgill, or what it said about a little girl, all gangly legs and wide frightened eyes in the arms of a man with a gun held to her head, he couldn't even begin to absorb. To do so would mean accepting the Thorgill answers. Deep inside he knew he had already done so, but he wasn't ready to say it out loud yet.

"I keep seeing her dead, my bullet," he blurted.

Gathers closed his eyes, but not before Leach saw the dread and pain there.

"It was a child, before, wasn't it?" Gathers asked. Leach gave a spastic twitch of his head, all the control he could muster for a nod, then realized Gathers wouldn't see.

"A boy," he admitted. "Katy's age, give a year or two. He hit our transport, killed one of my people. I thought he was going to kill me next, and I shot him." For a moment he considered lying, or letting Col think the best, that he'd only done what he had to do. But with Katy's solemn presence in every shattered fragment of Laura Simms' parlor, the truth would not be silenced.

"I was scared, yeah." He stopped, could find no right words to say it, nothing that would make it sound better than it was. "God, I was angry. I blamed that kid for Dunlop and for the bombed-out churches and the broken pavement I sat on while Dunlop screamed away his final minutes with a gut full of nails. I blamed that kid for sending me to Derry and for every terrorist bomb that ever hurt a London citizen, and I shot him in the heart because I wanted him stopped. Not just for the moment, not to stop him from throwing that last nail bomb. I wanted revenge for twenty years of war with that one bullet."

"Did it work?"

"You bastard!" Leach swung, felt his fist connect. When the haze cleared from his vision, Gathers was on his knees, weaving unsteadily.

"I guess it didn't." Gathers finished his fall, landing on his backside. He looked up at Leach, but the DCI couldn't figure out if that look had the depth of understanding he thought it did, or if Gathers were merely stunned by the blow.

He couldn't be more stunned than Leach was; he looked at his own fist, smeared with Colin Gathers' blood, and wondered whose hand it could be and how it had taken such action without his leave. God, he'd lost it completely this time. Best take himself off the case, go home, put himself on report for psych evaluation. He couldn't go on this way—it wasn't safe for the people around him.

Out of that distance only he could see, Gathers interrupted Leach's examination of his bloody hand.

"Sometimes, when we are fighting for our lives," Col said, "when we know that other lives depend on us, we do the wrong thing for other people's reasons. Sometimes the only choice is one we are not strong enough to make."

As absolution, it left a great deal to be desired. Leach wasn't even sure they were talking about the same thing. He owed Gathers an apology, though, but decided that an explanation might be more useful under the circumstances. In a war, and he was fast realizing that Thorgill was as much a war zone as

Derry, it was as important to know the weaknesses of your friends as those of your enemies.

"I regretted it the moment I pulled the trigger. Too late then to call back the bullet." The obvious answer, too flip, too easy to say when the doing hurt so much. His voice grew thoughtful. He hadn't dared before this to look too closely at what he was telling Col—he'd never admitted to any of it out loud.

"Sometimes I have nightmares. Once in a while, flashbacks. Not bad ones—the worst, until this case, were a couple months ago, when you got shot. It was my fault. I hadn't listened, and you almost died for it."

He waited for a response—surprise, denial, an admission of Gathers' anger—but Col just waited expressionlessly for him to go on. Finally, Leach did.

"Sometimes the two things would get confused, and you would be lying on the pavement in Derry and I'd be shooting the boy for killing you. Sometimes the boy would appear on the landing.

"Since we've been in Thorgill, the flashbacks have changed. I can't explain it. They're more vivid, more real. I think they last longer, but I couldn't swear to it. And now, sometimes I see you instead of the boy, dying with my bullet in your chest. Or I see Katy. I suppose you think that your local ghost is messing with my mind."

Col shook his head. "Anris has never shown that much imagination." Then, when he thought Gathers would hand him a way off that hook, the man sank the barb deeper: "It's your head, all right, telling you something. Warning you, maybe preparing you."

"For what?"

Col lifted a hand, let it fall again, as if searching for an explanation that Leach would accept and coming up empty. "I've got to get out of here," he said, reaching for the corner of the couch to drag himself to his feet.

Leach watched for a moment, almost afraid of what his hands might do if he tried to help. Anger still sent the occasional tremor through him, though why that anger seemed focused on the sergeant, he could not say, except that the man expected him to hand over logic and the beliefs of a lifetime as he'd handed over the Browning. He did reach out then, but Gathers warded him off with an upraised hand. "I'm all right," he said. "Just give me a minute," and he was on his feet, swaying slightly.

"Outside."

The police cars and emergency vehicles had gone, leaving nothing but the shattered glass of their windscreens to mark their passing. The glass crunched underfoot, punctuating the silence that seemed to hang expectantly over the dale. Leach wondered if the thick-shod hiking tourists on holiday ever felt that hovering tension when they followed their maps, staying on the marked trails so as not to damage the bracken that spread in twisted havoc over the high moors.

"I know how you felt, Leach. When you shot the boy."

Leach flinched, as if the words were bullets striking his flesh, but Gathers didn't seem to notice. Leach didn't know what the man saw when he stared off into that middle distance, but he figured Gathers would tell him in time. He wasn't sure he wanted to know it, but Gathers wasn't asking preferences right now.

"When I saw Anris holding Katy, I wanted to destroy him. I *would have* killed anyone in my way trying."

"But you didn't," Leach pointed out.

"Don't make me something more in your mind than I am walking this land, Leach." Col laughed, a dry sound with no humor in it. "If he'd killed her, DCI Powell's young officer would have died where he stood, his fault or no. Powell would have died. You would. By fire or wind or the earth itself rising up, this village would have died. I would have fought Anris on his ground, for all eternity, I suppose."

Leach recognized that rage, had felt it not just once, in Derry, but again watching Colin Gathers bleed on a landing in London. If the mind were a flame, London would have burned. He'd have been sorry later, but that wouldn't have brought the ashes back to life.

"He scares me."

Leach had to back up a moment, think. Who, he almost asked, but Anris, of course. A reasonable response, he figured, if the spirit did in fact exist. Leach had to admit he could find no other explanation for the baleful death that had looked out of young Mike's eyes today. He didn't even know the young man's last name, but he'd seen the confusion and dread cross the clean-cut features before the man had sunk to the ground. He wondered if Pankowitz had looked like that when the spirit left him alone with the body of his dead partner and the muscle memory of the knife in his hand hacking through flesh and cartilage and sinew. And Gathers was scared of him? What a surprise, and Leach told him so.

"If this thing exists, and I admit I can't come up with anything else that fits what I see, that's the most sensible thing you've said since we got here."

Gathers shook his head, and Leach realized that once more he'd missed something vital along the convoluted line of Gathers' reasoning.

"I know he can hurt me, kill me. I expect him to try tonight. That's what I was born for," Gathers explained.

He'd said it before, had kept saying it until it rattled around in Leach's head and made him too damned dizzy to protest. That didn't mean Gathers couldn't make his own destiny. Hell, most people didn't have a choice. But Gathers was talking again, and his voice shook with loathing.

"I'm not afraid of fighting him," Gathers said, "but of becoming him. If I'd done what I really wanted to do this afternoon, how would I be any better than Anris?"

They'd passed out of range of the broken glass here. With the soft grass that covered the dale smothering the sound of their footsteps, Leach could hear his own breathing, hear the sob caught and smothered in the throat of the man at his side.

"But you didn't kill anyone. Didn't hurt anyone. Wanting to isn't the same thing. Believe me on this one, Col." Leach closed his eyes against the sight of blood boiling from the chest of a skinny boy with a snarl turning into a gasped "oh" of surprise as he died.

"I didn't think I'd love them this much."

Almost a whisper, Gathers sent Leach's brain racing to keep up again, and, "Who?" Leach asked, not trusting his own mind to give him the answer.

"The children." Dry eyed, Gathers spoke from behind the wall of shock that protected him from his own words but did little to defend Leach from the sudden, gut-level understanding of how close the afternoon had come to Armageddon. "Kate and I never. I mean, she is my sister, and I care for her, but we never made the mistake our parents did. But I never realized how much I could love the children."

Which pretty much supported Leach's evaluation of Mrs. Jack Gathers. Not a loving mum. He wondered what Margaret would have been like if they'd had children, if he could have stood amid the chaos of his child's terror and thought only of his fearful love for her that would level mountains for her step. But something wasn't right—

"I thought there was only Katy?" It still made him uncomfortable to say it; Leach didn't want to think of Kate in her brother's embrace, and Gathers' claim that there was no love between them didn't help.

"Kate's pregnant," Col said. "She's carrying our boy."

Oh, God! Leach couldn't hold back the image of Kate spread out for her brother's taking on the tumulus under the stars. God damn it to hell, he could feel her moving under him, saw his own chest and belly meeting hers, while the chanting circled 'round them and the torches forced back the sky.

"Leach! Geoff!" Col's hand, on his arm, shook him hard, and Leach heard him calling while he gasped and shook from the power of the flashback. He was losing his mind in this Godforsaken place, and Col had something to do with it, but how or why he didn't understand, except that he couldn't, wouldn't believe that he had felt what he felt, had seen what he imagined because he wanted to.

"Leave me alone!" he growled and pulled his coat from Gathers' hold. "I've had enough of this place and all of its perversions. I don't know what you expect of me!" Leach turned and walked away as fast as he could, making for the road. He'd walk out to the roadblock and call for Jacobs to pick him up. He could be in London tonight—early morning at the latest.

"I don't *expect* a damned thing!" Gathers shouted after him, and he stopped. He didn't turn to face the man, but he waited.

"We need your help," Col said. "I'm begging for your help. I don't want Katy and her brother in my place fifteen years from now. I don't want them tied to Thorgill and its old ways. We've been wrong for five thousand years, Leach, and all we have to show for it is a dying town and children I can't ever call my own. Somehow, this has to end tonight. I can't do it without your help."

"You didn't want me here at all, boy," Leach didn't turn around, but he'd listened, and he had his argument ready. "Now you can't survive without me?"

He thought he was beyond surprise, but Gathers' answer pulled him back. "I said we would end it here, tonight, Leach. I didn't say anything about survival. That's why it can't be Kate or Barbara, why it can only be us."

"I'm here to solve a crime, Gathers, not be the guest of honor at my own murder."

"Who else, Leach?" Gathers was almost taunting him. "Who else gets paid to keep the peace? Who else can understand the mind of the brother of my line but we two, who have felt what it is to *be* Anris, to kill out of anger, to lie dying soaked in your own blood with nothing but adrenaline pulsing in your veins. We need you tonight, Geoff. Last chance, finish it or we're lost."

Leach stared at the man for a long moment, studied the hard glitter that held back the fear of death in his eyes. "You are mad," he said, and turned away.

He knew it wasn't true. Colin Gathers was sane, in the way that Thorgill had made him, and Leach, who was the mad one of the two, would do what he must because Gathers was right. He took a paycheck for keeping the peace, and once upon a time he had broken that trust. Time to pay up. But first he needed to be alone, to shake off the feeling of Kate Gathers' skin that clung to him like perfume, and to come to terms with his ghosts. God's honest truth, Colin

Gathers was enough of a weight on his conscience already. The fool wasn't, by God, going to add another ghost to his account, no matter what it cost Geoffrey Leach to make sure of it.

CHAPTER 28

Fire danced against the backs of his lids. Hot, seductive, the heated kiss of the flames leaping in the fireplace branded lips drawn grimly tight. Col rocked in his grandmother's chair by the hearth, but tonight the memories of lessons learned in this room, of childhood roaming the moors, would not come. Tonight he dreamed, awake, of fire.

He laid his hands along the arms of the rocker, clenched his fingers around the smooth wood, and felt the pain from the broken bone. Still as marble, he counted breaths—in, hold, out slowly, hold—and willed the flames in his heart to cool. Control. He needed control—couldn't afford to let the fire out when every villager would be on the moor, carrying their own bits of light. One of them would hold a knife at his daughter's throat, waiting for a mistake. Push back the dark, bind it deep inside the earth, or watch his child die; all choices ended badly.

"Col." Kate's voice. She wanted him to open his eyes, to look at her and tell her it would be all right tonight. But it would have been a lie, and she knew that as well. "You have to eat," she pressed him, and still he did not answer. He let her voice grow distant, until she could not reach him at all.

"Colin!" His mother, sharper than his sister. She shook his shoulder, and he opened his eyes then, so that she would stop. They stood over him, his mother in a simple dress and flats, his sister in jeans and a sweater, wearing matching frowns, though he detected more concern in Kate's and more exasperation in his mother's.

"I'm not asleep," he said, and his mother's annoyance pleased him. God-king, he felt larger than life and less than life—the fire loosed from its prison in the hearth, the sweeping hand of justice and retribution. Tonight he was dangerous, held barely in check, and he let her see all of that in his eyes.

Katherine Gathers lifted her hand quickly from his shoulder and stepped away. Col knew the smile he gave her, touched with stone, spoke more of Anris than the Finlay; havoc churned his blood with wild energy, with fire. His mother took another step back.

"None of this is my fault," his mother said, as if the words could quench the burning stone of his heart. "Jack tried to stop them."

She turned a chair away from the table and threw herself into it, the fingers of one hand tangled deep in her windblown hair. "I'd go into the tomb myself, but you are the king; no one else has a hope in hell of stopping him."

He detected bitterness in her words, and doubt. Gathers wondered if it mattered to her that he would die that night, or if she had convinced herself that, hurt and tired and shaken as they were, the villagers could hold Anris long enough for Col to escape alive?

Kate knew better. He saw that deep sorrow in her eyes. Their people feared the fire, feared their king unbound. If he survived the binding of the spirit, they would kill him to finish the cycle—roll the stone in place to seal the mouth of the tomb and chant their prayers while he choked to death in the airless place with the mad spirit and the bodies of the dead to watch.

"It's all right," he assured his sister, and meant he gave his life willingly, perhaps had wanted this two months ago, to put an end to generations bound in servitude to a heap of rock and a long-dead enemy. Too late now. He rested his hand on Kate's belly where his child grew, and she pressed her hand over his while her tears fell.

"Let this be the end," he told her.

"How?" she asked him. She fell to her knees then and rested her head against his broken hand lying on the armrest of the chair. Penance, he felt the sudden sharp pain to be, and embraced it, knowing worse awaited him on the moor above the house. When Kate looked up, her tears had stopped and she faced him in her anger.

"You see what he has done, how many have died. Do you think he would stop the killing if we weren't here to fight him? Who will stand against him next time, if not our children or their children?"

"And if they die tonight?" Col rested a hand on his sister's head, her hair so like Katy's under his touch. Katy.

"We don't have the right," he said, "not for any of it. Not to pledge our children's lives to a fight we should have ended millennia ago. And gods, what right have we to hold Anris tied to this land, this life? It's been five thousand years. Don't you think it's time we laid him to rest?"

"And what do you recommend?" his mother asked him. "Perhaps you'd like to line us all up for Anris' slaughter. Would that ease your conscience? Ah, but what conscience then, child of mine? You'll be dead like the rest of us."

"I'll be dead anyway, Mother," he reminded her. "At least my way, the children will be free."

"What way is that?" his mother asked, and Colin realized that Kate was watching him intently as well. If they really could find a way—

"I don't know yet," he admitted, "but we can't seal him into that tomb again." He remembered the feel of countless centuries flowing in his veins, filling his eyes with forests and his heart with the swell of fierce pride and the terror beyond madness of those centuries entombed in the dark.

"You can't imagine . . ." He stopped, caught his breath. He couldn't tell them of the afternoon he'd spent absorbing the emotions of the spirit as Anris experienced the living world with Col's body. He'd already endangered his children enough.

"Are you willing to trade the lives you were created to protect for whatever it is you imagine that we cannot?" his mother challenged. Col had no answer she would accept.

"Where's Katy?" he asked then, suddenly afraid.

"Taking a nap," Kate said, and their mother added, "She has to be rested for tonight."

Col looked at her with real threat in his eyes. He would have burned her to the ground, but Kate dropped a hand gently on his shoulder, reminding him to show restraint.

"She has to be there, Col."

His mother offered regret but no reprieve.

Gathers closed his eyes. "Gods, gods, gods." he whispered. "This is insane." He caught his breath, fought back panic while his hand went to Kate's and clung to her fingers. "Don't let them hurt our child."

"I know what you think," Kate began.

"That her own grandmother is holding our daughter hostage and that my soul is her ransom."

"Granny Finlay taught you better than that." Katherine Gathers rose from her chair and moved toward him but stopped at the threat in his eyes. "Do you think our Katy could live with that creature inside of her? With his thoughts and his memories crawling through her body? Katy's life depends on you, Col, not on the man who holds the knife.

"When Anris comes to you tonight, think of what he would do to Katy. Bind him to his tomb to save your daughter's life and the lives of everyone in Thorgill."

"It makes no sense!"

It wouldn't help to shout at her. His mother believed, like his grandmother before her, that the child king became the most vulnerable to attack, to retribution, if the old king failed. Better, he remembered Granny Finlay telling him when he was himself the child king, to die with love by the knife of a neighbor than in hate and torment at the touch of Anris. He hadn't believed it then, and he sure didn't believe it now, with his daughter's life in the balance.

"The old ways are hard, Col," his mother said, "but they exist for a reason—"

Col knew she talked not just about the coming night but about her brother as well. The gods had taken her brother because the two had come to the tomb with passion and not as a gift to earth and air. To let go of any part of the old ways, even if they meant the death of her own grandchild, would unravel the fearful meaning she had made of her life.

"—Gods only know what her power could do in his control."

"Whose power?" Leach stood in the doorway, an arm supporting Barbara Finlay. The terrible heat in the room seemed to cool with the entry of the newcomers.

"Katy's," Gathers said.

"Don't you ever give up, woman?" Barbara rolled her eyes with a disgusted snort that brought a sanity Colin desperately needed to the house. Kate rose from her place by Col's chair and went to help her half sister. She arranged Barbara comfortably on the settle, then sat beside her.

"There are worse things than a quick death," Katherine Gathers snapped.

"Like a grandmother willing to provide one," Barbara returned, and Col shut his eyes, willing the voices into the distance. He heard his mother leave the room, followed the sound of her footsteps on the other side of the wall and the snapping on of the stove.

"Gods." Kate let out a sigh that seemed to go on forever. "We needed you here, Barbara."

"What are they talking about?" From his place in the doorway, Leach sounded like the warning rumble of thunder before the storm hits. Col smiled.

Barbara Finlay shrugged and winced—bad idea, Col knew, with the flesh over her ribs torn up as it was—but she answered anyway.

"It's a precaution. Granny Finlay warned about it, said it was necessary, but none of us sees the sense in it. Except for dear old Mum, of course.

"Col is king," she explained, and Leach nodded.

"Katy is destined to be the next king. Her brother won't have half her talent."

"How—" Leach began, then waved off his own question. "Never mind. So Katy is the next king. Why is everyone grim as death about it?"

Katherine Gathers returned then with a pot of steeping tea. "Didn't I teach you not to air family linen in public, Barbara, darling?" she warned with an artificial smile as she set the teapot down and began pulling cups and saucers off their shelves.

"Nope. Tried, though." Barbara Finlay smiled at

Leach; Col recognized the grim savagery of it—more a showing of teeth than any humor. "Death is what they are talking about, DCI. They plan to bring Katy to the tomb tonight and hold her at knifepoint. If Col succeeds in trapping Anris, Mother Gathers will let Katy go. If it looks as though Col has failed, that he's died without actually trapping Anris' spirit, Mother Gathers, or another of the good citizens of Thorgill at her behest, will slit Katy's throat."

Leach looked at him for a moment, and Col waited, until the DCI shook his head. "That's a damned sick joke, Sergeant."

A reminder, that: Gathers might be a king to these people, but he was a servant of Her Majesty sworn to uphold the law to Leach, and the DCI didn't think this was one bit funny.

"No joke, sir," stressing the formal address, Col answered the unstated question. "According to Granny Finlay, it's necessary to save the child from the predations of the spirit and to save the village from the devastation a king's talent can create in the control of that spirit. I've always assumed it was more in the way of persuasion, myself. They take the king's children hostage in case he decides to do a bunk. If he does what that want, they let the children go. If he doesn't, they treat them like any kidnap victims whose loving family can't come up with the ransom."

Gathers noticed with some satisfaction that his mother had set the teapot down again and stood perfectly still beside the dresser. Leach stared at him, rubbing a hand through his hair, and looked from one to the other before resting his gaze on Col Gathers, unmoving in his grandmother's chair.

"I see," he said, and turned and walked past the chair to the hallway. Col heard the DCI speaking softly on the telephone, and a moment later the man returned but did not leave his place blocking the passage to the room where Katy slept.

"Jacobs and Spencer came back from Pickering to take roadblock duty at the White Rose. They'll be here in about five minutes to take the child out. They will be carrying weapons, so why don't we all just sit quietly, and when they've gone, you can explain to me what you plan to do that requires death threats to your own children."

"They can't come here tonight, Inspector," Kate said. "You saw what Anris did this afternoon—one of your men with a gun could kill everyone in this house, Katy included, and the gods know what he would do when we were gone. Your men are not protected against that kind of attack."

"Well, actually," Leach said, and rubbed his neck with a sheepish expression that Barbara Finlay picked up with triumph in her voice.

"I gave them both warding charms. Inspector Leach here told them it was a local remedy—vapors from the little sack counteracted the poison in the air. He showed them his, and they took the charms without a word."

"Actually," Leach added, "I have a notion that Spencer already had one from his own granny. They should be here any time now—"

The door opened without a knock, and Spencer stood there, Jacobs a step behind. Both had their weapons drawn.

"I don't think you'll be getting an argument, lads." Leach moved into the room to allow them access and gestured with a nod of his head in the direction of the back hallway. "The kid's in there. Don't scare her, but move as fast as you can."

Spencer nodded. He looked more certain of himself; Jacobs seemed not quite ready to believe anything he'd seen or heard in the past hours, but he dogged his partner's steps.

"Where do we take her?" Spencer turned around in the entrance to query the DCI.

"The White Rose has a room with a bed in the back," Col answered. "She'll be safe there. Someone should stay with her in case she should wake up frightened," he added.

Spencer nodded and disappeared down the hallway. A moment later he reappeared, a gangly bundle of blankets and half-awake child in his arms. "The White Rose. All right then. You'll be by in the morning, DCI?"

Didn't ask him, Col noticed, or Kate. Didn't take any of them into custody either, which was almost more than he expected. Jacobs held the door and followed Spencer out with a last, confused, half-frightened look back.

"Thanks," Col said to Leach when the door had closed behind them. The DCI gave him a sharp nod of acknowledgment.

Katy was safe. Until that moment, Col hadn't really let himself believe it. He let his head fall to rest on the back of the rocking chair; suddenly, he could think of nothing more interesting than the regimented thatch of the ceiling.

The scrape of chair legs on the floor pulled his mind back from the blank space where he'd flown for peace. When he looked, Leach was pulling the chair under him, face to face, as they had sat the night before. Again, Leach asked for answers.

CHAPTER 29

"I told the lads to start the paperwork on your husband's release," Leach said to Katherine Gathers, getting the easy part out of the way. "I told Bannister to make sure they typed slowly; I assume you don't want him here for whatever it is you have planned."

"You understand at least that much, Inspector," she replied.

Leach gave her a long, thoughtful stare. He'd have thought she would be like Kate, but he saw more of Col in her swiftness to judge, to move on her own resolve. He wondered if her frozen bitterness grew out of living with the results of judgments held at too dear a cost. Margaret had said that of him, once, before she left. Lord, how did it all turn out so wrong down the line like that?

"It's been a taxing day," Leach said. "I'm sure Mrs. Gathers needs some rest." He looked to Kate to pick up the unspoken message: he needed to talk to her brother, alone. "And I know Ms. Finlay would be more comfortable lying down."

"I'm fine where I am, Geoff." Barbara contradicted. Why didn't that surprise him? "And you called me Barbara when I was half-naked; I think you can continue to do so when I have my clothes on."

Leach could feel the heat rising in his face but couldn't stop it. He did better at keeping the burbled explanations and excuses behind his teeth. He *didn't* want to announce to the room at large that he'd rather have seen Kate naked. Again Barbara took pity on him, though, before he could sputter anything to make the situation worse.

"He held my hand while they patched me up," she explained. "I didn't think I'd be such a fool about it, but I started to shake when we reached Pickering."

"Shock," Leach murmured. Being held hostage and shot by a madman would do that to anyone. He didn't say it out loud, though.

"Probably," Barbara agreed, "but I was glad you were there." She gave a dry half-laugh. "I hate it when Col is right, but we do need you with us on this, Geoff. There's not a damned soul else in Thorgill who wants Colin to walk out of that tomb alive tonight. I'm counting on you to make sure he does just that."

"He's not the only one." Kate rose from the settle and detoured by Col's chair to drift a fleeting brush of fingertips across Gathers' neck before taking her mother's arm. "But I'd say they're all in this room. I'll be back when I have Mother settled upstairs."

She turned to Barbara then. "Don't let them start without me."

Leach flushed, somewhere between embarrassed and annoyed. He *didn't* want them treating him like one of their demented family. But Kate accepted him—pleasure at the realization pinked his ears— even if she had taken control of the situation right out of his hands.

"This was supposed to be a private conversation." He made a last attempt to regain that control before giving up completely.

Barbara smiled. "That's why Kate is taking Mother Gathers to her room."

"Fools, all of you," Katherine Gathers said. "You don't know what you are facing out there tonight!"

Leach dismissed the woman from his mind, focused wholly on Colin Gathers. Gathers said nothing, but something hopeless and wild churned in his eyes before he closed the knowledge away behind his lashes.

"You stay right here, Sergeant," Leach said, sharply. "Do not leave me hanging in the damn breeze while you tune out."

Col's head came up at the accusation, but Leach knew the anger tensing Gathers' jaw, had seen it there before, not like that glimpse just now into a hell that seemed to surprise the sergeant almost as much as it did Leach.

"We've a job to do here, Sergeant." Leach pressed the point. Col was a good cop, but he was shaping up as a lousy mystic, and Leach had no intention of following anyone with a death wish anywhere.

"I've seen enough in this village to realize that I need your much-vaunted local expertise. I'm wearing the damned sack around my neck and stepping over doorways instead of walking through them, and I've sent Powell and his men—who have the jurisdiction and could have thrown us both out on our asses—out of town on a fool's errand so that you can do whatever it is you have to do to put an end to these murders."

The phone rang, once. Leach stopped, waiting for it to ring again, and remembered the handset next to the bed upstairs. He hoped Kate had taken the call and not her mother, but he figured they'd let him know if he was needed. In the meantime he had Colin Gathers' attention, and he meant to keep it.

"I am right out on the limb with you on this one, *Sergeant*, and unless it includes slitting the throats of the locals or your daughter, I am willing to listen. But

we are not leaving this room until I know everything—and I mean everything—that you plan or
expect to happen tonight."

"Yes, sir." This time, the use of the formal address
seemed to signal real acquiescence. "I can tell you
what we expect," Col said, "but the plan . . ." He
sighed.

"We don't, it seems, have a plan." Kate Gathers
spoke from the doorway of the enclosed stairwell.
"DCI Powell called. Tut died tonight. Powell thought
you would want to know." She came into the room
and took up her mother's post at the dresser, pouring
tea. Leach noticed that her hand shook. "I shall miss
him," she said.

Leach waited out her thoughtful silence. He didn't
have the Gathers' history with the constable, but the
little he had seen showed the man to be formidable in
his own right. Solid, too. Leach found he missed the
man already. What Col saw behind those clouded
eyes of his boded ill for all of them tonight. For
Gathers, Tuttle had been more than a fellow law
officer, more than a family friend. Col had leaned on
the constable for some part of this night's work, and
his death seemed to put a period to some glimmer of
hope already gone south with Tut's injury.

Kate picked up her former train of thought then.
"Inspector Powell said he would send his officers back
into Thorgill if you needed the backup, Inspector
Leach. I told him we were fine as we were." She
handed him a cup of tea.

"Thank you," he said, for the message and for the
tea. He thought about asking her to call him Geoff, but
the news had cranked the tension in the room. He
couldn't afford the distraction of his name on her
tongue tonight. Tomorrow, if they lived . . .

"No plan?"

"Well." Barbara Finlay shifted uncomfortably on the settle. "There's a traditional way of going about this. It's supposed to have worked for the first Finlay, but with Tut gone . . ." She shrugged; it was pointless to speak out loud the obvious. Constable Tuttle would have no part in this night's work. "Col doesn't like that plan anyway, it appears."

No surprise there, to Leach. "It may have worked for everyone but the Finlay last time, but as I recall, the Finlay ended up dead."

"We *all* end up dead, Inspector." Barbara took her tea and sipped it. "That's why they call it the end."

Harsh words, but Leach heard the anger in them, not for Leach or for her half brother, but for the powers and traditions that would take Colin Gathers from them so young. Tradition said it was his duty, and the villagers waited for him to die for them. Barbara Finlay's hatred for that tradition edged her words.

"Not at twenty-six," he said. "Not on my watch."

Barbara Finlay smiled her small triumph. "It took me a while, but I figured that out," she agreed. "That's why I made you bring me back. I wouldn't miss this for the world. Which, by the way, we are putting at risk when we include an outsider in Thorgill business."

Solemn pleasure at her praise warmed Leach's gut. Cults were good at that, the cynical policeman in him said, and he wondered when he'd thrown his good sense away to follow the Gathers family into their personal insanity. But none of his old answers fit the case, and Gathers' answers, damn it to hell, did.

"What do we have, Sergeant?"

He thought Col would shut down again, but Gathers seemed more grim but on the job. He leaned back in the rocking chair, and Leach recognized the look: Gathers was searching his memory, organizing his thoughts. Never one to speak before he'd thought out clearly what he would say, Col made decisions, discarding, adding, data. The DCI let himself relax just a notch.

"And you can start with how I went from persona non grata to man of the year around here."

"Just in this room," Barbara Finlay corrected him. "The rest of Thorgill would consign you to hell with all the other outsiders."

"And we," Kate added, "will ask you politely to go to hell for us because we have come to trust you." She did not smile at him to make it a joke, but gave Col a cup of tea and took a place behind his chair. The hand she rested on Col's shoulder trembled.

Col caught his glance, held it as if he wanted to imprint the truth on Leach's soul before they went a step further. "With Tut gone, I wouldn't trust anyone else in Thorgill tonight."

Which was a hell of a distance to have traveled since the ride into town with nothing but suspicion and anger between them.

"I'm not sure I believe your explanations," he said, because trust like that deserved all his truth, "but I accept that it is nothing I've ever encountered before. And I'm willing to try it your way tonight."

"That much I can promise you—"

Leach didn't trust the grim smile that crossed Gathers' face—"You'll know for certain before this night is out."

"So talk."

"All right," Gathers said. "This is where we stand. When we came into Thorgill, we had a plan, worked out over five thousand years. Tut would wait in his office, unprotected. I would wait in the tomb for him. The villagers would wait around the tomb. Anris would take Tut's body and come for me, because I am the Finlay and the spirit of my ancestor-brother wants the Finlay dead—finally and for all time. So he'll try to kill me. If he succeeds, he will kill my children; the direct line will be extinguished.

"According to Granny Finlay, and her granny before her—"

"And Col's own dear mother," Barbara interrupted.

Col frowned at her before picking up his story. "My duty is to hold the spirit in his tomb long enough for Kate to order the entrance stone back into place. It doesn't matter, to tradition, who wins the struggle in the tomb. The Finlay is the lure, the battle is the distraction. The real savior of our people will be Kate, mother of the child king, who will order the stone rolled into place."

Leach stared at him for a long minute, absorbing the outrageous plan. "What about the part of the plan where we get out before the stone rolls into place?" he asked with a very sick feeling in the pit of his stomach.

"If I can convince him you are about to die—that I will kill you as the Finlay killed Anris five thousand years ago—I hope to drive him from your body, into the altar. When you feel his presence leave you, run like hell."

Col paused a moment, and Leach didn't have to ask what he saw in that middle distance. The tomb, cold and waiting, rose up in his own mind as well.

"Barbara will be leading the villagers to seal the space around the tomb with their bodies and their linked arms. Anris can't pass them because they will be wearing warding charms. But if you are free of him, you can pass, over or under their arms, and they will let you. Don't try to break through the circle; the gap would leave an opening for Anris."

"We'll drop to the ground," Barbara offered. "I'll be

in front—look for me, and jump over my arm. We're making this part up as we go along, Inspector, so don't expect Charlie White or Dick Morgan to react according to plan if you try a flying leap over them."

Leach sat back in his chair and winced as it creaked under his weight. Margaret was right—he should have kept himself more fit. He hadn't thought this job would call for hand-to-hand combat or leapfrog, though. He nodded anyway.

"Look for you. Leap."

Col suddenly looked more relaxed, but Leach noticed that Kate Gathers' hand had clenched around her brother's shoulder. The man didn't flinch, but Leach saw the awareness of the pain of it in the man's eyes, and the control.

"Col gets out the same way?" he asked.

He didn't bother looking at Gathers, who would lie with his eyes, but to Kate, whose anguish bled from every line in her drawn face.

"He doesn't get out," she said. "He shouldn't ask for your life—better to roll the stone as soon as Anris is inside the tomb—but I will hold off sealing the entrance as long as I can."

Leach stared at her, would have asked with his eyes what she wanted him to do, but her gaze had turned inward, already bearing the pain of murdering her brother. They wanted Leach to find a way out for Col, but he saw no hope that he would succeed.

"I can see why you have some problems with the plan, Sergeant."

Leach studied Col's face, looking for the tension in his body signaling the spark of battle that would mean Colin Gathers expected to live through this night, but he didn't see it.

"So what's plan B?"

Kate eased up on her brother's shoulder then. Col

looked grateful for that much at least. But Leach knew he wasn't going to like what he heard next.

"That was one of the things we were arguing about when you arrived, Inspector." Kate said, and added, "I don't believe I thanked you for getting Katy out of this."

"We prefer the moral high ground when we can get it," he answered, and winced when she took it for the censure it was.

Col seized on the exchange as an opening. "We don't have the right," he said. "If we seal our ancestor-brother in that tomb again, it means we haven't learned anything in five thousand years. It's time to set him free."

Barbara Finlay shifted uncomfortably on the settle. "I'm not happy about sealing you in a stone box with an insane spirit," she said, "but we can't give Anris the run of Thorgill. He won't stop killing until we are all dead."

"That's because he isn't free. Anris escaped his tomb but not Thorgill's hold on his soul. He can't leave; we have to help him find the way."

Gathers leaned forward in the armchair, speaking only to Leach, the inspector realized; Col handed him trust like a challenge.

"How?" Leach waited in the unnatural silence that descended upon the room. He heard the slow intake of air and knew that Colin Gathers alone of the four of them continued his regular breathing.

"Bring him to me, Geoff," Gathers said. "Bring him to me, and I will show him the way home."

"I can't," he said, and he knew that this night he truly would pay for his sins. The dying child in Derry flashed before him, wearing Colin Gathers' face. No surprise, though, but understanding and pity in those dying eyes. Harder on you, that face seemed to say;

my pain will endure for minutes, but you will carry the memory for all your long life.

"I'm a *peace* officer. How can you ask me—" Not quite a friend, he couldn't say that, but bound to this man by the blood that once had flowed onto his helpless hands "—to participate in your murder?"

"I have all of Thorgill to take my life," Gathers said, "but I can trust only you to give that death meaning. Don't let them seal the tomb. Let me do it my way."

"I won't let them seal you in there," he promised, because the thought of Colin Gathers, broken fingers leaving streaks of blood on the stone, squeezed the heart right out of him. "What more can I do?"

"Get out alive. Once you're out, don't interfere, no matter what you see," Col said, "and leave Thorgill and all its memories behind you when it's over. Know that it was my choice. Don't tie me to you nightmares, Geoff. Let me go."

God. Leach had been walking through a waking nightmare since they had arrived in Thorgill, and he knew that if he walked away from here alive, he'd carry a sackful of bad memories to replay in his sleep when it was done. But he couldn't add his fears to Gathers' burden. He pulled himself out of the chair, felt the breaking of some spell that seemed to have held time still inside the cottage while night progressed across the sky outside. He heard the rustle of booted feet in the grass outside and saw disembodied torch flames drifting past the window.

"They're here," Kate said. "Time to get ready."

CHAPTER 30

A knock sounded on the door, and Henry Tuttle let himself into the parlor, an expression of uneasy compassion on his face. Leach, Col noticed, had moved to the front window, where he seemed to split his uneasy watch between the darkness outside and the gloom in the parlor. Much to think about, his guvnor, and not a lot of choices, or time to make them. And Henry, he knew, would not make things better. Gathers stared into the fire, coming to terms with the only answers he had. Fire. The thought paralyzed him. Fire.

"I've come for Colin," Tuttle said, and stopped, his mouth open slightly as he groped for the next word.

"Henry." Col answered without turning his gaze from the fireplace, and Henry Tuttle slid past Leach to stand, hesitant but expectant, in the middle of the parlor.

"We heard about your uncle," Col said to fill the void, and, because he really meant it, "Tut was a good man. He'll be sorely missed." He did look up then, gave the man his sympathy.

"I miss him already." Henry's gaze slid away before he actually made eye contact.

No mystery why. They both knew that Tut's death this afternoon just meant that he wouldn't die tonight. The question, who would die in his place, hung over the minister like a shroud.

"Inspector Leach understands what is to be done. He will take Tut's place tonight."

"Are you sure? I mean—" Henry glanced back over his shoulder to where Leach stood at parade rest in front of the closed door.

"The inspector is certain, Henry, which is more than I can claim right now. Let it be."

The minister dropped his head. True Christian humility, Col wondered, or the natural fear all men had when facing the sacrificial victim in the moments before death? "I came—" Henry started, and Col noticed the Bible in his hand.

Ah, duty. Col would have thrown him out for the hypocrisy of it except that Henry really believed. Only Thorgill could produce a man so deeply committed to his faith and at the same time so accepting of Thorgill's pagan answers. It didn't mean Col wanted his prayers or his sympathy, but the man had suffered his own losses today.

"I thought you might need some spiritual support, Colin, for the night to come. If the inspector is to take my uncle's place tonight, perhaps he would like to pray with us."

Leach muttered a series of low expletives and slammed out of the cottage, looking, Col figured, for some solitude. No peace out there; Dick Morgan and the rest would be about, waiting. But Col still had Henry Tuttle to deal with.

"You've come to the wrong place, Henry; your God has turned his back on us in Thorgill tonight."

"He never turns His back, Col. This afternoon should have proved that to you. Katy is safe, Barbara alive."

"But not Tut, Henry. I didn't think your God demanded human sacrifice." Col turned once again to the fire. "Not like my gods."

Henry sighed. "God is merciful," he said. "It isn't God Who demands your life, Colin, but He understands and will hold you in His arms when you have given it to Him."

"Not until some poor sod comes along and opens that damned tomb again, Henry. Go pray for the soul of your uncle. There is no hope of salvation in this house tonight."

"It pains me to hear you speak this way when—"

"When death waits so close by, Henry?" He sighed, knowing Henry didn't deserve his wrath. Thorgill did, maybe, but a man could shatter on the cold stone of that tomb, could be forever lost in the tangled darkness of the moors.

"Go home," he said, "and comfort Laura. She's had a rough day, and she will need you tonight."

Kate slipped up behind him then; he felt her presence like the shield it was. "It's time to get ready," she said. "I'll help you."

Henry did meet Col's eyes then, his misery and confusion clear and sharp as a slap. Then the minister turned away.

"I will be with you tonight, Col." he said, and left, closing the door quietly behind him. No comfort tonight, Henry, Col thought. No rest, no hope. Just duty and a wrong that only the Finlay could set right. If only he weren't so afraid.

"I brought your clothes down with me. I didn't think you'd want to face Mother again tonight."

"She'll be there," Col reminded her. No way to keep Katherine Gathers away. She deserved his pity and not his anger—she'd lost a brother, a lover, already. But he could not bear to see in her eyes how small a part he played in his own death. Tonight his mother would sacrifice a son to Thorgill's unholy justice, penance and reparation for the sin of loving his father, but she would see only her loss, not his.

"Can't keep her away," Barbara admitted.

"But for now she will stay upstairs." Kate held out the clothing that would transform him.

Nothing to hide, he let his sisters undress him tonight, felt the trace of their soft fingers at the buttons of his shirt, sliding his trousers down his legs. He felt the doeskin leggings, soft on skin that didn't quite belong to him, the linen tunic, rougher, from the distance where his mind took refuge. Silk belt. He stood when they told him to, sat when they pushed him gently into a chair, and moved his arms, his legs, like an automaton, at the soft command of Barbara, who was hurt, he remembered, and should not bend so at his feet to slip the boots up over his calves. He lifted his arms at Kate's urging, her gentle fingers damp with tears. Somehow, his nightmares and his dreams all seemed to come to rest in the image of her tears.

Finally, he stood between them, the Finlay—the king—and the distance in his eyes embraced the clouds above the moors on a spring morning and the mist that filled the dale at dusk.

"It's time," he said. "Call Leach."

"I'm here." Leach stood in the open doorway, and Col wondered how long he had been there, what he had meant to see, or what peace he meant to leave unbroken. After a long moment, Leach stepped over the threshold. "What do you want me to do?"

Kate left her brother's side; he felt her passing, felt the lack of her beside him like a phantom limb.

"You wait," she said to Leach. "And then you try to live with yourself when we are through." She held the inspector's face between her hands, studied his features, and kissed him, softly and, damn them both, Colin Gathers, who could no longer feel his own body, felt that kiss and all the regret in it. "I would have wished our lives hadn't come to this," she said. "I would have wanted to know you without so much death to separate us."

Leach kissed her then; Gathers closed his eyes, but not soon enough. Leach's arms held Kate, his mouth found Kate's, and Col trembled with the effort it took not to hit the mantlepiece again. He couldn't afford any more broken bones, but he wanted to hurt the universe that would not give them peace. Don't let them die tonight, he begged that hostile universe and Henry Tuttle's God, if he was listening. Happiness was too much to ask, but to let them live, such a small thing in a universe so large, so full of the violence of stars and the calm of starless skies.

"We have to go," Col heard her say, and he opened his eyes again. Kate stood a pace apart from the inspector and lifted the charm on it's leather thong from around his neck. She led him to the rocking chair and nudged him into it. "Wait," she said, "and follow—you will know when."

She turned away and slipped her hand into the crook of Gathers' elbow. Barbara went in front of them, Col conscious only at a distance of the movement around him, through Granny Finlay's workroom, out into the night. Charlie White stood there, and Dick Morgan, Henry Tuttle with his Bible open and with Laura Simms at his side. More, deeper in the shadows, he could not see but could guess—they would all be there, clustered tightly in the flaring light of their burning torches.

He walked through the villagers as if in a dream, felt them take places flanking him, following. The night had begun dark, but now the clouds had passed and the moon, nearly full, shone cold light on the torches rising up the dale, ascending into hell. The moors lay cold and forbidding above him, and the torches burned a futile battle with the night, pinpricks of light that swept the hillside.

Brother-ancestor—he reached for the spirit of Anris with the love of a brother. The plan he had shaped in solitude would free him to show the tormented spirit the way home; together they would follow the path of smoke and fire. But gods, oh, gods. Gathers remembered, suddenly, the feel of death. He hadn't recognized it on the stair landing when the bullet took him—surprise, then, mostly, and shock that held the pain at a distance. Later, in the hospital, after they'd patched him up and before he could feed himself, the fear had hit with the sickening replay of falling, the part of him that thought and felt leaving his body to its swift and deadly pain. How much worse would tonight be? Col stumbled, and hands reached to steady him, flames dancing in the night wind.

The crest of the dale lay ahead in the gray light of the moon, the tomb a darkness that blighted the star-crossed sky. Torches flowed over, onto the moor, pushing back the shadows, circling the tomb, the meeting place. Henry approached him then, but Barbara blocked his way.

"The deeds of this night do not belong to your God, Henry," she said. "Stay at the bidding of your ancestors, but set your book down tonight."

Henry hesitated, but Colin Gathers gave him no answers. He had no answers to give but one, and that one ended in fire and pain. Finally Laura took the minister's hands and led him away like a sleep-walking child. Barbara held Colin close a moment, then let him go. He would have thanked her, but he could find no comfort in her touch, nor could he give her comfort in return. The words would not come, the gift of it as alien to him as all of Thorgill was becoming. Kate reached for him but stopped, and he saw her curl her fingers into a fist to keep from touching him. Wise Kate, who knew they only had each other's pain to share. Hard enough to endure his own.

"I won't let them roll the stone," she said, and he nodded acceptance. Whatever else happened, he would be free this night.

She reached then for the warding charm and he bowed his head to her, his queen, the mother of the child king, and she slipped the charm from around his neck.

"How can I let you go, Brother?" she said at the last, and he brushed the tears from her cheeks. "Even the Finlays have to end sometime, Kate," he said, and a last thought—"tell Katy I love her." He reached for her, placed a hand on her belly, where the child lay, and then stepped back, his hand dropping to his side.

"He's coming," Gathers said, and took a torch from one bearer and a newly chipped stone ax from another. Then he turned and passed through the low tunnel of the entrance.

His torch flickered and steadied again, and he pitched it upright into the soft earth and lay the stone ax at the feet of Anris' body. Then he stood, almost at rest, at the altar of the magician-king. Waiting.

CHAPTER 31

Alone in the old stone house Leach rocked and waited while the fire on the hearth burned low and died. In his mind he crested the dale with the torchbearers, but there his imagination faltered on the image of Kate in her brother's arms. His own arms tingled with the feel of her still warm on his skin. Not tonight, he knew. Death waited on the moors above the little house, but would he be the carrier of that death, as Col and most of Thorgill had led him to believe, or had they left him here with his thumb up his backside while they took their own justice on a murderer whose identity was obvious to everyone but him?

He wondered, with a certain bitter humor, what Margaret would make of him now. Awareness of his own vulnerability crept across his skin, raising the hair on the back of his neck. He shouldn't have sent his gun out of town. He realized it was more than his own nerves when he heard the voice; it chuckled softly in his ear, hungry and dangerous. He hadn't expected this gentle seduction of his senses, the caress of power and possession on his mind that some part of him reached for, embraced.

No! His hands clenched white against the arms of the rocking chair while he fought the thing that drifted like smoke through his surface thoughts. Curious, probing fingers of thought teased him, sending tiny shivers up his spine, into his crotch, tightening with a longing for something he could not express, but that the thing in his head promised him. He tried to fight it, to shut out the whispering voice and calm the pulse of sexual awareness that tightened in his body and throbbed, throbbed, more powerful than human, and he felt a part of himself float away. Arms outstretched, that insubstantial part of him reached for the earth, and he was taller than the ancient trees and wider than the forests that once marched the land, and he fell upon the moor and plowed the land with his body, earth pliant in his arms as he planted his seed in the fickle soil while voices screamed in his head.

Not him. Not Geoffrey Leach, who knew only concrete and small bits of garden tucked between the pavement and the front step. But he could not hold against the desire of the thing that leaked into his will and wrapped around his soul. Drained and exhausted, he gave his memories to the whispering voice and knew it was too late as his nightmares became the tools of the invader.

"Goodwife Margaret would not approve," the voice said, and violence blossomed in pain. When the part of himself that roamed free rose again, he saw his body clothed in blood and the land below him not the earth of the moor but a tangle of the dead, staring blankly into his eyes. Leach knew that the spirit fed him its own memories, but his mind lay open to the creature now, wracked by the images Anris fed with his own. He looked closer at the dead and saw Dunlop with a bellyful of rusted nails and slivered whiskey bottle while the child he had murdered fell, and fell again, his heart blown out. Blood from the wounds of his dead and dying stained the corners of his vision. Col lay bleeding on a cheap London stair landing,

caught again in that moment of frozen surprise while his blood flowed onto Leach's hands. So much blood.

"All our yesterdays lighting fools to dusty death," indeed. With all his own bloody death coming home to haunt his waking hours, Leach knew how that old Scottish king must have felt. And, he figured, he might as well throw in an "Out, damned spot" while he was at it.

The presence that curled its tendrils through his memory had no context for the referent, but Leach felt it grab hold of all the bloody murder that birthed the thought. Desire for Colin Gathers' death fed the greed of the spirit, and Leach could not hold against it. He fled to the part of his mind that was oblivion—unknowing, unfeeling. Anris shut that door, made him feel his own pain, self annihilated in the fierce possession of the magician-king. Then the pain drifted slowly into savage pleasure. Col dead was a thing to be savored, his blood like fragrant oils slick to his elbows.

"*Yes. This will do nicely.*" The voice hissed its pleasure in his ear.

Leach screamed, alone in the old stone house. He saw blood on his hands. Col's blood, flowing like a river down his wrists, disappearing beneath the cuffs of his shirt. Images twisted him out of the chair, visions of destruction, of savage waste and life ripped to pieces for pleasure. Margaret, staring at him with dead, accusing eyes, her throat slashed open, her body torn open like the photographs of Anris' first victims in this case.

Margaret was well out of it, gone to a new life with two suitcases and her precious Waterford crystal. But Kate Gathers was nearby. He could have her, could almost reach out and touch her, naked and screaming in the merciless power of his body dragging her down, and down.

The voice laughed at him while he vomited, beating his fists against the sides of his head to drive out the sensations of rape and torture and joy and murder, murder with one face burning at the center of the rage that overpowered him. The usurper king, Colin Gathers, who called himself the Finlay.

The thing inside him would destroy Col Gathers, have his sister on the altar of his tomb and kill her with the ax a Finlay had used to fell Anris—

"No!"

Through teeth clenched between locked jaws, Leach denied the thing that possessed him. He could not kill Colin Gathers, whose survival bound Leach in his flesh and bone. Gathers had walked into near certain death against his own instincts on the word of his superior, and Leach owed the man a life for the trust he had broken that day. This time, he would redeem the confidence Gathers freely gave him.

And God, he could not kill Kate, who saw to the bottom of his soul and cared about him anyway. The creature in his mind filled his body with the feel of flesh under his fingertips, flesh he took, and took while the pleasure curled in his gut and exploded behind his eyes. Rape her, rape her, and if she would give what he would take, he would break her, until she knew that her line, even to the child in her belly, died. The sensual press of the ax in his hand filled him. He felt it rise and fall, slicing flesh, and saw Kate's belly torn open, her bloody womb in his hand, even as he pulsed out his completion inside her dying body.

Leach gagged and screamed and fought the pleasure that spread like a sickness though his body, and he shook with the effort to contain the madness while his throat screamed itself raw. He would not hurt her, he would not hurt her, and the rhythm of the words matched the pounding of his feet. Leach was past the garden before he realized that he had left the house, fighting his way up the side of the dale, his land, his people, and the power filled him, ripped from the earth and the sky, while Geoffrey Leach fought to control the legs Anris used to pound his way upward, to the crest of the moor, and the magician-king laughed at the cowering spirit of the man who begged for oblivion he would never give.

"Watch, little man," he whispered to the cowering thing that was Geoffrey Leach. *"Carry in your fingertips the memory of murder for pleasure. For it does pleasure us, in our belly and our plow and in the wild fire that fills the universe with our lust, our lust, Geoffrey Leach, for I take my pleasures from your mind."*

Ahead, Anris saw the flicker of torches and the looming darkness of his own tomb. His rage tore at the mind of Geoffrey Leach: madness, madness. Leach felt himself curled abandoned in a corner of his own mind, rocking against the assault on his body and his soul. This was the thing that drove Pankowitz to drooling catatonia, that had flung a desperate archaeologist down a mine shaft. Leach would have turned away, then, the mine shaft drawing him more powerfully than the call of the torches, but Anris held him back. Suddenly they were within the circle of torches, ducking low to pass into the tomb that had held him captive for five thousand years, and Anris screamed in Leach's mind as the call of the Finlay, the king, drove him forward.

Memory of the endless centuries of darkness obliterated Leach's mind. Then Colin Gathers stood before him, as he had never seen the man before, and the light from the torch at Gathers' feet burned his eyes in the darkness where he whimpered for death to end the horror of the thing that held him.

"Help me," he gasped, and Gathers' serious nod shocked him.

"Today, we end it," the Finlay king said, and Leach would have wept, but Anris shed no tears.

CHAPTER 32

"He's coming."

Col heard his own words whispered at the entrance to the tomb, and the breath caught in his throat. Kate would hold back the stone, he knew, but would Barbara be strong enough to hold the circle against the fury of the magician-king in Leach's body? He watched the light from the torches that circled the tomb, felt the gray at the edges of his soul swallow him by inches as one and then another light flickered out. Finally the darkness was complete but for the single flame at his side—the flame that would draw Anris. No other light would shine until the spirit entered the circle, and then the torches would flare, drawing the circle firm and solid around them.

Colin knew he'd been born for this day, but he couldn't say he was prepared for it. Not this way, Hadley sending him home to do his bleeding for queen and country as though the twentieth century didn't even exist. He hoped Anris didn't have access to Leach's memories, but he couldn't count on it. Leach was a soldier; more importantly, he was a policeman with a sure knowledge of how Gathers would react in almost any policing situation. Col didn't even want to think about facing Anris' devious cunning twisted around Leach's expertise.

Anris was closing on the tomb—Col could feel his

presence, sense the blazing evil of him approaching like a storm. He reached for the charmbag at his neck and remembered, with the taste of bile on his tongue: Kate had it. Suddenly Geoffrey Leach stood before him, a dark mass in the entrance, and Colin's vision tunneled until nothing existed beyond the shadow-form of Anris in Leach's body.

"Help me," Leach gasped.

More control than Col had expected, but the losing struggle to fight the thing that possessed him wrote itself plainly across Leach's body. Col nodded, acknowledging a friend in battle. But he spoke to the magician, summoning all the power of the Finlay kings: "Today, we end it."

"Col." Suddenly, Leach was gone and the magician-king's rage burned in the inspector's eyes.

"Col." The tone was deceptive—loving, soft. The hands flexed. "Where's Kate? Shouldn't she be here?"

"Kate guards the door."

With the words, false dawn brightened beyond the shadowed bulk of Leach in the entrance. Family and neighbors set torches alight and raised them. Col's vision cleared as he drew strength from the reminder that he did not fight this thing alone. He drew a deep breath, feeling the circle tighten around the tomb. Col's way or Thorgill's, the killing stopped here.

But Anris did not attack as Col expected. The creature held Leach's body very still, a thoughtful, distant expression drifting across his face as if Anris listened to a far voice.

"He's not your friend, young Gathers." Anris smiled. "But there is something, not love, but more than duty. He almost hates you when he thinks about your dying. 'How dare you do this to me?' he thinks, and wonders how he can survive with your death on his hands. Takes it all a bit personally for a soldier.

How did the Finlay come to be in the charge of a soldier, boy?

"Not a soldier," Col corrected him. "We keep the peace."

Anris turned Leach's head in a single emphatic negation, lips curled in a lazy, seductive smile. "Not this one. His soul fairly reeks of blood. No peace here, boy." Leach started to move then, circling warily.

"Leach has been a soldier, yes. And you may take pleasure in those memories, but he doesn't," Col objected, matching the careful prowl of his adversary. "He knows blood and death, but he has sworn to protect the innocent."

Leach laughed with Anris' caustic irony. "There are no innocents in this village, Finlay king. Except you, or so your inspector believes."

Col raised an empty hand. "You are lying. He knows my flaws better than any man. He thinks I do not know it, but in his heart, for this time and place, Geoffrey Leach has put his soul in my keeping. I am his king, to spend him as I wish."

Leach's face smiled an epicurean appreciation as Anris rolled that thought around in his captive's mind. "You surprised him there—he didn't think you knew." Anris kept circling, and Colin let him.

"I knew. That is why he was chosen to bring you here. Together we will set you free."

"I am free." Leach's voice laughed at him. "Ask your sister, whose child I held at my mercy today. Ask dear Barbara. This time has interesting ways of dealing death."

"I mean, really free." Col eased further around the altar, keeping his distance from the magician-king. "Free to follow the sun home. Free to rest."

"How?" Leach stood very still, his head cocked to catch the words more easily.

"Come to me." Col opened his arms. The Finlay, Anris' king, he felt the surge of earth and sky in his blood, knew it called to his brother. "Let me take you home."

"No!" Leach stepped back, his eyes burning with Anris' mad light. "Now you are lying. It's a trap. I see it in his mind. You don't like it, but you are only waiting until this mule is free, then Kate will roll the stone in place. Don't think to fool me twice, Finlay!"

Leach's body leapt at him, and Gathers danced out of his way. "You are wrong about something else as well, old enemy, Geoffrey Leach is my friend, and I am his." Still keeping his distance, Col changed his tone, made it low and gentle, for Leach. "I'm sorry, Geoff."

Anris laughed. "Friend or not, he's going to kill you. All that bright red blood on his hands, the lovely ax falling. And you will die, here, tonight, whether you are friend to him or not."

Col met the hungry gaze calmly. "I won't let you have him." He stood at the side of the altar and watched as Anris, in Leach's body, moved to stand over the spirit's long-dead bones. Leach's eyes narrowed in the hunt.

"You've made one fatal error," Col said. "You thought he knew the plan. He doesn't."

"He's disappointed, Col."

That last wasn't true. If nothing else had convinced the DCI, Anris tramping though his mind surely had. Col had seen a fleeting glimpse of hope, which he was about to dash.

He ignored Anris' words, trying to keep the sound of Geoff's voice from working on his nerves, from lowering his guard. He made his own voice cold, burying the pain behind the walls he built inside his mind.

"It's Leach's job to protect the civilians with his life. He knew the risks when he bought in. So to take you, I will kill him. We owe each other that much. If he should kill me first, Kate has instructions to roll the stone into place. Either way, he is dead and you are trapped. Again."

Anris lunged for his throat. Leach's strong fingers trembling, almost a caress that exploded into crushing pain as they tightened their grip. Let it go. He had enough breath for the moment, relaxed the panic gasp that tightened the muscles against Leach's hands, and moved his forearms into position between his and Leach's elbows to ease the grip. Then his eyes caught those of the man he knew.

"You don't have to do this, Geoff," he gasped. "He isn't you, not any part of him. Fight him, and he loses."

The fingers at his throat loosened of their own accord.

"I can't hold him back. I'll kill you."

"Never." Col broke the hold and bounced out of Leach's reach. From around his waist he uncurled a short piece of rope with slipknots at both ends.

Leach seemed to have forgotten him for the moment. He knelt on one knee at the foot of the skeleton, then turned with a low snarl. "Where is it?"

"This little trinket?" Col held up the flint ax. "If you want it, come and get it."

He slipped the ax inside his shirt and moved into fighting stance, weight forward over the balls of his feet, knees slightly bent. His hands hung loose but ready at his sides. He took in the fury on Leach's face but did not let it hold his attention.

Leach's right hand flew at his jaw in a tight fist, the left aimed for a gut punch. Col rode out the left; he grabbed the man's right hand and slipped the first noose of the rope around his wrist. Leach's knee came up, and Col dodged it, realizing too late that the move put him in position for the left hand falling straight as a blade for the soft spot where neck met shoulder.

For an instant the expression of Leach's face was the man's own: comprehension and determination showed there. The blade hand closed into a fist and brushed past Col's shoulder. He took the opening Leach gave him and slipped the second noose over the left hand.

In a single leap Col was on top of the altar stone at the center of the tomb. He drew on the rope that held the DCI, pulling the man's arms over his head. Keeping the rope taut, he jumped to the far side of the stone, dragging Leach onto his back across the altar. He secured the rope over a spur of rock jutting from its base.

With his eyes he begged forgiveness, but he gave no sign of weakness. His was the face of judgment: not Colin Gathers, but the Finlay, performing a duty laid upon him five thousand years ago. Loyalty, trust, had no place here, but he knew he exploited it to win. He felt no guilt for that. If Leach were to survive, Anris had to believe that Col Gathers would kill and walk away. That meant Geoff had to believe it too. Col drew the flint ax out of his shirt before Leach could kick him out of the way.

"Is this how they did it the last time?" Col growled into the ear of the bound man. He pressed the side of the blade into Leach's throat. He could feel the broken rhythm of the carotid artery pulsing through the flint in his hand and he held it steady with an effort.

"Did the Finlay hold you down until your life's blood was gone, soaked into the stone like the hundreds you killed on this spot?" He angled the blade, drew a drop of blood from the small veins close to the surface of the neck stretched before him.

The life faded from the blue eyes for a moment, and Leach's own words slipped through barely parted lips. "Finish it, Sergeant. Better than having this thing in my head. Not your fault."

He didn't answer, didn't dare. Pain caught at his chest, but he fought to keep it hidden from those searching eyes. His hand shook and drew another fine cut on the throat stretched under his blade.

The eyes closed, and opened again on fear, but Col knew whose weakness that was. Anris. He turned a face of stone on the magician-king. "Remember how it felt, dying on your own altar, the blood warm against your cold skin. Remember fear. Remember death. You will feel it again when this body you inhabit dies. Drink your own death again, old enemy—"

Leach's arms pulled against the bonds, and Col lifted the flint ax for a lethal blow. Blue eyes darkened and suddenly cleared. Leach sagged, the tension leaving his strained muscles. A Geoffrey Leach smile crossed the man's lips—ironic, accepting. It was the sign Col had been watching for. The flint ax slashed down and cut the rope.

"Move, damn it!" He pulled the man to his feet and shoved him toward the entrance. "Don't break the circle. Jump!"

Leach stumbled, pulled himself back to his feet and ran, then he was gone; with the sudden flickering of the torchlight beyond the entrance to the tomb, Col knew that the inspector was beyond the circle, safe. He had no time to appreciate that small victory because the hardest part remained—and Anris was on him, in him, his rage and frustration beating Col against the walls of the tomb. His head rang with the blows and with the screaming hatred of the thing inside him. He fell to his knees, beat his fists on the ground, lost in the fury of the thing that threatened to tear him apart, body and soul.

No. No. He was the Finlay, and he had a job to do here, a destiny to fulfill. He reached for the altar, felt his hands seared with the power of the old blood that charged the place with power, and dragged himself upright. A foolish thing, needing to stand tall against the battering of his ancient brother-ancestor. A foolish thing, shaking his head, struggling for awareness to do this thing he had to do. Better to be done with it while confusion dulled his senses. But he needed control. Kate was out there, carrying his son. Barbara and Geoffrey Leach, the only witnesses who mattered, must walk away alive and whole, so he stood, embraced his brother's soul, and sought his own power, in flame.

Like the sun exploding from the center of his brow, the fire came. Stone resisted, but the altar, already steeped in the blood of Anris' power, caught first, then the roof above it.

"Fly," he whispered to the spirit. "Follow the smoke. Fly home." He felt it then, a lightening of his soul, a bright, sharp arrow of joy aimed at the dawn. And the flames enveloped the tomb.

Col screamed, fell to earth screaming. He hadn't known it would hurt that much and, laying there, arms splayed across Anris' bones in the bloody dirt, he cursed the gods of his ancestors and Henry Tuttle both because he was still alive with the pain and the smell of his own burning flesh in his nose, until the heat seared his lungs and strangled the sound in his throat. Then he prayed, but to Kate, not to his gods. Hold back the stone. Beyond all fear save one lingering horror that still sparked in his dying mind, he prayed: don't seal the tomb.

CHAPTER 33

He fell, took the skin off the palm of his hand but managed to keep his face out of the dirt, and then Kate was beside him, pulling at his shoulder.

"Get up, Geoff. It isn't safe."

She tugged at his arm and he flinched away from her, Anris and the filth of his desires still singing in his nerve endings.

"Get away," he managed to choke out. "I'll hurt you." But she didn't seem to be listening.

"You're free of him now, but you've got to get outside of the circle."

Leach remembered Colin Gathers' words, the same as Kate's. He had to get to the other side of the circle. It was important, though he didn't remember why. If nothing else, it would put distance between himself and Kate Gathers, so he dragged himself to his feet and moved toward the torchlight that seemed to dance just above the bracken ahead. He caught his ankle on something, heard a grunt with pain in it, and tumbled again, but the light was rising out of the moor, a circle of light. Don't break the circle. He almost had: he realized only now, face down in the brambles, that he must have snagged his foot on Barbara Finlay's arm. Shot on that side this morning, too. God, he'd be lucky if she didn't turn him into a frog. But he was outside the ring of torches now, and

Barbara Finlay had risen up with the rest of them. She'd hung on, and hadn't let him break a path for Anris to follow him.

A distant part of him realized that he was weeping, but no clutch-at-his-breathing sobs alerted him, just a slow, steady trail of dampness running down his face that refused to stop no matter how many kinds of fool he called himself. He felt dirty—wanted to stand under a shower forever and wondered how in God's name he would ever feel clean on the inside, where that creature had been. How could he ever look into Kate Gathers' eyes again, with the images Anris had left in his mind of her spread before him, torn and dying with his prick buried deep inside her? Sick bastard, and now Geoffrey Leach carried that sickness inside himself.

He tried to lever himself up, but his shoulders screamed their objection—he'd dislocated the left one struggling against Col's ropes. Shouldn't have struggled, he realized, should have died on that altar for the sins that *thing* had planted in his soul. Couldn't have done that to Gathers, though. Too great a burden to leave to any man, murder of a friend. Friend.

Col. Didn't think he'd ever seen agony like that in a man's face before, not even in Derry, and that's when he knew that Gathers really would kill him. The blade taking slices out of his neck was just window dressing; until he saw that look, he believed Col meant for him to escape this thing. Then he knew Anris was going down, regardless of whom he took with him. That's when the spirit figured it out too.

He lay there in the dirt, waiting for the driving madness that had taken Pankowitz and the archaeologist, wondering how much longer he could hold onto his sanity and if he were sane, and, if this was sanity, did he want to keep it? And where was Colin Gathers? He should have been right behind Leach.

"Col," he whispered, then louder as the dawn seemed to find them from the wrong direction. Fire! "Col!"

Flames snapped in the entrance to the tomb. Impossible. Stone, the tomb was nothing but stone and beaten earth, nothing that burned, but yet it did burn, and then he heard the screams coming from inside the tomb.

"Colin!" He was up, then, running, the shoulder forgotten until someone grabbed him, pulled him up short by the injured arm. He added his own agonized scream to the cacophony—couldn't help it—but the arm snapped back into place, and Leach managed to shake off his captor, but more of the villagers grabbed at him. Colin Gathers' voice rose in a steady crescendo of pain, and Leach tried to shake off the hands that held him.

"You can't, Geoff." Barbara touched his arm, gently; her other arm she held tightly to her side. He'd hurt her, he remembered, saw her pallor in the pale light of that false dawn, saw the fire reflected in her eyes. "You can't help him now."

He didn't listen, couldn't listen. Couldn't carry the sounds of Colin Gathers' screams into his nights, couldn't bear the weight of one more death on his back. He broke away, knowing he'd hurt her again, but he couldn't wait, or the screams would die and it would be too late to do anything but burn with the man for no reason but his utter, last, and complete refusal to drag one more death through even an hour more of his miserable life.

"Don't you do this! Don't you die on me you son of a bitch!" He shouted as he ran, mad, now, not Anris' madness, but his own, and Kate was there, and the stone was moving. He'd broken the circle and didn't care if Anris killed them all if he could just reach Col in time. With a last, bloodcurdling shriek, the sound of a man burning inside the tomb—stopped. Nothing remained but the crackling of the flames and their blood-red reflection on the stone.

"Don't you die on me!" and he was at the mouth of the tomb. Kate said something he did not hear, but the stone stopped moving. At another word the flames fell back, and he ducked his head and entered the tomb, shuddering with reaction and memory and fear of the fire. Colin lay on the beaten floor atop the broken and scattered bones of the skeleton that had rested undisturbed through so many centuries. Blood streaked the man's forehead, the heat blistered his skin, but at the center of his own conflagration, the Finlay still lived. Leach shook him and heard Gathers mumble, "Give my spirit to the dawn. Don't seal the tomb."

"Not today, Sergeant," Leach growled the words deep in his throat, trying not to breathe. The fire had pulled away from him when he entered the tomb, but it raged in a furious circle around them nonetheless. Not natural, he knew, and figured the fire itself owed little more to nature. Still, if someone was holding back the flames, they'd doubtless be grateful if he hurried. Colin Gathers was in no condition to cooperate.

Shit. There was nothing to hold onto that wouldn't break cracked and blackened skin or tear away flesh melted to cloth. Leach knelt next to the man and grabbed his arms, then cringed away from him as skin split and peeled away in his fingers. He'd seen men burnt before and so he hesitated now. The pain would never stop. At twenty-six, the best Gathers could hope for was a short life twisted around that pain. At worst, he faced fifty years in a scarred mockery of the body that had walked into that tomb. Better for Col to let him go.

But Gathers still breathed in short, painful gasps, and Leach remembered the one thing Gathers had asked of him. Don't let them close him up in the tomb. So Leach curled him over his left shoulder, because he needed his right arm to do the dragging, and groaned when he tried to stand up. Sweat beaded on his forehead, and the tomb spun and tilted, but he took aim at the entrance and staggered toward it. Ducked, and nearly came to grief as the pain in his shoulder dropped him. Then hands were there, pulling Gathers off him, and Leach let himself go. Consciousness, he decided, was highly overrated.

"DCI, can you get up?"

Who? Henry Tuttle, for Christ's sake, dragging at his damned left arm again. What was it about these people? Why couldn't they let him rest in peace? But there was no peace; he heard the flames behind him, and Barbara, leaning over him, spoke softly, her voice too dry: "Inspector, can you hear me? Col wants to speak to you. He's holding on, but I don't know for how much longer. . . ."

Where were the tears? A day ago he would have believed she didn't care, but now, he wondered, dimly, as he roused himself and tried to sit, if any of them would ever cry again. Something else was missing, though. The night had returned, with just the gray of a true dawn shrouding the horizon. The fire had gone out—

"Don't close the tomb!" he cried, knowing despair, that he had not succeeded at this one request.

"It's all right, Geoff. You pulled Col out of there." Kate. He would have recognized her by the touch of her fingers on his forehead. He didn't know how one woman came with the power to heal all his hurts but the last, and that one made him pull away. He didn't want to think about her the way Anris had, when her fingers felt like cool water on his neck. He didn't dare think of her at all, or he'd be vomiting on her shoes.

"There isn't time to explain." She waited, not touching him, but asking, "Can you get up?"

Col needed him. Son of a bitch couldn't write parking tickets without getting himself half killed. He struggled to his feet and realized that they were alone. She reached for his arm and he moved a step back, afraid of her touch, afraid to follow her, but all out of options. "Where is he?"

"There." She nodded in the direction of a circle of villagers, with Barbara Finlay and Katherine Gathers kneeling at its head. Not far. He headed toward them in a staggering jog and fell sickened at Gathers' side. Col shouldn't be alive in that condition, and Leach knew he'd done the man no favor dragging him out of the fire. No more than a minute, maybe, and Col would have asphyxiated in there—the tomb could never support the oxygen for a fire that hot. But he'd made a promise, damn it, and he'd kept it.

Colin Gathers saw him then—no, sensed him somehow, because the cataracts burned over his eyes wouldn't let him see. Leach cringed away from the hand that groped for him and fell, leaving streaks of congealed blood on his jacket. He couldn't let him die like that, so he took the hand, as gently as he could, and tried to deny the feel of bone, fragile through the skin, that clutched weakly in his grasp.

"Geoff," Col whispered through cracked lips, and Leach bent closer to hear. "Thank you."

"It wasn't enough," Leach answered.

"No!" Gathers shook in his grasp. "We both did what we had to do. Now let it go. Let *me* go."

"I can't." Leach wanted to weep but couldn't,

couldn't find any way to escape the enormity of *now*, not with hallucinations or unconsciousness or simple grief; nothing rescued him from the infinitely present pain of denying Colin Gathers his death. Oh, God, oh, God, why did it always come down to blood on his hands, his heart?

"It hurts." Petulant, like a small child, Gathers stated the blindingly obvious, and Leach felt the convulsive shuddering of the man's pain.

So, "Go," Leach said as the day created the moor with its murky light. Light the path home, Col had said, and Leach bowed his head over their clasped hands and waited for the tears that would not fall.

"He's gone, Inspector. There's nothing more you can do."

Barbara, he realized, as she reached over his shoulder and gently uncurled his fingers from around Col Gathers hand. He wanted to resist, but his hands were cold, numb like his mind unwinding slowly at the end of the road Col Gathers had put him on with a promise demanded and given. Col was free, not trapped for an eternity in Anris' tomb. He hadn't thought past the moment when he'd told Gathers he could go and found himself hating the man for leaving him behind with a head full of memories that would fuel his nightmares forever.

"Son of a bitch," he muttered, "son of a bitch."

"You need attention," she said. "What hurts?" Leach realized that she asked it for the benefit of Henry Tuttle and Dick Morgan, who stood solicitously by.

"Nothing," he said, and meant everything.

Barbara nodded and rose to her feet, and he followed her, lightheaded, and staggered slightly with the change in position. He heard Kate's voice behind them, directing the placement of the stone to seal the entrance to the tomb, and the feel of her blood washed his tongue while he rubbed his hands convulsively on his jacket to clean them of Col Gathers' dying. He had to get away from the sound of her voice and the smell of burning flesh and the murmuring shock of Tuttle and Morgan and White and Laura Simms, and Katherine Gathers, who had sacrificed her only son to stop the thing that had tainted his world forever. He had to escape the concern of Barbara Finlay, who should have hated him because he hadn't saved her brother.

But he would have stood and done his duty as Her Majesty's servant if not for Kate. He couldn't hear her voice without wishing he had died in that tomb instead of Colin Gathers, just to stop the visions that played out behind his eyes. He turned and ran, then, catching on the bracken and tearing away, losing all sense of up or down until the ground reached out for him and he fell, forever, into his own darkness.

CHAPTER 34

"Geoff? DCI Leach?"

Barbara Finlay. Tough bitch, but loyal as they came, he remembered, then wondered what she was doing in his bedroom.

"Guvnor?"

What the hell was Jacobs doing in—oh. Memory caught up with Leach in a jumble of images. Fire, and Colin Gathers burning, and himself running, or stumbling, away from the sounds of Thorgill cleaning up after exacting its pound of flesh. He remembered falling, alone, unconscious on the moor. Which didn't explain where he was now, or how he'd come to be lying on a bed with a pillow under his head.

"Where am I?" he asked, and winced at the cliche of it.

"The back room at the White Rose, sir," Jacobs said. "We found you out on the moor and brought you down after they put the fire out."

Leach's arm still throbbed, but as long as he didn't think, he felt alert and physically unharmed. He couldn't help thinking, of course, and that dragged him into a bleeding despair. But Jacobs, much aggrieved, continued to natter at him, and Leach tried to focus on what the junior inspector was saying.

"Knew you needed backup, but Spencer wouldn't

let me come until the fire was out. Said some things don't need outsiders mucking about in them."

"Spencer is a good man." Leach struggled to sit up, made it. "He told you right."

"Um, they weren't sure how much you remembered." Jacobs glanced away, at Barbara Finlay, whose eyes would have told him anything he'd been lucky enough to forget. Leach didn't want to hear it. "I remember it all, Ben," he said, though he, too, looked at Barbara Finlay when he said it, "until I passed out."

It should have been him dead; he'd lived longer, burdened with more dead on his soul then he could carry. Had no children to mourn him, nothing but more memories to shatter his nights.

Jacobs just shook his head. "They moved Col to the church, mucked up the crime scene, which has DCI Powell breathing fire"—he paled at his poor choice of words; Leach figured they'd be tiptoeing around their own words for a long while and might as well get used to it now.

"Powell wants to talk to you before they take him, Col that is, back to York. Cause of death and all that."

"He bloody burned to death, Ben, what does he think?"

Jacobs didn't answer. Didn't need to. They both knew forensics would want an autopsy. They were still looking for a drug at the bottom of the slaughter, and Leach had nothing better to give them. Nothing Powell could take to his super.

"I told Powell he'd have to wait, you need to be in the hospital, but she "—Jacobs motioned at Barbara Finlay—insisted . . ."

"I'm fine," Leach protested.

"If you say so, DCI. But I've got the car here to take you to the hospital."

"It's Ms. Finlay who need a hospital, Jacobs." He

ran a hand through his hair, pulled it out smeared with ash. "All I need is a bath and twenty-four hours of sleep."

"If you are well enough to speak with him, DCI Powell is waiting. He said to tell you they have a standby emergency vehicle waiting," Barbara Finlay said. "But he's not letting any of the family leave the White Rose until you are conscious enough to clear us of Col's murder. We can't go to him, to Col, until you explain."

"I was about to tell you that myself, DCI." Jacobs sounded put upon, but Leach didn't have time for it.

"And what, precisely, do you expect me to tell him?" Not to Jacobs, but to Barbara Finlay, who understood.

"The truth, as far as it goes. He died in the fire, trying to save the village." She paused. "We'll never forget what you did out there."

"Neither will I," he answered her, with all the bitterness he couldn't express in words with Jacobs looking on, confused and unhappy and mourning a friend. Hell and hell again. Time to get it over with. "Where is Powell?"

"The public room," Jacobs answered. He's there with Col's family, waiting for you to wake up. And for the hazmat team to come back."

Leach nodded. "Let's go, then." He made it to his feet with some surprise that he didn't fall back down again.

"Geoff."

He stopped in midstride, realizing Barbara Finlay hadn't used his first name since Jacobs had arrived. Why now?

"Your men are holding Katy."

"You left me no choice about that." And he still wasn't happy about it.

"I am not reproaching you, Inspector. You did exactly what I had hoped, but now it's over."

He nodded, once, abruptly. "Right," he said, and turned to Jacobs. "Clear it with Spencer, Ben. Have him turn the girl over to her mother." He couldn't say Kate's name, or the child's—couldn't risk the flood of memories that the words evoked. "Tell Inspector Powell that I will be out to answer his questions in a moment but that he can let the family go now. They did nothing actionable."

"Yes, sir." Jacobs gave him an acknowledging tilt of the head but left with obvious reluctance.

When they were alone, Barbara Finlay touched him gently on the arm. It didn't even hurt the shoulder, but the words cut deep.

"You can't leave without seeing her."

Kate, of course, and he damn well could.

"I can't deal with it. Not any of it. I wouldn't believe it had happened, even now, except that I couldn't live with myself if those feelings I had tonight were really mine."

He waited out the shudder of revulsion. "You don't know. I can't think of Kate without wanting to fling myself down that mineshaft to make sure I don't hurt her the way he wanted to hurt her."

"It wasn't you."

"If it were just the images—" He shrugged, regretted it. "He took pleasure in it, you know? Physical pleasure. His thoughts but my body. And I responded. It would have been my body doing those things to her. When I think of her, I think of him, and my body still responds to the pleasure he felt. So, no, I can't see her. Take care of her, though, won't you? And Katy? Don't let that old witch get her talons in. The kid doesn't need this sort of thing."

Barbara Finlay shook her head. "We asked more of you tonight than we had any right to do," she said.

That was his job, though, to protect the innocent. Or even the not-so-innocent. "I failed her, you know. Failed Colin. I couldn't save him."

"You didn't fail anyone." Too much knowledge in her eyes, and he knew they reflected the same in his own. Some things human beings weren't meant to see or feel or touch in this world, and they'd bulled their way through all of them last night. "He only ever asked one thing of you at the end. To set him free. It was more than anyone else could do for him, but you pulled him out of Anris' tomb.

"Col died free, in the light of the morning. His children will live free of the old traditions—Katy won't have to go up the hill with her brother, won't have to face Anris in the dark. So don't ever think you didn't do enough. If you hadn't been here, we'd all be dead, or trapped forever in the cycle of the Finlays."

"It's not enough."

"Sometimes it has to be, Inspector." She left him, and he heard the murmur of her voice in the pub, and the deeper tone of George Powell objecting, finally capitulating. When the murmur died down to one or two voices, and then to silence, he left his sanctuary.

"Inspector."

Katherine Gathers. He hadn't expected to see her, felt ambushed by her presence in the room. He'd thought they'd all gone.

"I asked DCI Powell if I could have a moment."

Well, wasn't that just fucking wonderful. Did she want to thank him for getting her son killed, or for not raping and murdering her daughter like he'd planned when he came tearing up the hill? He didn't hide a bit of his anger from her, but she didn't flinch. The old bitch had backbone if nothing else.

"Jack called. They've released him. Thank you for that." Each word sounded like the ratcheted unwinding of a spring wound too tight. "He wanted to drive up, but he's had such a trying time in that prison that I told him to go home. He can come up tomorrow, or the next day, when they return Col to us. There will be a service, of course; you are welcome . . . ."

Leach turned his back on her; he couldn't face the taut need she had to tie him to Thorgill with her words. He'd be here, all right, in the uniform that had been too tight the last time he'd attended a policeman's funeral—old Marshall, who'd had a heart attack while questioning the victim in a convenience store robbery. But that didn't mean he was giving a part of his soul to the damned village. Duty. That was all.

"They had to seal the tomb last night to put out the fire, but Anris is gone. It was a foolish stunt Col played there. Risky."

Better the two of them locked up in the dark forever, fighting each other and the evil thing between them, Leach figured she meant. Tough, tough old bat. But her voice broke at the last.

"I couldn't have left him there alone, you know, Inspector. Only Kate knew. I would have joined him, at the last, rather than leave him alone in the dark." Katherine Gathers' voice was tight, and her face, when Leach turned to look at her again, was ravaged by the horror of the night before. "He was my son, you know," she said. "My son."

Leach didn't know what she wanted of him. He couldn't give her absolution, that wasn't his line. He couldn't tell her what a good mum she'd been, or that he forgave her. None of it would be true, and he'd been pushed past his limit for polite fictions. So he scrabbled in his pocket for a crushed but otherwise unblemished handkerchief and waited while she wiped her nose and eyes.

"I think DCI Powell wants to speak to me now," he said, "So if I may . . ."

Powell entered the pub then, followed by three figures in environmental hazard suits, one with her helmet tucked under her arm. Beth Newton. Leach remembered the archaeologist from their earlier introduction. The other two carried equipment which they set on a table before tugging off their helmets. The hazmat team, Leach guessed, and they didn't look best pleased.

"Beth." Katherine Gathers held out a hand but the woman in the hazmat suit ignored it.

"I know, dear." Newton wrapped her cumbersome arms around Col Gathers' mother. "How positively awful for you."

She looked as though she hadn't slept, and George Powell didn't look much better. "I was with Jack last night," Beth Newton explained, "At the prison. He was worried for you out here, and of course he was devastated when he heard about Col. But we think we figured it out."

"What?" Leach wasn't tracking. If anyone outside of Thorgill knew what had killed Colin Gathers, his stepfather certainly would. Leach didn't know about Beth Newton, but he hoped she wasn't about to spill Thorgill's family secret onto George Powell's shoes. Leach had a feeling the DCI would not take it well.

"Coal gas. The fire pretty much clinches it. Kate says they haven't really put the fire out but merely contained it by sealing up the tomb again, which is pretty common with this kind of thing . . ."

Powell finally stepped into the discussion, but no more intelligently than Leach had: "Coal gas?"

You'll have to do better than that, Inspector, Leach

mused to himself, or you will find yourself trying to explain rampaging spirit possession to your guv. Fortunately, Beth Newton had enough force of conviction for all of them.

"It was the mine, you see. You set us onto it, actually, Inspector Leach, when you asked where one of the tunnels in the mine went. I was in York when the call came in, and we took a look at the map. Sure enough, the tunnel works its way under the tomb.

"When I talked to Jack, we realized that coal gas must have been leaking into that tomb for centuries. When the team opened it, they were exposed to a mix of the gas and probably other toxins from the old mine workings as well. It effectively poisoned them. The rest was suggestion.

"With all that activity around the site, a fire was a foregone conclusion. You know, there are whole towns in Pennsylvania, in the States, where the mines have burned for decades. Every once in a while a house collapses into a pit, or a fire erupts in the middle of the street. They seem to think nothing of it. We shouldn't see anything like that around here, of course. The workings were nowhere near as extensive as that, and the fire doesn't seem to have spread. Of course, I've had to rescind the recommendation for an open dig here. Even if we hadn't discovered the place was unsafe, we'd have had the devil of a time mounting a second project, given the experience of the first."

"We took some samples." The senior member of the hazmat team didn't seem happy with the explanation, but Leach didn't figure he was ready to accept the only alternative on offer either. "We'll run some more tests back at the lab. But if Dr. Newton's guess is true, there won't be anything to find this morning, except for what may have bound to the residue of the fire, of course."

"Well, Inspector Leach," Powell interrupted, "swamp gas would seem to leave your sergeant off the hook."

"Coal gas," Leach corrected. "And lying dead in that particular way doesn't strike me as being let off any hook."

"Sorry," Powell conceded. "Coal gas. Of course."

Too many feelings too raw still for either man to approach the subject rationally, Leach knew. As if the rational could help in this case. Powell still believed Colin Gathers had been responsible, somehow, for the deaths in Thorgill, if for no other reason than his need to put a period to the death of his officer, the emotional ruin of two others. Leach recognized the feeling, was holding on by a thread himself because there'd never be an explanation to rid him of his own guilt. But Powell had to see, if not any truth on the table, at least the pressing need to free another dead officer's family of the shame of murder. Whatever Gathers had done, he'd paid for it now. Whatever.

The third space-suited figure, this one with a red cross on his chest, pushed his way forward. "The lady outside said you needed medical attention, sir. Do you need a stretcher, or would it be easier to walk?"

Quite suddenly, Leach realized that he'd been standing far too long, that his shoulder was in open rebellion, that he had no idea what time of day it was, or even what day of the week, and that if he didn't get himself prone right quick, he was likely to start blubbering all over the red cross hazmat suit from simple exhaustion.

"I'll walk," he said anyway, though he hoped that emergency vehicle was parked near the door.

"We'll still be doing a house-to-house, of course."

Powell stopped him, waited. People seemed to be doing that a lot to him today, though he had nothing left to give them. "If there is anything you'd like to discuss now."

"Nothing," he said, and turned at the urging of the medic.

Powell's voice stopped him again. Not threatening this time, or challenging, the voice spoke volumes about sleepless nights and the guilt a man carried whether he should or not.

"Someday, when this is over, I'd like to know what really happened here, Geoff."

"Someday, George." And because the man shared losses with Thorgill, he let the masks fall away, let him see his own pain and horror stark on his features.

"Like that, is it?" Powell looked away a moment and Leach let him recover his composure. "I thought it might be."

CHAPTER 35

The churchyard was small, with thin slate headstones bearing the names scratched into them of families who still populated the dale. Gathers could have had a hero's funeral, but Kate had wanted him put to rest quietly here, next to Henry Tuttle's green Methodist church with its tin roof and plain windowpanes. The lights were out now, the Finlay curse ended, and the most recent mound sunk with six months of mist and quiet rain.

He should have brought flowers, Leach supposed, but he hadn't felt much like sentimental gestures when he'd decided to come back here. Face down his ghosts, that was it, and a man didn't do that with flowers in his hand. Leach stared at the small stone marker for long moments and wondered what to say to the man whose death he carried like a scar that only hurt when a man could least afford the pain. *You were a good cop in a bad situation? Sorry I couldn't stop you from burning like a torch, but at least I didn't let them wall you up alive in your own tomb?*

He sank low on his haunches, closer to the man beneath the stone, and tried to come up with words for the feelings. But "Bastard" was all that came to mind. So many dead on his hands. Dunlop, in Derry, and the boy. Col Gathers. He just didn't have the strength to carry them around on his back anymore.

"Do you ever see the others, Gathers?" he whispered. "The 'Geoffrey Leach put me here' brigade? If you should see that boy where you are, would you tell him I am sorry? Tell him . . . tell him sometimes good men do bad things for reasons that stop making sense just the other side of too late. And if you meet up with Dunlop, and they've got good ale in heaven—must have, how else could it be heaven?—sink a few for old times. And keep a bench warm for me."

Leach rose to his feet and dusted off his hands. He didn't feel freer, or lighter, or any of the things he figured a person was supposed to feel when he made his peace with his dead, but he figured that someday, now, he had a chance of waking up in the morning without Col Gathers bursting into flames in his shaving mirror.

"What was it for, Col?" he asked. "What was the point of it all?"

He didn't want an answer, really, but Thorgill, never a forgiving place, wasn't letting him get away that easily. He scanned the churchyard, avoiding the longer view onto the moor, where the tomb, sealed again, crouched over the village, and caught sight of the child, Katy Gathers. She leaned on the corner of the church, one foot tucked up on top of the other. She recognized him—he saw that in her eyes. And she'd been watching him, still was, in that steady way she had when faced with a knotty problem, like an outsider who knew whose child she was.

He considered, briefly, calling to her, but almost as the thought formed, he saw her slip around the corner of the church, out of view. Bad idea, he agreed, silently. He'd have asked about her mother, and he wasn't ready to face that yet. Probably never would be. Some things die before they are born, and you just have to let them go, he told himself. But there on the brink of leaving, he wished he'd brought flowers for the grave.

Camille Bacon-Smith

☐ **THE FACE OF TIME** UE2707—$5.99

Tracking down a serial killer in the town of Thorgill, two New Scotland Yard officers are about to enter a whole new territory of police investigation. And though one of the detectives and the townspeople know what is really going on, no one's willing to let his partner in on the secret. But as ancient rituals begin to be fulfilled, the two officers find themselves drawn into an unholy war—facing an enemy more powerful than death itself. . . .

☐ **EYE OF THE DAEMON** UE2673—$5.50

All the wealthy Mrs. Simpson knew was that her half brother Paul was missing, and the ad she was responding to had been lying on top of the ransom note she found in her dining room. But these were private investigators of the immortal kind—and this kidnapping was about to lure them into the heart of a demonic war. . . .

Buy them at your local bookstore or use this convenient coupon for ordering.

PENGUIN USA P.O. Box 999—Dep. #17109, Bergenfield, New Jersey 07621

Please send me the DAW BOOKS I have checked above, for which I am enclosing
$_____ (please add $2.00 to cover postage and handling). Send check or money
order (no cash or C.O.D.'s) or charge by Mastercard or VISA (with a $15.00 minimum). Prices and
numbers are subject to change without notice.

Card #_____ Exp. Date _____
Signature_____
Name_____
Address_____
City _____ State _____ Zip Code _____

For faster service when ordering by credit card call 1-800-253-6476

Allow a minimum of 4-6 weeks for delivery. This offer is subject to change without notice.

Tanya Huff

☐ **NO QUARTER**   UE2698—$5.99
Trapped together in one body, the assassin Vree and the body
snatcher Gyhard seek a solution to their dilemma in Shkoder, the king-
dom of bards and healers.

☐ **FIFTH QUARTER**   UE2651—$4.99

☐ **SING THE FOUR QUARTERS**   UE2628—$4.99

VICTORY NELSON, INVESTIGATOR:
Otherworldly Crimes A Specialty
☐ **BLOOD PRICE: Book 1**   UE2471—$4.99
☐ **BLOOD TRAIL: Book 2**   UE2502—$4.50
☐ **BLOOD LINES: Book 3**   UE2530—$4.99
☐ **BLOOD PACT: Book 4**   UE2582—$4.99

THE NOVELS OF CRYSTAL
☐ **CHILD OF THE GROVE: Book 1**   UE2432—$4.50
☐ **THE LAST WIZARD: Book 2**   UE2331—$4.50

OTHER NOVELS
☐ **GATE OF DARKNESS, CIRCLE OF LIGHT**   UE2386—$4.50
☐ **THE FIRE'S STONE**   UE2445—$3.95

Buy them at your local bookstore or use this convenient coupon for ordering.

PENGUIN USA P.O. Box 999—Dept. #17109, Bergenfield, New Jersey 07621

Please send me the DAW BOOKS I have checked above, for which I am enclosing
$_____ (please add $2.00 to cover postage and handling). Send check or money
order (no cash or C.O.D.'s) or charge by Mastercard or VISA (with a $15.00 minimum). Prices and
numbers are subject to change without notice.

Card #_____ Exp. Date _____
Signature_____
Name_____
Address_____
City _____ State _____ Zip Code _____

For faster service when ordering by credit card call 1-800-253-6476
Allow a minimum of 4-6 weeks for delivery. This offer is subject to change without notice.